EVERYTHING
IS BEAUTIFUL AND
EVERYTHING
HURTS

T0155441

EVERYTHING IS BEAUTIFUL AND EVERYTHING HURTS

A NOVEL

JOSIE SHAPIRO

ALLEN&UNWIN
SYDNEY•MELBOURNE•AUCKLAND•LONDON

First published in 2023

Allen & Unwin
Level 2, 10 College Hill, Freemans Bay
Auckland 1011, New Zealand
Phone: (64 9) 377 3800
Email: auckland@allenandunwin.com
Web: www.allenandunwin.co.nz

83 Alexander Street
Crows Nest NSW 2065, Australia
Phone: (61 2) 8425 0100

A catalogue record for this book is available from the National Library of
New Zealand.

ISBN 978 1 99100 644 8

Cover design by Christa Moffitt
Internal design by Kate Barraclough
Set in Adobe Caslon Pro and KG Happy Solid
Printed and bound in Australia by the Opus Group

10 9 8 7

MIX
Paper | Supporting
responsible forestry
FSC
www.fsc.org   FSC® C001695

For Willa and Marnie

CONTENTS

PART ONE

THE RACE

THICK SEA FOG ROLLS IN before sunrise. The water isn't far away, but it is as though it isn't there at all. I close my eyes for a moment, and I hear it, the slapping of the tide against the rock wall.

I watch the other competitors move through the whiteness, coming in and out of focus. Some jog around, warming their muscles, hyped up with anticipation and fear. I can almost smell it, bitter and sweet. Legs kick knees high; brightly coloured sneakers squeak on tarmac. My own legs quiver with the chill of a spring morning. I bounce, once, twice. My feet, clad in the lucky pink socks, feel like dead weights; I'm unsure in this moment if I can make even one kilometre. How to make it through forty-two? Well, the hay is in the barn now. I rub my calves, dig my fingers into the muscle, not too hard.

A quick glance at my watch. Five minutes to go. The competitors clot together. Dawn is only minutes away. Above the hushed pre-race chatter: the haunting call of a tūī, high in the pōhutukawa bordering the shore.

I slip around the side. I want to be much closer to the starting line, nearly at the front. Older men glance at me as I weave in front of them. They take in my not-quite-five-feet stature, my boyish hips, legs like chopsticks, long brown ponytail. I know their type. Don't like to be beaten by a girl. I ignore their stares and their judgement and move away.

The golden light of the sun's first rays brightens the morning. Not too far ahead: a pace runner. It could be the one I want. Two hours 30 minutes. Quick enough to qualify for New York, quick enough to prove a point. He's a tall, gangly man in a bright green, tightly curled wig, wearing aviator sunglasses and a tee-shirt with his pace time printed on the back. He doesn't look at me when I push in next to him, but the group around him — more men — eye me, size me up. I take off my long-sleeved yellow top. I raise my arm high and toss it over the heads of the other runners. I'm in my favourite singlet now, the white one with blue panels, and I run my fingers along the edge of my race number, checking the pins. Shoulders up and down, head roll to loosen my neck. A deep breath through the nose, hold it: then exhale. I can't resist another look at my watch — one minute to go. There's a shifting in the crowd. A cold sweat breaks out down my back, and I fold my hands into fists.

Everyone begins to inch forward, squeezing up the space between us. Closer and closer. I'm only three metres from the front … now two. The professional runners are right there. If I wove my arm between the bodies in front of me, I could touch them. I recognise most of them — Olympians and New Zealand representatives: Dylan Freeman, Ruby Bright, Marcus Sheehan. Others I don't know. I can tell they're professionals by the way they move, by the shape of their muscles. They don't look back at the mass of runners crowding behind them.

The pacer beside me lifts his sunglasses and winks. My body relaxes. It's Ryan! He turns back to face the starting line, and there's no time left to think of anything other than the moment — there's a long beep of a horn, then the gun sounds. We're off.

ONE

THERE WAS NOTHING IN MY childhood that suggested I'd be a good runner, let alone a great one. My mother, Bonnie, was an intensive-care nurse, ambivalent about sports in general; my father, Teddy, was a journalist who fancied himself an eloquent man of letters, and whose attitude to all sports other than cricket and rugby was one of simmering hostility. Neither of them encouraged me towards athletics. Bonnie was loving but preoccupied with my older brothers and sister — the twins, Helen and Kent, and Zach. My father, well, he wasn't there to direct me in one way or another.

My mother told me I was late to walking, that I crawled like a crazed bear cub until I was eighteen months old. I refused to take a step, even with Bonnie, Zach, Kent and Helen all cajoling me to get up and toddle to their open arms. By the time I did take my first steps, Teddy was in Auckland, living with his new girlfriend. Once I was up on two feet, I didn't stop moving. 'You're responsible for all these grey hairs, Mickey,' Mum liked to remind me. 'One for every time you did something you shouldn't.'

I was born with big ears, and Bonnie said I made snuffling squeaks exactly like a mouse. My birth certificate might say Michelle Joan Bloom, but everyone called me Mickey.

WE LIVED IN NGĀMOTU, ON a small section near the beach. Three bedrooms, one bathroom, everything the same since the day it was built decades earlier. The carpet was thin and starting to fray, the linoleum in the bathroom was peeling up from the floorboards in the corners. The kitchen light fitting constantly blew its bulb. None of this mattered, though. With the noise and the mess of four children, it felt like a home.

I shared a cramped, yellow-wallpapered bedroom with my older sister, Helen. We'd lie in bed and sing, or tell each other secrets, and when I woke from a nightmare, she'd whisper, 'It's okay, Mickey. It's just a bad dream. Everything's going to be okay.' Our hands would stretch out and touch, and I'd fall asleep again, my hand still in hers.

Bonnie worked long hours at the hospital, managing her shifts around the menace of school and kindergarten drop-offs and pick-ups. When the weather warmed, she'd pack a bag with towels, sunhats and a box of homemade ginger crunch, and we'd walk together across the domain to the river. There was a secluded swimming hole she'd known since childhood, and she preferred it to the dumping waves of the beach. I loved it too.

I remember the day she took us there when I was five. Us kids ran ahead, Helen and Kent streaking to the front on their long legs, Zach not far behind. The grass in the domain was long, dry and tough. It felt to me like a wide, tussocky plain, and my short legs struggled to wade through it.

'Wait for me!' I screamed, and I remember my voice floating up towards the high and dusty-blue sky. They didn't slow, the lure of the river too strong.

'I'll walk with you, honey,' Bonnie called. I didn't want to walk with

Mum, at her leisurely pace, strolling through the heat of the afternoon. I hungered for speed, for wind in my hair, and I shot on ahead of her. By the time I reached the river, my body was stiff and slimy with sweat. Helen and Kent were already on the far side, clambering up the bank to the rock where they'd jump, slicing their bodies down into the deepest part of the bend. Zach was in the middle, in the thick of the current, his arms working to swim against the undertow, refusing to let the green pull of the river rip him downstream. I was furious they'd got in without me.

Bonnie's one rule about the river was that until you could swim freestyle from one side to the other and back without help, you must be always with an adult. 'You can't tell what the river's thinking,' she would say. 'She's a moody one. It's not worth taking any silly risks.'

That day I ignored the rule. I splashed into the water alone. My feet slipped on the mossy rocks; my skin pimpled from the shock of the cold. I lunged toward Zach, and then found I couldn't touch the bottom. I paddled frantically, my hands slipping through the water, my head dipping under. I struggled, kicking my legs, and my head popped up above the surface for a moment. 'Mickey!' I heard Bonnie screaming my name. There was time just to sip in a mouthful of air, and then I was down again, into the viridescence.

It was quiet down there. My chest tightened as I dropped deeper. Then hands gripped my chest. Kent heaved me up, and onto his back. When he made it to the rocky foreshore, Bonnie rushed over to us, her face pale.

'She's all right, Mum,' Kent said, lowering me to the ground. His arm stayed fast around my shoulders. 'I wouldn't let anything happen to her.'

'Mickey, my dear.' Bonnie shook her head and put her hand on my cheek. 'You're going to be the death of me.'

'Stop it, Mum,' I said. 'Can I get back in?'

She glanced at Kent, who nodded.

'Okay,' she said. 'I'll be with you in a minute. Keep her close to you, Kent.'

THE SUMMER I TURNED SEVEN, the pocket of grass in the back yard of Rutherford Street changed from green to deepest brown. There was no rain for weeks, and the days had a thin, parched feeling to them. I wanted to spend every day at the river, drifting in the coolness of the ice-melt, but there was no time for what I wanted — Helen and Kent had a volleyball tournament at the YMCA; entire Saturdays were lost to Zach's cricket; and because the others loved to read, we had one afternoon a week at the library.

'I don't read,' I said to Bonnie. 'Can't I do something else?'

'You'll never to learn to read if you don't read,' she replied, passing me a pile of books that I knew would remain unopened.

The summer holidays evaporated in a haze of sunshine and boredom. On the first day back at school, Christian, a boy I sometimes played with at lunch break, told me he was going to the free athletics on Tuesday afternoon. 'Down at the rugby field near the beach,' he said. 'We do these running races and long jump. Sometimes we throw a ball — that's the best.'

Running. Throwing a ball. It sounded so much better than sitting at the library, surrounded by books full of nonsensical code I couldn't understand. I begged Bonnie to let me skip the library that week.

'Zach and I can walk from school,' I said. 'You can get the books from the library without us.'

Bonnie slapped the tea towel she was holding onto the bench. 'Reading's important, Mickey,' she said. 'I don't know about this.'

'It's free,' I said with a grin, and this seemed to be the clincher. We were allowed to go.

THE FREE ATHLETICS RAN FOR five weeks. There was always a mix of activities — running, jumping, throwing. Kids came from all over — some were students I recognised from Nikau Primary; others were from the Catholic primary school on the other side of town. The community group who organised the event said it was about having fun and participating, so the races weren't timed and they didn't fuss over winners.

The final session was in late March, just before Easter. The volunteers placed neon-orange road cones to mark out the sprint, the long jump, the long throw. I couldn't wait for the sprint, my favourite event, and kept imagining my toes on the line and holding my breath until I heard the whistle, the wind whipping my hair away from my eyes.

Viv, the ruddy-cheeked leader of the volunteers, sucked in a shrill call between her teeth and waved her arms. The kids swarmed around her. I stood near the back of the group, near some of Zach's classmates.

'Move over, dwarf,' one of them said, and pushed me into the child in front, who turned and glared. I stared back, almost daring him to hit me. I was fearless sometimes, to the point of reckless. The older kid stuck out his chin and faced forward again, just as Viv began to speak.

'Today we'll finish with a relay.' She paused to wipe sweat from her forehead. 'Tony will put you into teams once we've finished the games and we'll explain the rules.'

Tony, a man with long, greasy hair and raggedy Canterbury shorts, led the older kids to the high jump and long jump at the far end of the field, and the younger kids stayed with Viv for the sprints. Zach usually joined in, but that day he sat with the school bags under the pōhutukawa beside the rugby club rooms instead, his body grey with shade, thumbs buzzing on his Tamagotchi.

Viv sorted the younger kids into age groups and spread us out, ten across. I watched the kids in the group ahead of me race to the finish line. I felt excited, kind of high, and I bounced from foot to foot, ready for action. My group moved forward, and I inched my toes to the line, just as I'd imagined. I pressed my tongue into my teeth and held my breath. Viv hollered, 'On your marks, get set ...' and then she set her lips just so, letting loose her piercing whistle to start the race.

Ten little bodies leapt from the line. I pushed forward with them. The wind was warm on my cheeks, my heart beat fast in my ears. Above me, the sky was bright and streaked with long flat ribbons of cloud. Seagulls soared through the wide blue, and I imagined I was flying with them, chasing the clouds. The other children drifted behind me, and soon I couldn't see them at all. I crossed the finish line — and looked up at the sky as I breathed heavily, trying to calm my body. The dwarf insult no longer bothered me. My brain melted into the blue, sweet and soft.

My group moved to the high jump. Tony dropped the height of the bar when it came to my turn, and some of the other kids laughed. We took our turns, then followed Tony to the long jump. On my first attempt, I landed short of the pit. I thought I heard a hushed sneer.

Tony knelt down beside me. 'You have the speed,' he said. 'Just need to get those feet working in the right order. Then you might fly.' He lifted my legs, his calloused hands rough on my ankles, his movements helping me mimic the steps I should take in the moments before I jumped. 'Good try,' he said. 'You're a natural.'

At first I didn't understand what he meant. I wasn't used to compliments. My legs tingled with warmth, and I looked down at them as though I'd never seen them before.

Viv whistled three short blasts, and we gathered around her again. Tony sorted us evenly into six teams. I stood in the second team. Beside me, in the third, was the older boy who'd insulted me earlier.

He leaned down, his wet lips pink and full. 'Don't even bother trying to win, loser,' he said. 'Midgets like you can't keep up with me.' He waved his freckled arms. I pressed my finger into my mouth and bit the edge of the nail where a sharp edge grew. I stared at Viv, who was explaining the rules of the relay. *Pass the baton to your teammate, hold your arm behind you to receive like so, hold the baton in front of you with arm extended like this*, each instruction delivered with a gesture to demonstrate.

'Before we find our places around the race course, I wanted to thank Tony for his help this year. What fun we've had! And to all you children, thank you for making Tuesday athletics such a wonderful time. Give yourselves a round of applause!'

Sixty sets of sticky, dirty hands clapped, then the runners split up, one person from each team taking their place at a traffic cone. No one told me where to go, so I stayed where I was, watching as my teammates took the first nine spots, leaving only the last place, the anchor leg. The other final runners stared at me as I approached — they were all ten- and eleven-year-old boys. No other girls.

'What are you doing here, Mickey?' It was Sam. He'd come to Zach's birthday party last year. 'This is supposed to be your team's fastest runner.'

'I am our team's fastest runner,' I said, even though I knew it wasn't true, and the boys sniggered.

'What a smart-arse,' one of them said.

Two cars sped along the road that bordered the far side of the field. Their engines revved, and the howl of tyres echoed around the grounds. Hidden in that noise, I knew, was Viv's whistle. Her upraised hand dropped, and the first set of runners started around the track.

Three of the kids started to pull in front. At the first handover, four of the teams dropped the baton, and two teams stretched their lead. I hopped on one foot then the other, bouncy and sure-footed. Everyone was screaming, cheering their teammates on, and I shouted too, without words, simply a long, electrifying cry. My team was in second place, just a beat away from the leaders at the second handover.

The baton moved to the next runner, then the next, and soon the second-to-last runners were powering around the field towards us. Beside me, the boy running last for the leading team stood facing his oncoming teammate, holding his hand out in front, not in the way Viv had shown us. Face the finish line like so, she'd said, hand at your back like this. But still, he was away running before I had my baton. I kept my hand behind and then, there it was — in my grasp. Quick feet, toes into the scratchy grass, the sun on my face: I was away.

The sound of the waves and the squealing cheers of the other kids seemed to amplify in my head. My tongue stuck out the side of my mouth. My arms pumped, elbows out. I rounded the corner of the track, closing in on the older kid ahead. Zach wasn't sitting on the school bags any longer; he was on his feet, yelling my name. I could hear his voice and the snap of his clapping hands above the dry heaves of my breath.

Closer — each stride drew me closer to the boy in front. His legs were slowing, his shoulders bunched to his ears. I was flying, it felt like flying. Three steps, two, then I was in front, I was in the lead, and at the finish line the rest of the kids gathered, jumping around, feverish with the thrill of the Easter long weekend and the sight of the youngest Bloom child overtaking Evan.

I threw myself into the waiting crowd. It felt as though my heart would burst through my chest, it was beating with such force. Then someone's arms were around me, and my feet were off the ground. It was Zach, holding me high and tight. All the races I'd won throughout the athletics season — 20-metre sprints against a random selection of kids my own age — meant nothing compared to this. This was winning when everyone expected I would lose. The midget, the shrimp, the little Bloom taking out the race. A magical, tingling sensation spread from the soles of my feet to the tips of my fingers.

WHEN WE ARRIVED HOME, I rushed inside to tell Mum about the relay. Bonnie pulled me into her, and I lingered there a moment, my face buried in the creases of her uniform, the stench of hospital disinfectant and lemons caulking my nostrils.

'I'm so proud of you, Mickey,' she said, and she kissed the top of my head five times. 'I'm not sure I always get things right, but I'm trying my best. It's lovely to see you so happy.'

'Tell us again,' Helen said, her eyes wide, so I repeated the story.

'She was like a rocket.' Zach whipped his hands around to imitate the speed of my body. 'Zoo-zoo-zooming around the field. You wouldn't believe it, Helen, she just blew them up like dynamite!'

'Special dinner tonight to celebrate,' Bonnie said. 'We'll have custard for dessert. And let's call your dad. It's not every day we get to call him with good news!' She winked at me as if to say we were doing this together, the good times and the bad.

I knew what she was referring to. We usually called Teddy once a week, on Sunday afternoons, and she often spoke to him about the difficulties I was having at school. I could still barely read. She's disruptive at mat time, the teachers said, creating a challenging learning environment for other students; she has difficulty making friends.

Kent picked up the phone and punched in the 09 to call our father. I wasn't the only one who wanted to speak to him: Zach was busting to tell him about his new cricket bat. But Kent went straight on in and spent ten minutes explaining the plot of See Ya, Simon. I waited my turn until at last he handed me the receiver.

Athletics, the cicadas, Viv, the whistles, the older kids, the relay — the words spilled out. 'I won the relay!'

'I think you mean your team won the relay,' Teddy said. He sounded distracted and far away.

'No, I won,' I repeated in a loud voice, to be sure he heard.

'Congratulations to your team. Sounds like a fun day.'

'No, Dad. I *won* it. By a mile.'

'It wasn't a mile,' Zach said. 'But you did win it.'

'It was,' I said. It had felt like that to me.

Teddy spoke to someone in the background, and I held the receiver with two hands, gripping it firm, as though to hold him as well. When he finally spoke again it was as if I'd not mentioned the race, or the win, and my words were only air to him, warm air without meaning.

'Put Helen on for me, would you?'

They talked for a long time, my sister explaining again the name of her teacher, the maths equations they were working on, the books she'd got from the library that day. I lay on the couch, half listening, furious with my father but unable to understand exactly why. I watched the ghostly spectacle of light on the ceiling as the net curtain waved in the breeze. The smell of dinner cooking in the kitchen grew thick. I heard saucepans, the tap going on and off. I decided I would go and tell Bonnie the story again, see her smile, but then I heard Helen giggle and say, 'We won't forget!'

I sat up. There was something in her tone, the way she glanced at me, that made me certain they'd been talking about me. She set the phone down.

'We won't forget what?' Kent asked, putting aside his book.

Helen lifted her eyebrows in a smirk. 'The baby, of course.'

Zach and Kent started laughing as if she was the comedian of the year, and Bonnie, walking through the lounge to take out a salad bowl from the buffet, smiled too, saying quietly to herself, *the baby*.

I felt my face grow red, my cheeks hot to touch. I kicked the couch. Everyone ignored me.

The joke was, they *had* forgotten the baby once upon a time. Teddy's sister Marguerite had invited the family to stay at her bach in Awakino. In the hours before we left, the house was in a fluster: people rushing around, gathering beach towels and jandals, packing bags with clothes and food. I sat in my high chair, occupied with a handful of crackers, removed from the chaos. The story goes: they were in the car, boot full of sleeping bags, cricket bats for Zach, *An Artist of the Floating World* for Teddy, a sun hat for Helen, Weet-Bix for Kent, and it wasn't until after the car had reversed down the driveway and was picking up speed along Rutherford Street that Bonnie spun her head around, mouth open slightly. They were about to turn on to Rimu Street when she cried out, 'We forgot the baby!'

FOR A FEW WEEKS I re-enacted the relay in the back yard. Bonnie helped me make a fake baton with rolled-up newspaper, and I tossed it from hand to hand, playing the roles of all the team members. As the weather began to cool, and the leaves started to brown and drop on the Japanese maple at the corner of Rutherford Street and Harley Close, other things crowded into my mind. Reading recovery homework, and the nightly fight with Bonnie about it. Another fight, about badminton — I wanted to do athletics, only the season was over and the badminton season was beginning. I had the sensation of being dragged along helplessly in the current. I was caught in the family's slipstream, pulled to Helen's jazz dance class and Zach's football practice and Kent's weekly library visits for more and more books. Soon, the relay race was nothing more than a cute anecdote that everyone grew tired of hearing.

THE RACE

NO ONE HAS TOLD ME what it feels like, running at the front of a marathon. There's a surge behind me, a powerful force of energy rising and pushing: akin to panic, to the feeling of a large wave lifting you from the sea bed and threatening to drop you into the shallow water below, the whitewash pressing you down. For a moment I fear I might never escape the turbulence of the pack. My legs won't move the way I want them to. They're stiff and empty. The surge behind me swells larger, the excitement builds inside my chest—

I'm away. Feet on tarmac, through the last vestiges of fog. Boats anchored in the waters beside the start line bob on the incoming tide. We run towards Torpedo Bay. I smell fish. Across the harbour, the flickering lights of Auckland twinkle in the dawn. Strands of the fog curl around the Sky Tower's point. Someone nudges me, gently, as the group sorts itself into order at high speed. I take a moment. I can't let this fluster me. Take a breath through my nose, exhale. Trust my legs to find the pace.

The front pack is about thirty runners strong. Other runners trail from the end of the group, desperate to stay in touch with the leaders.

Long sinewy legs and bright racing sneakers flick in and out of my vision. Quickly the course turns left, away from the waterfront. In the window of an art gallery on the corner I catch a glimpse of the group: most are men, wiry and muscular in that lean way of professional runners. There's one guy to my right who's gasping a little, too flushed in the face this early on. Not even a kilometre in and he's made the mistake of trying to keep up. He's overestimated his fitness, and he'll be lucky to last the distance.

There are three other women in the front group. Two I don't know: one looks to be my age, early thirties, the other even older. Both have the same clenched jaw, the same concave chests. Ruby is the other woman, and she's the youngest. She wears only a sports bra and running shorts, her smooth, tanned torso exposed to the cool dawn air. Her blonde hair is braided in two long plaits, and she's running up with Dylan and Marcus, the three of them forming a line at the front of the group. It's clear from their timing, the relaxed lean of their shoulders, that they are comfortable running together there. They like to lead.

I know that I'm not a leader. I prefer to hunt.

The course curves up through the colonial streets of Cheltenham, past the rugby field and an empty kindergarten. A few hardy families are outside their houses, standing in the shadowy glow of pre-dawn. 'Go go go!' they shout. One woman shakes a tambourine.

The road weaves up and around past Fort Takapuna. There's a beach to the right, and across the water stands Rangitoto. Then up a hill and onto a long street where the leaders put on the first real taste of speed. Only a slight acceleration — they're already running well under 4-minute ks. It will take more than this to rattle me.

A left turn and there it is on the right, the first support station. My bottle's there, my water with electrolytes. I swerve to pick it up — drink, gulp — drop it to the ground. I think I hear someone calling my name. I don't turn to look.

It's right here that I realise Ryan isn't with me. He's not in the group. Is he behind me? Or in front? I can't remember the last time I saw him.

I keep running. There's no need to panic. I can do this by myself.

TWO

IT WAS A WET SATURDAY in September 2000, the rain falling in thick silver sheets. The first daffodils had opened only a few days earlier, and their bright-yellow trumpets now lay flat, collapsed under the ceaseless onslaught. We were waiting for Teddy. It was his first trip to Rutherford Street in three years. The twins had returned from university in Wellington especially, and the house was full of the clutter and noise I'd missed in the months since they'd left: Helen playing The White Stripes at an obscene volume, her architecture textbooks vibrating to the sounds of Jack White's insouciant twang; Kent's voice coming from another room, the novels from his English literature course piled up in the lounge. Zach and I sat twitching our thumbs. After lunch, Teddy had said, I'll arrive sometime after lunch.

It was already after lunch.

I heard Kent speaking to Bonnie in the kitchen: '—and then Trudy fell over the curb, and I said, Lady! Keep your feet on the floor and your eyes on the prize!' Zach didn't budge. He didn't seem to mind as much as I did that the twins seemed so different. Helen wore dark eye makeup and black boots, and Kent was constantly referencing people and places we didn't know.

Zach propped his feet on the coffee table. At eighteen he was over six feet tall, a giant beside me. I could see the door frame, the one where we'd marked our heights since the moment we could stand. Mine was way lower than his — 'Mickey' was printed next to a mark for 150 centimetres. For the past six months, I'd prayed for another growth spurt, one last gasp at height, but now I had to accept that this was it. I was short, minuscule — at fifteen, no bigger than many children much younger than me. So I wasn't only useless academically. I was too short for basketball, unwanted for any netball team. My thrilling win at the community athletics eight-and-a-half years earlier was nothing more than a whisper, a faded colour. It seemed that nothing special ever happened to me, and nothing ever would.

The day dragged on. The twins joined us in the lounge, and Kent held up a deck of cards, shaking them like a maraca. 'Want to play gin rummy?'

Kent dealt the round, slapping the ten cards to each person with quick hands.

'No cheating,' Helen said, and Kent let out a gasp. 'I don't cheat!'

Zach and I laughed. Helen shook her head, and said, 'Tell your lies to the man above, my friend. Ain't a person in this room believes a word you say.'

A sweet warmth filled me; life was so much better when we were all together.

We played two rounds. The rain didn't stop. Still no sign of Teddy.

'Do you think he's coming?' Helen asked, discarding a six of spades.

'Of course he's fucking coming!' Zach's mouth was set in a sulk, and he smacked down his hand and knocked the discard pile so that a fan of cards spilled over the carpet. Kent, Helen and I sat in silence, looking at his red face and shaking hand as he stood, gripping his Nokia phone, and stalked off to his room.

'Looks like someone misses his daddy,' Kent said then.

Bonnie's voice rang out from the kitchen. 'Before I get started on the corned beef, who'd like to help me make the custard?'

Corned beef. Silverside. I hated it — I called it 'suicide'. That hearty, fatty meat was Teddy's favourite meal. I wondered why she bothered trying to please the man who'd left her. Custard, though — custard I could get on board with. Mum made it from scratch. It was her favourite meal. 'Good for breakfast, good for lunch, and perfect for dinner,' she liked to say.

'I'll help,' I called back, and Helen threw down her cards in disgust.

'Dad's right,' she said. 'You can't commit to anything, Mickey. Not even one simple game of cards.'

THE CUSTARD WAS COOLING AND the rain set in even heavier. Zach came out from his room and turned on the television. Still no Teddy. He stood every ten minutes to check out the window.

'Got ants in your pants, Zachary?' Bonnie asked.

'Where is he?' Zach's voice was now a whine.

'He'll be here soon,' Bonnie said, though I could tell she was worried. She stood up and headed toward the kitchen. 'I'll get dinner on the table. Can't put our lives on hold just for one man, even if it is Teddy Bloom.'

The light leached from the day, leaving the lounge dim. The darkness suited the prickly feeling inside my stomach. Still no Teddy.

'Do you think he doesn't want to see us?' I asked Helen.

She turned from the television screen and squeezed my hand. 'Sure he wants to see us, Mick,' she said. 'He probably got caught up in roadworks around Mōkau.'

Helen and Kent followed Bonnie to the kitchen, and Zach went back to his bedroom, slamming the door. On the television, the six o'clock news started. Suddenly, headlights swept the room. A black car had pulled into the driveway. I stood on an angle at the window so I wouldn't be seen, and watched the windscreen wipers flick in a limping beat.

Teddy's face was aglow in the reflection of the headlights. His mouth was wide in a toothy grin. He held his cellphone to his ear with his shoulder, and as he spoke, his hands lifted from the wheel to gesticulate, his movements both graceful and emphatic.

After a moment, he put his phone down and killed the engine. When he climbed out of the car he glanced up at the house, his face set in a peculiar grimace, one I couldn't understand. I moved away from the window further into the darkness of the room, and heard Zach's bedroom door open. He rushed past me into the hallway, and I almost felt embarrassed for him showing such need.

I stood in the doorway between the lounge and the hall. Teddy opened the door without knocking. He shook his head, trying to dislodge the wet strands of hair that were stuck to his forehead. Drops flew all over our jackets in the hallway and onto the small canvas painting of the mountain that hung crooked above the light switch.

'Son—' He pulled Zach into his arms, closing his eyes, seemingly transported elsewhere through the touch. 'Getting tall there, boy,' he said, pulling away from Zach. 'I've still got an inch on you though.'

I pressed my thumbnail between my teeth. Teddy removed his wet coat and hung it on the rack beside the door, and water dripped from the sleeves to the floorboards. The kitchen door swung open, and Helen and Kent rushed out: 'Dad!' He held them close, slapped Kent on the back a few times, smiled at Zach again, and then turned to me. His tongue slid over his lower lip and he nodded. 'Michelle. Nice to see you.'

He was right there, and yet he couldn't have been further away. *Michelle.*

'Dad,' I said. 'It's Mickey. Come on.'

He gave a half-shrug. 'You're too old now for Mickey. Your grandmother always refused to shorten her name, and I can see why.

It's a beautiful name.'

He opened his arms to hug me. *Michelle*. I wanted to hug him, I did — but I couldn't. I extended my right hand. Teddy looked at it as though it were a snake, my palm its fanged mouth open to bite.

'All right,' he said. 'If you insist.' His hand was large, and wet from the rain. I tried to keep my hand strong and firm, like Mr Todd, my vertical form teacher, had shown me. Not limp and flat like a dead fish, he'd said.

The twins laughed and Kent said in a thin voice, 'You're shaking hands? What on earth!'

Teddy let go of my hand and looked at his fingers. 'What have you got on your hands, Michelle?' He wiped his hand on his jeans.

I didn't look at my hand, or wipe it. There was nothing there; he was making it up.

'Everyone calls me Mickey.' I needed him to understand. *Mickey*. I put my finger in my mouth again, cast the nail over the tooth, and bit. The rough blade cut into my gum.

Teddy sighed. 'Chill out, darling. I just want you to act your age.'

Bonnie came out of the kitchen then. 'Teddy,' she said. 'You're just in time for dinner.'

He scratched between his eyebrows and looked down at his feet. 'I think I might head over to the motel first,' he said. 'It was a long trip. Those roadworks through Mount Messenger, bloody hell. I need a Panadol and a beer and then I'll be back.'

'You could shower here, Dad,' Zach said.

I looked at my hand as they spoke. It seemed clean. I wiped it on my sweatshirt anyway, while no one was looking.

'We have paracetamol and bath towels,' Bonnie said. 'No need to rush off when you just got here.'

Helen took Teddy's hand, told him she'd drive to the shop down the road and buy him beer, and he said no, no, no. He wanted to go to the motel, and nothing we said could persuade him to stay.

I washed my hands in case he came back. I looked at myself in the mirror. A new pimple had erupted on my chin, red and vicious, and I turned away. Even though I knew for certain that my hands were now clean, there was a lingering feeling of dirtiness that I couldn't wash away.

AT 8.30 TEDDY HADN'T RETURNED. Bonnie dished up the dinner. Corned beef, potatoes with butter, mustard sauce. 'Never too late to eat a good meal,' she said, though it was terribly overcooked, the meat like rubber. The clock on the wall ticked in the spaces of quiet while we chewed, each sound an acknowledgement of a second passing. Zach ate quickly, knocking his fork to the floor. I picked at the food until Bonnie said we could leave the table.

The four of us sat in front of the television again. Two more hours passed, lost to mindless channel surfing. At 11 p.m. Bonnie said it was time for bed. 'At least for you two younger ones.'

Zach lifted his hand in the air and groaned. 'No!' he shouted. 'For fuck's sake. I don't need you telling me what to do anymore.' He kicked the couch, the way I'd done as a child. His foot almost hit my leg, and for a moment nobody spoke. I didn't move, uncertain of the right thing to do. I didn't know how to help him.

'Fine,' Bonnie said. 'You can stay up and wait all night if you want. I'm going to bed.'

Zach sat down on the carpet and stared at the television. I stayed with him for another minute. An advertisement for PAK'nSAVE turned the room yellow, and I left without saying goodnight.

WHEN I WOKE, THE LIGHT was blue under the curtain. It was too early to get up, only it was impossible to sleep again. I kept thinking of my father, and the feeling that had sat in my stomach when we shook hands. I recalled his face, the curled lip, as though he were disgusted by my body. I was still angry that he insisted on calling me Michelle, as if by language he could transform me into someone he wanted me to be.

Across the room Helen was sleeping, and I realised then how much I'd missed her, missed the sound of her breathing in the mornings while she dozed. Under the covers her body looked like hills, a series of curves and undulations, so different from how she'd looked under that same duvet as a child. I still found it awe-inspiring how our bodies could change simply with the passing of time.

I walked quietly to the kitchen for a drink. Through the doorway to the lounge I saw Zach asleep on the couch. His mouth was open, the muscles around his eyes relaxed. He looked younger, less like Teddy. More like our mum.

IT WAS STILL RAINING WHEN Teddy returned the next morning. He left his shoes on, tracking wet prints into the lounge, and he collapsed onto the couch next to Zach, their two large bodies taking all the space. I sat on the floor near their feet, fingering the pimple on my chin. The conversation wandered from books to rugby to living in Auckland, all topics I had no opinion about. Zach was moving to the city in the new year to start an electrician's apprenticeship, and he peppered Dad with questions about where he should live, did he need a car. I tuned out in spite: I didn't want Zach to leave. I wanted him to stay.

Bonnie came into the lounge with a coffee for Teddy, and he took it without thanks and sipped. She sat on the floor next to me and ran her fingers down my cheek. 'Are you feeling all right, honey?'

I nodded, then shrugged. I felt a churning of feelings, nothing explicit and yet everything all at once.

'What's that on your face, Michelle?' Teddy stared at me as though

I'd suddenly become visible — but for just the briefest of moments, because within seconds he glanced away, not waiting for an answer. He balled his hand into a fist and coughed into it. 'I've got something to tell you all. Kent, Helen, could you join us in the lounge room, please?'

I touched the pimple again. It felt tender and ready to erupt. It was disgusting. I was disgusting.

Helen came in and sat on the armrest beside Teddy, placing her hands on his shoulders. She looked so comfortable with him, and he with her.

Teddy cleared his throat and said, 'It probably won't surprise you to know that Sera and I have been talking about starting a family.' He looked from Zach, to Helen, and then smiled when his eyes met Kent's. I waited for him to look at me. He didn't. It was as if I wasn't there. *Starting a family,* he'd said, as though he hadn't already started that a long time ago. 'We're expecting our first child a few weeks before Christmas. It's exciting, we're excited. I think you should be excited too.'

'A baby?' Helen said. 'Dad, that is so cool!'

'It's a girl, Helen, you're going to get a sister.' Teddy took her hand in his, holding it carefully.

'She already has a sister,' I said. 'I'm her sister.'

'People are allowed to have more than one sister, Michelle,' Teddy said. 'Sera's doing great. The pregnancy's been easy so far, and we look forward to you all meeting her soon.'

'Congratulations, Ted,' Bonnie said. 'That's wonderful. Tell Sera to give me a call if she has any questions about children.' I felt as though I'd been slapped — Mum seemed happy for him. 'God knows I've had enough of them.'

'Will do.' Teddy clapped his hands on his knees.

They continued talking — Helen asking twenty questions a minute — and I glared at the television. My cheeks were hot. I was seething, and couldn't understand exactly what I was angry about. Another sibling — why should I mind? I loved my brothers and my sister. Now there'd be someone else to love. Only this child wouldn't live with me here in the house we grew up in. This child wouldn't eat the special custard made by Bonnie on Sunday mornings in the orange kitchen; it wouldn't follow trails of ants to their hole in the ground in the lawn out the back with me after school. It wouldn't learn to walk on the green linoleum floor like we all did. This child would live with Teddy.

'Aha!' Teddy shouted, pointing at the television screen. 'The Olympics! That's Sydney!' He launched into his old stories: how he'd lived there in his twenties, working at a small suburban newspaper, living in a house in Rose Bay. I fixed my eyes on the television, refusing to listen. The camera was high above the streets, and a man's voice said it was a warm, sunny 23 degrees, not optimum weather for a marathon.

Teddy laughed, then said, 'It's funny how I can't stand sports and yet every four years I can't get enough of the Olympics.' He began describing all the insider information the sports reporters at the *Herald* had relayed to him, hearsay about athletes and antics at the Village. Parties and condoms, boozing and fun.

Nothing he said interested me — but the women on the screen were mesmerising. They stood on a road in a group, all wearing white sneakers and brief two-piece outfits that exposed their long, lean thighs and taut stomachs. They shook their arms and adjusted their sunglasses and hats. Each had a number and name pinned to her top. The commentator mentioned the name of a Kenyan runner, Tegla Loroupe, and said she was considered the favourite. *She won London and Rome this year, and Berlin last year.* I didn't understand: had this woman won the cities? Or other Olympics? They were only every four years, weren't they? The group bunched together, their clothes a mix of blue and yellow and green and white and then—

The starter's gun sounded.

I was aware of everyone talking, and I sensed Mum climbing from the floor to prepare lunch. I didn't turn away from the screen once.

The women burst into movement.

The race wound down through North Sydney to the Harbour Bridge, and the woman in the lead, *Marleen Renders from Belgium,* led the group up the incline of the bridge, a grey clothes hanger slung over the silver-blue water. She had spindly arms and blonde hair, her running style jerky. Behind Marleen was a mass of white shoes, the feet of the other runners flickering, hovering, hunting.

The race was spellbinding. The camera switched back to the viewpoint high overhead. 'That's shot from a helicopter,' Teddy said. From above, the runners' legs criss-crossed like matchsticks, ready to spark a flame. There were no cars; the everyday world seemed to have stopped in that city, all to let them run. Flags fluttered along the side of the course, and occasionally a spectator would sprint alongside the competitors, only to fall away, unable to compare. These women were strong, undeterred by the heat and the distance. They were beautiful.

The bright, harsh glare of the Sydney light filled the room. Kent and Zach were still talking with Teddy about someone called Salman Rushdie. I blocked them out. I wanted to pretend I was in Sydney; I wanted to believe that I was there. In some strange way it seemed as though this magical race was happening to me. My heart was pumping, my skin was clammy with sweat. The drama of the race filled me with a nervous energy, and I felt odd. More alive.

By the twelfth kilometre, Renders was pulled back into the pack, and the dynamics shifted. Three Japanese athletes were now at the front, Eri Yamaguchi, Ari Ichihashi in her Olympic debut — *only twenty-two years old, 157 centimetres tall* — and Naoko Takahashi. They looked so tiny, like figurines. Takahashi wore sunglasses, and I wondered what she looked like without them. If I could see her eyes, would I be able to understand how she could run so fast?

Mexico, Romania, Australia, Ethiopia, Kenya, Japan — women

from all over the world, all running and racing together. Gritting their teeth and doing something immensely difficult, and not giving up. Their skeletons seemed almost visible, and the only curves on their bodies were those where the skin wrapped around their bones.

Takahashi has been training in Colorado, where the world's best runners go. Colorado, El Dorado, gold dust. An hour of the race passed, and Ichihashi strode out with Takahashi to the lead. She looked both fragile and unbreakable. I squinted my eyes and imagined it was me, moving up to the lead.

'You know, I could walk five kilometres in an hour if I was really putting my mind to it,' Bonnie said, coming back into the room with another coffee for Teddy. Helen laughed. 'Why would you want to do that, Mum?' I did the maths in my head, kilometre splits: these women were running 5 kilometres in about 17 minutes. I couldn't understand the pace they were going, how that might feel. I only understood the beauty of it. It almost looked as though they were flying.

I didn't move the whole race, even when Helen and the boys left to eat lunch. I stayed on the floor, my head tilted to the screen, basking in the light. It seemed impossible for anyone to run that far, it seemed otherworldly. And yet, there they were.

Two hours and 20 minutes later, Takahashi ran down the wide avenue to the Olympic stadium in Homebush. Crowds were massed along the balustrades, cheering and screaming, waving flags and signs. *The Olympic record is within reach,* the commentator said. *She came here saying she wanted to leave proof that she exists in this era.*

Maybe, I thought, maybe she felt the way I did: invisible, unreal.

Maybe she ran to feel seen.

The noise when Takahashi entered into the stadium must have been deafening. A prickling sensation ran down the back of my neck. Naoko Takahashi ran on, stretching out her legs to a wider stride, her elbows wide from her body, her mouth slightly open. She crossed the line in Olympic record time. The best in the world, the commentator said.

I turned around and looked at my father for the first time in hours. He was the only person still watching the race with me.

'Impressive, isn't it?' he said. 'Bloody impressive.'

We sat there for a few minutes in silence as the other runners entered the stadium.

'I'm going to do that,' I said, before the thought had even crystallised in my mind.

Teddy gave a short laugh and ruffled my hair. 'If you do that, Michelle, then I'm a father of a boy named Sue.'

THE RACE

WE LEAVE THE SUPPORT STATION and head down a slight hill. If I look up, I can see across Shoal Bay, the edge of the Harbour Bridge creeping into view. We'll be there soon enough. I remember Marleen Renders leading the pack over the Sydney bridge, alone in the front, her jerking style with arms swinging out and back, her red shorts and her blonde ponytail slapping her neck.

That day will remain with me forever. Fifteen years old, completely lost in the wilds of hormones and emotions — and then bang: that Sydney Olympic marathon changed my life. Here I am. Running a marathon. The city has stopped for us — roads are closed, the bridge is our domain. Is Teddy proud of me? Or am I a boy named Sue?

My throat feels dry, even though I've just drunk water. My feet clap on the pavement, and I sit in the tailwind of the leaders around the corner and into the straight of Lake Road. Ruby isn't too far ahead — close enough to reach out and touch — and Dylan sets the pace down past the grand building of Takapuna Grammar and up the hill to Esmonde Road. Huge pōhutukawa showing the first sprinkles of red lean over us.

Small groups of people line the course now. They clap and shout, but it's not enough. I want the overwhelming screams of a stadium. The enveloping wave of noise that brings tears to your eyes and makes every hair on your body zap and sting.

I wonder if Teddy is watching. You never know — he might be there somewhere along the course. He could be any one of these people, and I wouldn't even know. Quickly I scan the faces of onlookers. After a moment I realise I'm not looking for him. I'm looking for something else. Someone else.

The 6-kilometre sign looms. I'm properly warmed up now. Settled into the pace. It feels good to feel good. Nobody from the group has split off ahead or dropped back. Dylan's pace is steady — I could watch the beat of his orange Nikes all day. There's something in the curve of his neck to his shoulder, the graceful sweep of the muscle to the throat, that reminds me of Niall. The geometry of desire.

The sun grows higher in the east and thick yellow light pours over the world. More people take to the streets as we near Takapuna. A small brass band in multicoloured sombreros stands on the side of the road playing 'La Cucaracha'; further along, teenagers in white coveralls beat on bongo drums, the noise mimicking the thrum of my heart. The eyes of the crowd are glued to Dylan, Ruby and the rest of the group, including me — they know they're watching something special. Not your ordinary runners.

At first I feel overexposed. These people are judging, critiquing my movements, noting the way the cellulite ripples my thighs on the down step. Ruby's all sculpted muscle, model legs, unblemished skin. I can almost feel them surveying her body for what it looks like, not for what it can do, and the same for mine.

I need to get a grip. My body is just that: a body. Any body is a runner's body, it just needs to run. I tell myself to pull my focus back to the true moment: breathe through the nose, inhale to a count of four, exhale same length. Notice the things around me. The orange shoes in front; the burbling cheers from the crowd; the noises of the runners around me. I key into the feeling of my body moving through the air. Flick my eyes to the other two women running with us.

I relax my torso, keep my neck soft, my shoulders down. My legs swing and thump and push. I am dancing, I am flying, I am beauty.

THREE

I SAT ON THE DUSTY floor at the back of the school hall, surrounded by the entire Year 12 of Mangorei College — a rippling sea of green shorts and polo shirts. It was our Wednesday Physical Education class, and nearly ninety students sat waiting for our teacher to speak.

Mr Reihana clapped his hands. 'This term, our focus will be cross-country running.' He paused as the auditorium filled with a collective groan. 'We'll be training for five weeks. Race day will be July the first, and you'll race against the Year 13 students.'

My heart skipped a beat. I thought of the women flying, legs slicing the air as they crossed the Sydney Harbour Bridge, a vision of white and green and yellow under the soaring blue sky.

Someone in the crowd shouted, 'Five weeks of running? This is bullshit.'

Mr Reihana ignored them. In his low voice, he explained the course we would run that day. It would begin on the field, near the hall. We were to race twice around the field, clockwise, and then another half lap until we were on the far side, where we would exit through the gate between the trees and head down to the river. The river was normally out of bounds for students: there was a surge of whispered excitement at being allowed out of school grounds.

We'd cross the small footbridge there, Mr Reihana told us, and run along the path on the far side of the river for nearly three kilometres. When the path curved down to meet the river at a shallow point near the rapids, we were to cross through the cold, ice-melt water and then go up the riverbank to the farmer's field. You can take the stile, he said, or you can leap the fence. Your choice; please don't hurt yourselves. Run over the field, pass through the gap in the hedge that takes you back onto school grounds, and run alongside the swimming pool, down the footpath to the field, and there will be the finish line.

We headed outside to begin our first training run. As we set off, I stayed at the tail end of the group. My head felt tense, my breath short and shallow. I ran slowly, careful not to trip on the tree roots on the riverside path.

The water at the river crossing bubbled over mossy stones, and some of the students ahead of me stumbled and fell in. I hesitated before splashing to the other side, then glanced back over my shoulder. I wasn't coming last: I wasn't the worst. But I would need to go faster than this if I wanted to win.

Because that was what I wanted, even on that first day.

I wanted to win.

WE TRAINED FOR CROSS COUNTRY two days a week. It was unbelievable that this was school — I'd hated almost every moment of it till then, even PE. Hockey, volleyball, basketball, tennis: all horrible. Team sports were a misery, I'd decided, relieved that I'd been spared this hell as a child, when I'd begged and pleaded for my own after-school activities. The exception was swimming in term one when we were allowed to free swim in the manky concrete pool behind the home economics building. I loved floating in the water on a scorching day, diving to the bottom, the water in my ears, a sense of freedom from myself, from gravity, a delightful charade of weightlessness.

But no PE session was as bad as English. That term we were studying Shakespeare, and after cross-country practice I went straight to Mrs Ingalls' classroom. We sat at our desks with *King Lear* texts flat open before us, taking turns to read aloud.

'Michelle, you will be our Cordelia,' she said that day, fixing me with a pointed glare. There was no time to puzzle out the words in private, to navigate and understand the structure of the sentence so I could announce it clearly and eloquently — the two words Mrs Ingalls insisted describe our 'speaking aloud' voices.

I put my head down and started to read, the words coming out mangled and unintelligible.

'I love your … Mah, jesty, according to my duty as a daughter. No more, no less. My hon, honour … able lord, you have … con, conk, conkeev—'

'Conceived, dear,' said Mrs Ingalls loudly. 'The moment of conception in the uterus.'

Somone let out a hissing snigger. I took a deep breath, felt the burn of thirty pairs of eyes on me. 'Conceived me, raised … me up and loved me. I return those duties … as is fair — obey you, love you, and hon ... honour you entirely.'

Mrs Ingalls shook her head. 'That was … interesting, Michelle.'

A few people started giggling. I could feel my cheeks flush punch-red, and my hands started to tremble. I pushed the book off the desk and marched to the nearest open window. Holding onto the sill with clammy hands, I climbed out and dangled several metres from the ground.

'What in the lord's name do you think you're doing, Michelle, get back inside right now!'

I heard the whoops and hollers of the students — 'Go, Midget!' I dropped to the ground and ran home.

The house was damp with cold and too quiet: Bonnie was at work and Zach had moved to Auckland, the twins to Wellington. I wasn't sure if it was any better at home than it was at school.

ONE LUNCHTIME IN THE MIDDLE of June, a group of girls from my statistics class surrounded me, sitting too close, smiling too sweetly. One of them patted my hair, another fired off questions: How old are you? How tall are you? How much do you weigh? Have you had a boyfriend?

The cloying warmth of their bodies around me, the attentive looks: to be seen in a place where I was usually so unobserved was strange. I answered their questions, unsure of why they tittered and giggled. My words seemed to encourage them to ask other, more personal questions. Do you get your period? Have you had sex? Have you given anyone a blowjob? I picked up my lunch and walked away. Their attention wasn't what I'd thought it was, what I'd wished it was. A girl with thick lips and a dark mole above her right eyebrow tried to pull me back, pleading that I shouldn't be upset, it was only a question.

Truancy was a habit that was verging on addiction: no one could stop me leaving. I collected my bag from my locker and left school again. I wanted my mum, but she wasn't at home. She seldom was. A note sat on the kitchen table in Bonnie's writing: *Sorry honey. Taken an extra shift. I'll be home at 6.*

Bonnie seemed to be working more and more, despite having fewer children to keep. I needed her home right now. I hated being there alone: the sound of the second hand on the kitchen clock echoed through the silent rooms, and the cloudy day shrouded everything inside with bleakness. There was no music, no mess, no soul — it didn't feel like a home, just a house. I couldn't stay there a moment longer.

Returning to school was out of the question — I couldn't face those girls or another class with Mrs Ingalls. Mum wouldn't want me at the hospital, so I trudged across the sports field, where seven-year-old Mickey had streaked to her meaningless win, and then over the sand dune to the beach.

Near the point, a man was walking his dog, their bodies blurred in the thick salt spray. Above us, gulls walloped and glided in the wind gusts. I kicked sticks and stood on shells, breaking them until they were nothing more than tiny shards. Late-afternoon darkness seemed to leach in, filling my mind with ink. The wind picked up, the onshore blasts biting through my thin sweatshirt. Mum would be finished work soon. I was longing to see her, to be comforted by her, so I wiped my red eyes and went home.

The front door stood open. Mum was back early, and I thought then that everything would be okay. I sat on the front step and kicked off my sneakers. My right sock was wet and dirty, and I checked the shoe — there was a hole in the sole large enough for my pinkie finger to press through. If Mum was in a good mood, I could ask her for new running sneakers for the cross-country race.

A light was on in Bonnie's bedroom, pooling out into the darkened hallway. She was talking on the phone. I paused near her door. I could see her reflection in the dressing-table mirror. She sat on her bed, her slippered feet tapping the floor.

'As I said, I only called to see if you wanted Mickey to visit you in the holidays.' She ran a finger along her eyebrow. 'It's been a while since she saw Cleo, and she hasn't spoken to you in, what, six weeks?'

Teddy's voice was sharp and unexpectedly clear: 'What about a holiday programme? Don't send her up here.'

'Ted, come on. Why can't she come up? It would be good for both of you.'

I couldn't hear what he said next, but I heard him grunt, and then say, 'So you can spend all your time with that new man of yours?' I held my breath. Mum had a boyfriend?

Teddy continued: 'Get her a tutor, sort out her reading once and for all.'

When Mum spoke next, her voice was spiky with impatience. 'I've asked you to help pay for a tutor for years, Ted, so don't make out like this is my fault.'

'Never said it was your fault. Michelle's lazy. She doesn't know what it means to work hard. She needs some boundaries.'

I tongued the nail on my middle finger and bit down on the thick edge. Bonnie must have told him about what had happened in English, how I'd jumped out the window and wagged the afternoon classes. They didn't know I'd skipped off other days too, and I wasn't going to tell them.

Without waiting to hear what Bonnie said next, I ran out the front door. There was only one thing I wanted to do. I stuffed my feet into the tattered shoes and started running.

The sky was clear now, all the winter cloud blown away in the fresh-gusting breeze. A three-quarter moon sat plump over the horizon and the world was coated in its delicate silver light. I felt the asphalt on my foot through the hole in my shoe. It wasn't uncomfortable. I inhaled deeply, and the cool night air and adrenaline cascaded through my body.

I headed away from the beach this time, running in the direction of the hills that surrounded the town. I let my legs hang loose. My body seemed to fall through the darkness. The sound of my footsteps ricocheted back like gunshots. A woman who'd been out jogging had gone missing in these hills in the late eighties. Zach had told me about it, how her body was found lifeless in the dank bush, naked in the rotting leaves. It was stupid to be out there, sixteen years old and vulnerable. But I didn't want to stop. I ran away from everything, and towards everything. Running alone at night seemed no more dangerous than staying at home, listening to my parents talk about me.

At one stage I thought I heard steps on the road behind me, though every time I turned there was no one there. Faster I ran, longer, up into the dark hills, and nothing had ever felt so good.

I STARTED RUNNING AFTER SCHOOL. Before school. On the weekends. Always seeking that high, the clear mind that comes after the discomfort of exertion. Mum was rarely home — I presumed Teddy had been telling the truth: there was a new boyfriend she was hiding from me. Though it also seemed that life was crowding in around us, an eternal busyness that kept her occupied and distracted. There was never a quiet moment when she could ask where I was or what I was doing. I desperately wanted her to ask. I felt forgotten. *Don't forget the baby!*

At school on Monday and Thursday mornings, we ran no matter the weather. I relished any opportunity to be outside the classroom, to be on my feet. Mr Reihana waved us off each time: 'Enjoy!'

And I would. Even when the wind was biting cold or icy rain chopped down like knives I'd finish the run with beet-pink cheeks and a smile, my soul on fire. The pain of it was worth the joyous calm left in its wake. I wanted to run more, run longer, run faster.

Very soon I could. Day by day the runs became easier. On the training loops, fewer students were ahead of me around the course, and all of them were boys. They took their running seriously, pounding out the steps as though their lives depended on it. Their bodies were strong, well used to movement and action. They'd stomp past me through the river — unless I was passing them. On one training run in late June I overtook Nick, a boy from my biology class, and I heard him say softly, 'Fucking bitch.'

By the end of the five weeks of training, only one person in Year 12 could beat me around the course. Benji Jameson. We were in the same school house, Tupare, though we'd spoken only once or twice. I also knew him from English class; I'd felt his stare the many times I'd sat, centre of attention, grappling with the text. On the last Monday before the race, during our final training loop, I watched him run ahead of me. He had an easy gait, legs hooked slightly like a wishbone, arms relaxed at his sides, neck straight and head high. He ran as though he was born to do it. I was in awe of his talent. I wanted to run like that, exist like that: as though it was easy.

When I rounded the path beside the emptied swimming pool, I saw him standing alone at the finish line, half bent over, his hands on his knees. He lifted his head as I approached. He'd watched me as I struggled as Cordelia, but this felt different. Something more like respect. I stopped near him, and we stood together in silence for a moment.

'Have you been secretly training, Michelle?' he asked. His hair was matted with sweat. I could smell his body, that rough funky scent of teenage boys. It wasn't beautiful, yet there was something about it I liked. It was the smell of movement, mud, rivers. Things I liked. He brushed the hair from his forehead and said, 'You never used to run this fast.'

'What? No.' I didn't want anyone to know I'd been running after school, before school, all the time. It seemed desperate. Masculine. Girls at my school didn't run — they sat around at lunch break tanning their legs. My panting breath caught in my throat and I knelt, pretending to fix my shoelaces. When my lungs were calm and full, I stood and asked, 'Have *you* been training in secret, Benjamin?'

He straightened, leaning over me. He was almost a foot taller than me, and I had to tip my head up to see his face. There was a moment — only a flicker — when I wondered if I should feel scared of him, or if I should fall in love with him. But then other people started to run through the gap between the swimming pool and the hall, and on to the field, and he looked away.

'I don't know if you'd say it's a secret,' he said. 'I'm running cross country for Birchfield Athletics. You should think about joining us, if you're really this good.'

'Maybe.' I heard the way it sounded — flat and uninterested, a tone Teddy used when he spoke to me. A deadened tone that made me feel invisible and unimportant. I don't know why I answered Benji in that way, because even though I wasn't sure I understood what Birchfield Athletics was (or what it meant to run for them), if it meant more of this — the wind in my hair, my legs flying, the world flashing past — then of course I wanted to join. With the buzzing energy of the run still coursing through my veins and into my bones, I said quickly, 'You can call me Mickey.'

'Like the mouse?' He shook his head and let out a short laugh. 'Okay, if that's what you prefer.'

'That is what I prefer.' I wanted to scream then, make loud all the things I did prefer: racing through the air, my body in motion, no reading, no writing, no sitting at a desk. No boredom, no shame, nobody watching, nobody judging.

He didn't take his eyes from me. For a moment I wondered if he might ask, What else do you prefer? I felt enormous. The smell of him seemed to grow stronger. Apart from Zach and Kent, I was unused to being the object of male focus, and for once it wasn't about my height, or lack of it. Benji was looking at me as though he could see something else, something that no one had been aware of until then, not even me. One of the other boys, a pimpled kid with blue socks splattered with mud, bumped his shoulder into Benji and the moment was over.

I walked to the changing rooms, dragging my feet, ignoring the conversations of other runners, and pressed two fingers into the groove under my jaw. My heartbeat was slower than I thought it would be, the pressure gentle under the tips of my fingers.

A LIGHT DRIZZLE FELL ON the day of the race. Our shirts were coated in a speckle of wet as we stood on the field in a tense huddle near the starting line. I had come late from the changing rooms, and stood near the back. As I was trying to push my way nearer the front, a Year 13 boy leaned down and spat onto the ground near my feet and then looked up at me. It was obvious to me what he was thinking, what they were all thinking. I glanced around, waiting for someone to make a joke about me, or say something cruel, but no one was watching. They were focused on Mr Reihana. Only Christian caught my eye; he lifted his hand and gave me a thumbs-up. Someone elbowed my chest, pushing me back, so I stopped trying to move forward. They didn't know that I would soon be running past them, leaving them all behind.

From inside the huddle I couldn't see the spectators. Bonnie had said she would come if she could switch her shift with another nurse. I stood on my toes to look for her, and saw only a bobbing sea of umbrellas. Mr Reihana blew his whistle and explained a few course rules, but it was hard to concentrate on what he was saying. I thought I saw Benji standing at the front and was glad now that I wasn't up there with him. From here I could pick off the other runners one by one, move ahead, hunting my prey. Heat spread through my chest and stomach. It was as if I knew I would win, and the secret was an ember inside me.

'On your marks,' Mr Reihana shouted. 'Get set—' He lifted a small air horn. One second, two, then its blast drilled a spark down my spine. The group began to move, a seething multi-pedal beast. Feet on mud, the front line sprang out, the quicker runners making fast into the first loop of the field. I wove through the group, heading to the front, and by the end of the first loop I was in the top ten.

Temptation called like a siren: run out of my skin in the next loop, and make it out the gate before them all. But I held back. Kept my breath steady. There would be time to get ahead. There was a pleasure to be found here, following their steps, responding to the rhythm of the leading group. I passed a few more of the runners — the easy pickings — before they made it to the gate. The screams from the watching whānau quietened as we rounded to the gate, and then fell away as we crossed into the bush of the riverside.

The trail was lit by a pale light. I heard the rain pattering down on the leaves. Pīwakawaka flitted around and ahead of me, and the thin winter sunlight glinted off the green river water. Heavy rain in the past few days meant it was swollen high. It would be much higher for the crossing, possibly over my knees. I tried not to panic. There was still a long run to complete before then. I needed to focus on the present. Be careful not to slip and fall on the muddy track. Watch for the tree roots bending up, ready to pull you down.

Benji was in front of me, and four others ahead of him. The trail was too thin to pass there — it dropped away to the river on my right — and the thick undergrowth of the bush to my left kept us running single file. After all my secret training, the many afternoons I'd snuck down to run around and around this path, I knew the track like the creases on my palm — up ahead it twisted left and a kānuka grew isolated from the bush in the centre of the trail. The path split there, one side cleaving closer to the riverbank, the other curved around the kānuka to the left. That was my only real opportunity. There could be no mistakes, only quick feet, a brave heart.

There it was. The tree up ahead. I sped up, sitting right on Benji's heels. He and the other four boys all took the path that went straight, the path of least resistance, hugging to the water. I stepped left on my toes. Into the bend. Around the tree, onto the toes of my right foot and back into the straight. I almost collided with Benji, missing him by millimetres.

'Hey! Hey!' I felt the heat of his breath on my neck. 'Fucken watch yourself, Mickey!'

I said nothing, concentrating instead on my feet. One of the boys in front misstepped a chunky pōhutukawa root and sprawled over, legs wide. The boy behind him jumped clear and continued running. I did the same, leaping over him and landing back on the path.

'Get out of my way!' Benji shouted to the boy on the ground. It didn't matter. I could sense he had fallen off the pace, sulky and ego-bruised, losing the will to keep up. All because a girl got the better of him. His footsteps grew fainter. If I'd had breath to spare, I think I might have laughed.

There were three in front of me now. The river crossing would be the time to take another.

The slate-grey clouds let loose a spray of harder rain. It landed on my skin like a cool gauze. The leader increased the pace, I could feel it, the tempo registering deep in my bones. I wasn't bothered — I could run forever. The feet of the boy in front of me kicked up stones and mud, and I stepped back slightly so it didn't bounce up and hit my face. The trail veered imperceptibly to the right, and I prepared myself for the crossing.

The first boy splashed into the river with high knees. His name was Struan. He had vivid orange hair and arms sleeved in freckles. We'd built castles in the sandpit together as kids; there was a photograph of us sitting side by side in a kindergarten graduation picture. I hadn't spoken to him in years. The second boy entered the water — Trent. He had a long rat's tail that shimmered on his back as he ran. The flooded river water splashed up over their knees.

The third boy, the one I knew I must pass here in the water, was Hugo. He'd been Zach's friend for a while. They'd played Dungeons and Dragons in the lounge room on searing hot afternoons, their concentration so intense that not even a fly buzzing and landing on their hands could distract them. I watched him slow down in the river, unsure of his feet on the rocks. I trusted my feet, kept my pace quick. But the water was deeper than I'd expected, and I had to swing my hips wide to shift my feet forward. My sneakers filled and became heavy. I wasn't sure I could do it. The current was strong, pulling, pulling me.

A splash. A body in the water. Trent had slipped. He sat in the freezing green for a moment, then stood, the earthy-smelling river water gushing from his tee-shirt and shorts. Hugo slowed even more to watch him, some sort of zombie spectator. I didn't miss a beat, crossing the river, wet almost to my waist. Then I was out. I clambered up the opposite bank only seconds behind Struan.

My wet sneakers slipped on the muddy bank. The hole in my right shoe was bigger now — I felt the rocky trail through my sock. Struan lifted the pace once again. My heart thumped in my ears, in my eyes, my throat. My legs were tight and starting to tire, the wet socks and shoes a real burden now. I was in second place, so damned close to first.

We neared the stile. Struan was tall enough to vault the wire in an effortless leap, but on the landing he stumbled on the uneven paddock. I jumped to the high step of the stile and, with all my power, took off from the top and over into the paddock beside him. He straightened, and pumped his arms to pick up speed. Together we sprinted over the field, dodging crusted cow pats, aiming for the tree line that bordered the school.

I remember the sounds of our bodies working and moving in the rain: shoes squeaking on the long wet grass; his breath heaving in ragged and uneven bursts. The world felt vivid and disjointed, all my senses on hyper-alert.

Concentrate. The turn ahead favoured me — through the trees we would turn right, then along the footpath beside the Year 13 common room, alongside the swimming pool, and then, finally, onto the stretch of the field to the finishing line. There was such a short distance left, yet I might not be able to beat him.

But then the rain stopped, and a light wind blew on my face. A duck flew overhead, a drake, the emerald head bright against the steel sky. I could do it, I could.

We reached the trees at the same moment. I slipped through, tucking myself into the cramped space between Struan and the nearest trunk. My arm grazed on the bark. I was dimly aware of blood, scratches, but felt no pain. I was in the lead. I'd hunted, I'd caught my prey. Nothing but open space now between me and the finish line. Shouts and cheers reverberated in the space between the buildings, dipping into the hollow of the empty swimming pool, and I smiled.

The field was a kaleidoscope of coloured umbrellas. I pounded my arms, my legs. My brain screamed, telling me to stop, to give in, it was too hard. I didn't stop. I would never stop.

In those moments, there was only one other concern. Was Mum there? Had she come? Then I saw her — Bonnie's arms in the air. She stood in the rain with no umbrella, her hair plastered wet on her head. She was jumping up and down and shouting, 'Mickey! Mickey! Mickey!'

Mr Reihana held the finish tape on the far side. We were closing in on it. Struan was at my elbow. I heard the gutsy rumble of his inhale, the grunts he made too, as though the sound would make him faster. My legs burned. The metres flashed by, three to go, two, one, until I was there, at the tape, it was on my chest and breaking, and I ran through and fell to my knees.

Struan didn't look at me after he crossed the line. He lifted his arms and roared. He moved around in a shuffling victory dance, and it seemed as though he didn't care, or understand, that I'd won and he had come second. I wanted to tell him to give it a rest. But then Mum was there, helping me up from the ground. The world began to fall into place again, the colours dimming, the sounds quietening. I felt Bonnie's arms around me tighten. She rocked me from side to side.

Mr Reihana patted me on the back. 'Didn't know you had it in you, Mickey,' he said, and nodded to Bonnie. 'You should be proud of your daughter. She's at a bit of a physical disadvantage and she still pulled it out of the bag. I've not seen a performance like that in a long time, if ever.'

He stepped away to congratulate the other students. I looked at Mum, and was about to ask her what Mr Reihana meant by a physical disadvantage when I saw Benji walking towards me.

'That was some bolshie bullshit you pulled out there,' he said. 'So you going to join the club or what?'

I looked at Bonnie. 'Can I join the athletics club, Mum?'

Bonnie turned from me to Benji and gave a weak smile. 'Let me talk to your dad,' she said.

THE RACE

THE COURSE VEERS LEFT THROUGH the shops of Takapuna. Flashes of our reflection bounce along beside us in the darkened windows. There's a stillness to the group right now. The breath of the older woman comes in long sighs. Someone's shoes squeak as they hit the road. We're calm in this moment, though I know the pressure can pick up at any time. We turn left and head down to a roundabout. I grip my hands into relaxed fists and swing around, taking the corner as quickly as I can, my sneakers pressing on the tarmac, my body leaning into the turn and then righting as I career straight ahead.

Marcus is in the lead, his legs stretching out to longer strides. Ruby and Dylan sit behind him, their bodies moving in time. Then, up ahead, on the sideline, I spy a grey singlet, with red writing, and my breath catches in my throat. In a second we're past it, and I'm unsure if it said Birchfield Athletics or if it was simply a trick of the light.

I hear magpies in the trees, their melodic, fruity call high above the road. The air is cool on my face. I do a check on my body, a check on my feet: the new shoes worn in enough not to hurt, still full of bounce; the pink socks bringing me all the luck Niall promised they would.

No blisters. Even if I get them, I'll channel Allison Roe running the Tokyo Marathon in 1980. New shoes on her feet, gathering blisters that bled red on the road. Allison didn't stop running. I won't either.

Is that proof of my strength or my stupidity? The lies I've told to get here, the hurt that others have caused me: none of it matters right now. All that matters is this breath, this foot in front of the other. Nothing else exists in this moment but the next step. Not the future, not the past. Only this inhale, that exhale, the ceaseless beat of the heart.

FOUR

'NO,' MUM SAID. 'I'M SORRY. No more wagging, better marks, then maybe we can talk about you joining the club.'

I bit my fingernail with a savage rip. It was so unfair. My dream of running in a bright-coloured racing kit had shrivelled before it had time to blossom. I bit again, too far, and the sharp stinging pain of exposing the nail bed brought tears to my eyes.

'This is Dad's idea, isn't it? He's telling you to say no.'

Bonnie shook her head and put her hand on my shoulder. 'This is both of us, honey. We want you to succeed at school and we feel that joining athletics would be too much of a distraction.'

I stormed to the lounge and phoned Teddy. He didn't care for my reasoning, my pleading: he said my attitude was a piece of shit, excuse my language, and maybe they would reconsider next year if I showed some improvement at school. I hung up before he finished, and I saw Bonnie watching me, her face sad in the meek glow of the lamp. I didn't speak to her. The slam of my bedroom door was my only response.

I couldn't sleep that night. I blamed them, I blamed myself. They were doing what they thought was right, what was important, but I couldn't give up. I thought of Naoko Takahashi, and imagined myself in her place. Surrounded by the crowds, everyone cheering my name. I was the one whose dream was coming true.

The decision to lie came easily. I saw an advert in the local paper for people to deliver pamphlets. The idea came fully formed: I would tell Mum I was saving up to visit Helen in the holidays, but I would use the money to join the club.

'Are you sure it won't take up your homework time?' Mum said when I told her. 'There was a reason we said no to the running club.'

'You won't regret this,' I said, and gave her a hug. 'I can do it all.'

The following Monday, a man driving a dirty white van delivered the pamphlets to our house in large brown boxes. I was expected to have them in letterboxes by Thursday, so I spent the next few days folding supermarket pamphlets and Toy World flyers, placing them into bags for delivery along my route. The job was harder than I expected. It required a special technique to slot the wads of paper into letterboxes, and the weather hampered things too. On the fourth week of the job, in early September, clouds packed in dense and thick, and I trudged the streets soaked through, my skin soft to the bone. Both of my shoes now sported large holes, and my toes rubbed inside my damp socks, blisters threatening on the spongy skin. I tucked Mum's raincoat around me to keep the bag dry. My wet hands, clumsy and numb, fumbled with the papers. It was miserable. Still, I wouldn't give up. The reward would be the club, the running, the glory that I was certain awaited me.

There had been some glory already. After winning the cross country, my reputation at school shifted subtly. Kids began calling me Michelle instead of Midget; some of them even called me Mickey. Benji sat next to me in our English class. It was enough to spur me on. I kept running as often as I could, and when I wasn't running I was daydreaming about it: I envisioned myself older, stronger, fitter, flying.

Whenever I thought about the fact I was lying to my mum, keeping my plans a secret, I let this vision fill my mind instead, and the guilt subsided.

MRS BADDITCH, THE SCHOOL GUIDANCE counsellor, had an office next to the sports shed. Her room was cloudy with incense smoke, and the sunlight that made it through the dirty windows was sallow and green. She smiled when I came through the door. A thread of wool from her lilac mohair sweater was stuck to her lipstick.

'You must be Michelle,' she said. 'Come in, take a seat.' She gestured at a white plastic chair.

It was as uncomfortable as it looked, its hard grooves cutting into my legs. I scuffed my toes on the carpet — my legs were too short for my feet to reach the floor.

'Now, you're probably wondering why you're here, Michelle.' She held a pen that she jabbed in my direction with every word she said. 'Let me reassure you that you're not in any trouble. It's policy to bring in senior students to discuss their study choices to ensure a smooth transition to life post-school, and to talk about any other issues that might be troubling them.' She leaned forward and said in a loud whisper, 'I remember being a teenager. It's a tough gig.'

Mrs Badditch paused for a moment, as though waiting for me to respond. I had nothing to say to her. I felt sticky and restless, and I wanted to go outside.

Mrs Badditch sat back and reached for her computer mouse. With one touch the computer screen lit up. She replaced her reading glasses and peered at the screen. 'You've had a bit of a bumpy ride, I see. A few behaviour issues, minor truancy. Hmm, okay. Bit of a difficult year for you? Let's take a look at your load for this year, and then we can talk about the future.'

That was an understatement: a difficult year. There'd been too many changes, too much adjusting and altering. Zach leaving home, Bonnie's enigmatic boyfriend I wasn't sure existed, Cleo the sister I both hated and loved but who I hardly got to see. There was the feeling of my first crush, the weight of it like the name, the way the air pressed from me when I thought of Benji, or saw him. I was lying to my parents, saving money to do something they'd told me was not allowed.

I didn't tell her any of this. I looked down at my feet. A small electric heater clicked on, emitting stuffy warm air.

'Now, I can see you have a full NCEA Level One load. Great choices. English, biology, statistics, design, computing. What are you thoughts about your subjects for next year? I see you did well at the cross country. Would PE be something you might choose to explore next year?'

I kept my eyes on my shoes and bit my fingers, working in at the loose skin around the edge of the nails. I didn't want to think about what came next. Any answer seemed to be an agreement to endure another year of school.

'All right, then.' Mrs Badditch turned her body to face me. 'Why don't you tell me about what you want to do when you finish school?'

There was no mistake about what I wanted to do. 'I want to run in the Olympics.'

Mrs Badditch nodded, her chin bobbing up and down for too long, the brownish moss of her hair bouncing around, then her fleshy cheeks rounded in a smirk.

'That's a nice dream, my dear. What's your real plan? How are you going to pay the bills? And, statistically, most girls quit sports completely by the time they finish school, so it's a good idea to really give it some thought. Money doesn't grow on trees, I'm sure you've figured that out.'

Quit? I hadn't even begun running yet. This time next year I would be almost finished school for good, and this woman was suggesting I give up my dreams based on what, exactly: statistics? She kept talking — something about teachers college, polytech. 'Nursing,' she said. 'Have you considered nursing? What about beauty therapy?'

It was just noise, sound spewing from her mouth. Noise that had nothing to do with me. My neck tightened and I felt a flaming heat in my head.

I leaned forward. 'Why do they quit?'

Mrs Badditch removed her glasses and rubbed her eyes. The strand of wool on her lip wobbled when she spoke next. 'What was that, Michelle dear? I'm so sorry, I'm a bit deaf on this side.'

'My name is Mickey.' I pushed off the plastic seat, my feet now flat on the carpet. 'And I'm not quitting.'

She glanced back to the screen, squinting at my file. 'Well, I like your optimism. In all seriousness, you do need to consider your options. Life has a habit of upsetting even our strongest of intentions, and I'd hate to see you struggle in the future when we have an opportunity now to plan.'

BIRCHFIELD ATHLETICS' CLUBROOMS WERE NOT far from home, ten minutes if I cycled along the river path and cut through behind the strip of shops. In late October I rode my bike there. A man putting out empty crates behind the dairy looked up as I came through: 'Get out of here!' I pedalled harder, bouncing over the long tails dropped by the Norfolk pine overshadowing the lane. The scent of the roast shop made the air almost viscous, and my stomach twisted in hunger. I couldn't stop. I had something important to do.

The clubrooms were an old two-storey weatherboard building. Rust and lichen dotted the roof, and several windows on the second floor were broken. It looked derelict, though the sign above the door was new: *Birchfield Athletics Club, Est. 1955.*

Inside it was quiet. Sunlight filtered through the windows, making dust motes sparkle and dance in the beams. Rows of black-and-white photographs in dusty frames lined the walls, one for each year since 1955; further down the hall they shifted into colour. The very last photograph, with the year 2000 printed on the bottom, showed over a hundred people in the group, their faces tiny, almost blurry. I picked out Benji with ease, and felt my cheeks grow hot.

There would be another image soon, framed and hanging next to it, and I would be there too: part of the history of this place, part of something bigger than my family, my school. A whole world was opening up, welcoming me into the rest of my life.

'Hello, dear, can I help?'

I glanced around to see a square-shouldered woman sitting at a desk in one of the rooms off the hall.

Nerves pulled on my breath, and I could barely get the words out. 'I'm here to join the club?'

For a brief moment she gazed at me without speaking. I fingered the thumbnail on my right hand, but before I could lift it to my teeth, she smiled and asked for my birthday.

'Twenty-fifth of January.'

'And how old will you be on your next birthday, dear?' Her pen was poised above the membership form.

'I'll be seventeen.'

'Oh, you look a lot younger,' she said, winking. 'Could enter you in a different age group and you'd likely clean up. Ach, no point breaking the rules, I suppose. Are you track or field or both?'

All the things I didn't know swamped me — track, field, what that even meant. If only someone else could answer for me. Mum, or Zach. Even someone like Benji, someone who understood all this. There were footsteps then — I heard them, soft sounds from the hall. I turned, but there was no one there, only the rows of photographs, eyes and smiles following me down the hall. I took another step closer to the desk. The beginning of everything always starts with the first small step.

'Track,' I said. 'I'm a runner.'

'Righto, then,' and the woman passed me a form to fill out. Name, birthday, address, medical history. Events for competition: 100 metres, 200, 400. Eight hundred. Longer: 1,000, 1,500, a mile. Three thousand, 5,000, 10,000. Then came some words, and it took time to nut them out: hurdles, and another I wasn't sure I could understand — steeplechase? I thought I'd read it wrong, and glanced up. The woman was fiddling with her phone. I must have read it wrong. That was a horse race, wasn't it?

The numbers swam around on the page. Some were short, and others were long, and I had no idea what I should be doing. I closed my eyes briefly, and imagined the cross-country race again. The feeling of my chest burning, the kilometres ticking over. Pulling in the competitors one at a time. The list reappeared and I ticked the longest I could see: 10,000 metres. I slipped the clipboard back over the desk, and the woman looked up.

'You can choose more than one, dear.'

The paper in front of me again. I gripped the pen and ticked next to the 5,000, the 3,000. The woman flicked her eyes over the form again and nodded. 'Some big races for such a little girl. Are you sure you're going to be able to handle those distances?'

I pressed my tongue into the roof of my mouth so I wouldn't shout, and nodded. The Eftpos terminal lit up and I pulled my card through, punched in my PIN. That was my savings cleared out. Eleven weeks delivering pamphlets and my money was all gone. New shoes would have to wait.

The woman held out a grey singlet and red shorts. Across the singlet's chest the club name was printed in red letters. Birchfield Athletics. The material was silky to touch, and light. 'You can train and race in this,' she said. 'It should fit you.' She looked me up and down. 'It's the kids' sizing. If it's not right, bring it back and I can replace it. Here's a list of some of the other gear we have for sale too.'

The list was long, and I couldn't read it all. Shame throbbed in my temples and I chewed at the skin under my nails. *Sweatshirt,* I decoded haltingly, $80. How many pamphlets would I need to deliver to pay for that? To pay for the all other things on the list? Hundreds, maybe thousands. I looked down at my feet. I needed new sneakers more than a sweatshirt. As I walked away, the uniform scrunched into a ball under my arm, I wondered if the woman heard the sound my shoe made with each step, the left sole flapping on the hard wooden floorboards.

THE RACE

I INHALE DEEPLY THROUGH MY nose, taking the oxygen from the outside in. From my lungs to my blood to my muscles. This air, this very same air surrounding me and powering my body, once filled the lungs of all those who lived before me. How many people ran a marathon before I was even born? Thousands? Millions? At one point in time there were none, and then one person started it all.

We aren't far from the second support station. There's a buzz inside me, a feeling that it's all going well, it's all feeling good. Excitement about what's up ahead fizzes around my brain, spreading to my fingers and toes.

Ruby's body moves with a grace that's almost painful to watch. I don't want to lose her. Keep close to her, Philippa had said, so I do. I find myself cutting my eyes to Ruby again and again, studying the swing of her legs. She's not sweating yet; instead, her whole body glows with a golden light. I might feel good, but I know it's madness to pretend I have any chance of beating her. It's a good thing I'm a bit mad, then, I suppose.

We're cruising along together, the group moving in a bobbing mass through the streets. We're swerving left back onto Taharoto Road when I feel a clipping tap on my ankle. I glance down to see the laces on my left shoe have loosened. With another step, they undo completely and the shoe begins to soften around my foot. My heel lifts — and I almost step out of the shoe. Stumbling, I knock one of the women running beside me.

'Watch it.' Her voice comes like a hiss, and she doesn't take her eyes from the road ahead.

My foot slips out once more, and again I wobble, trying to keep the pace as well as ensure I don't lose the shoe. The laces tangle and my legs buckle. The man running behind me swerves and moves ahead, and I'm forced to stop.

There's never been so much pressure on a shoelace before. I thought I'd double-knotted it before I set off, I thought I'd checked the shoes before the starter's gun. My fingers feel thick and clumsy, as though they belong to someone else, and I'm working to perform the fine movements of over and pull, one loop, another loop, sweep one loop around the other and knot. I sense the seconds slither away, the leading pack edging out of my reach. Something as simple as a shoelace, only eight kilometres into the race, might be enough to derail it all.

The shoe is on my foot again; the laces are tight, too tight to let anything come between me and the road. Ruby's 50 metres ahead, 55.

I've caught up to the chasing pack when I get my legs going again. I set my lips into a line. Bugger it all — I kick into a gear I hadn't planned on reaching until much later. Hunting them down. Pulling them into my orbit, close enough for me to touch.

It's hard to catch this prey: they're professional runners. Olympians. They are used to being chased, and they know how to escape the hunter with ease. I push, legs starting to burn a bit, my chest filling with the fire of hard work.

Closer, closer, and then, there. I pull away from the chasing pack, and I'm near the leaders. Someone on the sideline calls out, 'Get it, girl!' and that's enough, that one lonely voice ringing in my ears, to get me into the leading pack once more. I pull in and take a moment to let my breath steady, my heart rate soften. In a few seconds, I've settled into the rhythm of the group and I'm fine. I'm still here, uninjured. I'm still in the race.

Up ahead: the second support station. Hilary's there, next to the table covered in cups, her lips drawn into an anxious grimace, though her face relaxes into a smile when she sees me coming along with the leaders. 'One gel, like you said.' She reaches out and passes me a salted caramel gel sachet. Dylan stops for a moment to drink and talk to his support crew. The rest of us keep moving. Hilary yells out behind me, 'Own it, Mickey!'

FIVE

ONE LIE LED TO ANOTHER. On the evenings when I wanted to go out running and Mum was home, I lied. I told Bonnie I was going to the dairy to buy lollies, or to Christian's house to hang out, even though I'd not spent time with him for most of the past year.

At the start of November, I told Bonnie I was going to the beach after school and felt the familiar thrill of lying laced with guilt. Part of me wished she could tell I was lying, the way she had when I was little. When she knew me better than anyone else. She didn't notice: she simply nodded and said she would be out as well — dinner with a friend. I couldn't tell if she was lying too.

Instead of heading to the beach, I rode to the athletics club, the new uniform stuffed in my backpack, old shoes on my feet. I cycled down the shortcut behind the shops, over the lumpy Norfolk pine tails. The old man wasn't there this time, only the stack of crates and some faded newspaper rustling in the breeze. It had been an unseasonably warm start to the summer, and the sun was striking white through the patchy clouds. I took my time locking my bike. Now I was here, I didn't want to go inside.

The clubrooms were deserted. It was bizarre: I'd expected buzz, people arriving in their running gear, a sense of purpose. The square-shouldered woman was nowhere to be seen. Nor was there anyone in the changing rooms. I put my bag down, heard footsteps, but no one came in. I changed into my Birchfield singlet and shorts, and went outside.

A line of trees stood sentinel at the far end of the tangerine-coloured track. The white lines of the lanes were stark on the orange, and a stack of hurdles sat square and intimidating on the outside lane. Inside the track the grass was lush and knotted with weeds. Three people stood there, a teenage boy and girl, and a young-looking man. Blond hair swept up from his face. He had legs with muscles like a diagram on a doctor's wall. Perfect posture, his neck long. I'd never seen anyone stand like that before, hadn't seen a body make that shape. Comfortable and confident. He looked at me, and continued his conversation. The girl kicked her legs up as though she were doing the cancan, her shorts riding up high on her hip, and I turned away. It seemed private somehow, and my neck felt stiff. Someone called my name from inside, and I turned around.

'Come on.' It was Benji. He wore the same kit as me, the red shorts, the grey singlet. Together we looked like Schwarzenegger and De Vito in *Twins*. He glanced down at my feet. 'Nice shoes.'

INSIDE THE CLUBROOMS, OTHER KIDS my age stood around talking. Aside from Benji, I knew none of them. No one looked at me, and I bit my nail in disappointment. I'd imagined this might be the place where I'd fit in.

It wasn't just that everyone was taller than me. That wasn't unusual, though it still made me feel out of place. Their skin glowed fresh with beauty and youth and health. When someone did glance my way, taking in my height, my long unbrushed hair, my old dirty shoes, I felt my neck tighten, my stomach pressing into my throat. I needed a drink of water. I felt conspicuous and invisible at the same time.

I found a seat near the door, and smiled at a group of nearby girls. They were talking about people I didn't know, discussing their wardrobe and their dog and their boat. All of them wore makeup — lip gloss and mascara, two of them thick foundation like cake icing. Several of them had their hair plaited into elaborate patterns, the ends of the braids snaking down their backs, and although they wore the same uniform, they didn't look as though they should be on the same team as me. Their tee-shirts curved to fit their bodies; mine hung loose on my narrow chest. Eventually, one of the girls turned to me and said, 'You know this is the under-19 training.'

'I know. Thanks.'

She smiled. 'I mean, are you supposed to be in the under-14 group? I think they train tomorrow.'

Before I could answer, the blond man I'd seen on the track came in. The kids stopped talking and looked up at him as he went over to a whiteboard at one end of the room. He looked relaxed, tanned and smooth. I recognised him then. Daniel Merriweather. I'd watched him run at the Manchester Commonwealth Games only a few months ago, the 5,000 and the 10,000 metres, and he'd competed at the Sydney Olympics too, though I didn't recall seeing his race. His body had seemed so small on the TV screen. In real life he was luminous, bigger and stronger than I'd imagined. I understood the awed silence in the room now. He was the real thing.

He spoke slowly without pausing. The summer ahead, he said, would follow a training schedule like this — and he started writing on the board with a blue marker, detailing runs and drills, using words I didn't understand. A-skips. Tempo. VO2 max. Dynamic stretching routines. Foam rolling. He wrote down the rules he expected us to abide by while at the club and at competitions. No smoking, no drinking, no drugs.

The season would run as follows: interclub meets around the Taranaki region, before the North Island Colgate Games in January and then, at the end of April, the National Track and Field Championships. The list of events trailed down the board, each one another opportunity for deceit. I ripped off the edge of my thumbnail and gnawed at the skin. How would I go to all of these events, most of them on the weekends? I could never pay for it all, the entry fees, the travel, let alone how to get there. Sneakers, too — I couldn't race in these things. There was blood in my mouth; I'd bitten too hard.

Then Daniel told us to stand, and run five laps of the track to warm up. I waited, watching the other kids leave. I wanted to run at the back and figure out how it all worked. I'd never run on a track before, didn't even know which direction to go. I'd imagined this would be different somehow, easier.

Daniel followed the last of the kids out and paused at the door beside me. He smiled, and said, 'Are you training with us today?'

'Yes,' I whispered.

He looked down at my feet. He went to speak, then stopped. After a moment, he said, 'Let's go then.'

THEY WERE FAST, BUT I was surprised they weren't faster. We ran as a group, legs moving in synchrony, five laps around the track. I hovered near the back. The pace wasn't out of my reach but I was happy to watch the others. The muscles in the shoulders of the leading boys looked clenched tight, their arms stiff and bent at perfect 45-degree angles. The group of girls I'd sat near in the clubrooms were between me and the leading boys. I watched their braids flicking around, curling up as though animated themselves. Next to me, a boy with ruddy cheeks panted; he was obviously unfit. Yet it was clear he wasn't going to slip behind without a fight.

Five laps finished and we stopped. A group of older athletes were setting up the high jump in the grassy centre of the track. Two boys who had gone to school with Zach were there, and one of them waved when he saw me. I waved back. Would he tell Zach I had been there?

'Is that your boyfriend?' one of the beautiful girls said.

'No,' I said. 'He knows my brother.'

'Oh, right. I didn't think he looked like a paedophile.'

I wasn't sure I'd heard her properly. A paedophile? She didn't laugh, so it wasn't a joke. I watched her face until she turned back to Daniel. Half the group would stay with Stacy, he said, and he pointed to the girl I'd seen him with on the track earlier. That group would stay here and do some shorter track training. He read off a list of names. I wasn't one of them. 'You're the sprinters,' he said. 'And the sprinters will stay with Stacy. The rest of you are coming with me.'

I followed him out onto the road. We were to run a four-kilometre loop around the streets and back to the clubrooms. An easy one to get started, he said. I tucked in behind him at the front of the pack, my cadence four steps for his two. Footsteps clapped behind me — other runners who wanted to be there next to him, as though his achievements would melt out with his sweat and transfer to us. I didn't slow or move out of their way. Someone clipped my heels, pushed their shoulders into me. I didn't give in: I wanted to stay close to Daniel. I wanted to learn how to run like he did.

AFTER THE RUN, DANIEL LED us through a short stretching routine. Hamstrings, quads, glutes, calves, hip flexors. I didn't usually spend time stretching, and I watched the others so serious in the business of legs akimbo, bodies like pretzel bites. It seemed important to them, a ritual. Afterwards, most of the athletes wandered inside to shower and change. I stayed sitting on the clubroom steps, looking at the flapping heel of my sneakers, trying to figure a way I could buy new shoes. It was past six o'clock, and the evening chill hung lightly in the air. My legs ached, in a good way, fatigued from use, and my body felt calm. I would find a way to go to some of the competitions. I would sell something or hitchhike. I'd lie.

Daniel sat next to me and said, 'You're a good runner. The fastest girl in the bunch, I think.' He tipped his head to the side and gave a half smile. 'I admit I didn't think you'd be up to much. How old are you?'

'Sixteen. I'll be seventeen in January.' I stood and he did too.

He gestured at a girl walking down the street, away from the club. She was the one who'd made the weird paedophile comment. Her backpack was slung over one shoulder and she was talking with some of the boys. Benji was with them, laughing, his hands in his pockets. Seeing them together filled me with a peculiar, thrumming pressure.

'Emma's your age,' Daniel said. 'She raced with me last summer. If you have any questions, ask her.'

'Okay,' I said. I had so many questions, though I knew I would never ask her. 'I don't even know what races I should compete in.'

'I think you should focus on the 10,000, and also race the five. You'll have to race with older girls in the longer distances but I think you can handle it. You aren't a sprinter — can see that from your body. Hurdles would be a hiding to nothing for you. How much do you weigh?'

I didn't know why that mattered. He was looking directly at me, this Olympian, so I assumed it must be important. 'Forty kilos.'

'Speed is all about the strength-to-weight ratio,' he said. 'We need to get you stronger as well as lighter. You'll need to get to a gym and do some strength work.'

I took my bag and walked with him down the steps. The street was quiet and still. Everyone else had gone home. His arm touched mine and he moved away, clearing his throat. Then he said, 'Michelle, you must know you're at a disadvantage. Longer legs mean longer strides — that's just physics. You're going to have to work twice as hard. If you can do it, if you can do everything I ask you to do, you might be a great runner.'

A great runner. I wanted to be the best. I would do anything, everything he asked. I thought of the long lean line of Emma's legs, the way she glided around the track. Her perfect face, the long braids flicking back like whips. I could beat her. I knew it, somehow I did. I turned to Daniel and said, 'My name is Mickey Bloom.'

'Mickey Bloom,' he said. 'It's a pleasure to meet you.'

I rode home along the streets I'd just run, streets I'd known all my life, and perhaps it was a trick of the light but they looked different. Longer, wider. I saw new opportunity in them: an invitation to run. Back over the bumpy monkey tails, standing on the pedals, past the dairy and the roast shop, along the river path where ducklings trailed their mother in the lazy green current, and home to Rutherford Street. I assumed it would be another long night watching television by myself, but Bonnie was there, waiting for me. 'My shift at work changed at the last minute,' she explained. 'So I've made us a proper dinner!' A roast chicken with crispy spuds and minted peas, a chocolate pudding for dessert. It was almost perfect, the two of us together, and I wished I could tell her all about my first night at Birchfield Athletics. When she asked about my afternoon, I told her I was delivering pamphlets, another lie to fold into all the others.

THREE WEEKS INTO THE TRAINING, Daniel told us to stay late for a special workshop. Twenty-three of us sprawled over chairs or flat on the floor, freshly showered and lethargic. Through the windows, strands of pink sky slipped into darkness. The square-shouldered woman from the reception popped her head into the room and told Daniel she was leaving now and he would need to lock up.

'All good, Ngaire.' He stuck a laminated caricature of two people — one stick-slim, the other bloated and round — to the side of the whiteboard, then turned to face us. 'I'm not a nutritionist. I'm not a dietitian. But I do have the experience of training as an elite athlete for over a decade, and I didn't get through that time without understanding how to fuel my body. I'm sure you'll all be familiar with the food pyramid.'

He handed out computer printouts, diagrams and information boxes, line drawings of figures and foods, fact sheets detailing fats and proteins of common foods. Some of the kids didn't look at the sheets, others slid them into notebooks and scribbled down every word he said. It was all the girls writing frantically; none of the boys. He drew a basic pyramid on the whiteboard and punched the pen tip into the sliced triangle: 'Carbohydrates, vegetables, fruits. Your proteins — meat, fish, eggs, tofu. Milks, cheeses. Oils, salts, sugars, fats.'

The lecture continued. Kilojoules, calories, sodium, sugar.

'What you eat is important,' he said. 'And how much. Let's shine a light on this, so you can all feel informed before you prepare a meal.'

A boy near the front covered his mouth and called out, 'It's all right, coach. Got the girls to do that for us.' There was muted laughter, and I saw Benji had joined in. I felt hot and irritated at both him and the joke.

'Moving on,' Daniel said. 'Some of you could do with losing a few kilograms. Not going to lie. Keeping in shape is part of your job as an athlete. Especially important if you're a runner. A five percent reduction in your weight will improve your racing times, and it makes sense that a greater increase in weight reduction will lead to greater speeds across longer distances.' He looked at us, pen raised in the air. 'Now, who can tell me what they understand in terms of your diet and your energy availability?'

The information came like a tidal wave. I sucked at the words, frantic to remember them — I knew I would never spend time deciphering the printouts. Daniel stalked around the room. 'With each impact,' he said, 'each footstep, your joints — your hips, your knees, your ankles, your feet — will bear the full force of body weight and acceleration.'

I understood what he was saying. There was a direct correlation between the weight of your body and how fast you could move it and the stress of impact on your joints. I saw that running wasn't separate from life, from my body. It was connected. Running with my legs changed my mind, my heart, my metabolism, my joints. My whole body began to feel soft and wide, as though it were slipping outside of the boundaries of my skin. No one else seemed uncomfortable.

I also knew what Daniel was really trying to say. Lighter meant faster. Be as light as possible. I would lose weight until my body almost lifted from the ground.

SIX

I PULLED AT THE HEM of a polyester navy dress. It was too short, and the cheap fabric chafed my skin. My whole body felt scratchy, though I knew it wasn't just because of the dress. 'I should've worn jeans,' I said to Bonnie.

We were sitting in a bar in town that Helen and Kent had hired for their twenty-first birthday party. We were early — the twins wanted to be sure everything was ready before the guests arrived. I watched them fidget as they discussed the bar tab with the wait staff, and then saw them argue as they moved the birthday cake to the other corner of the room.

They'd come home a few weeks earlier, filling the house with noise and fizzing excitement for both the party and Christmas, which was only a week away. They talked about the party all the time, what canapés to serve, what music to put on the playlist. Helen's stereo blared at all hours, and Kent sat in the kitchen drinking coffee, pretending to read the palm of whoever sat down next to him. 'I see great adversity in your life, Mick,' he said, holding my hand tight in his, running his finger over the lines. 'Many people coming and going, and two great loves. Very interesting.'

At training two days earlier, breathless and red-cheeked from a sprint around the track, I had invited Benji to come, even though I wasn't sure it was a good idea. Now a nest of nerves laced itself into my chest at the thought of him meeting my family. Meeting Teddy. But how bad could it be? I was sixteen, no longer a baby. I could handle myself.

I tugged at the hem again, regretting the dress. 'You would've been too hot in jeans,' Bonnie said. 'You look nice! Come on, I'll get you a fizzy drink.'

Guests began arriving, strangers from Wellington in black dresses and boots and jeans, and I gave Mum a look. *See, jeans.*

My aunt Marguerite, Teddy's sister, jostled in with her children, my cousins Franca, Lukas and Hans. Zach came late with Riley, his new girlfriend. He approached Bonnie with a shy smile, and introduced her to us quietly. He hugged me, and it was unexpected. He seemed even taller, and wider, more like a man, and he smelled different, a new cologne, and I snuck glances at him, trying to see the brother I remembered. I didn't feel like I'd changed at all. I still looked like a child. I still felt like a child.

The room filled up, and the walls bounced back snatches of burbling conversation. The staff opened the wide doors into the private garden at the far end. I couldn't see Benji anywhere, so I sent him a text.

r u coming

There was no answer. Music started playing over the bar's speaker system: the Sugababes, their saccharine voices gritty through the cheap speakers. I heard Helen say, 'He's here!'

I'm not sure why I thought she meant Benji, but I was confused for a moment when I looked up and saw Teddy. He wore a red-striped shirt, and his dark thick hair was curled around his face. He hugged the twins, and went on for a while about how it seemed impossible that a young man like himself could have such old kids. He shook Zach's hand, then Riley's, before he put a rigid arm around my shoulders. 'How are you, Michelle?'

I ignored the question. He peered at me over the top of his glasses. I would answer him when he called me by my name.

Bonnie hugged him and said, 'Nice of you to come, Ted. How's Cleo?' Teddy took his phone from his pocket and flipped it open, showing Bonnie and Helen small grainy photographs of a baby's face. I leaned in, too, thinking how odd it was to be looking at this small person on the screen of a phone. She was related to me, and yet I didn't really know her.

My phone buzzed: **I'm inside. Where you at?**

I spun around. I was surrounded by a wall of bodies — the twins had a lot of friends — but when someone shifted slightly I saw him by the entrance to the bar. He stood stooped, his face to his phone and fingers tapping out a message. He didn't notice me walk up to him.

'Thanks for coming,' I said.

He looked up. 'Mickey, hi. Cool party.'

'Come and meet my family,' I said, beckoning him to follow.

Benji was taller than both Kent and Teddy, who looked at him with his jaw set. Helen's boyfriend Bryn hovered on the periphery of the group. He pushed his dark glasses up his nose with one finger and reached out to shake Benji's hand. 'Welcome to the family,' he said.

Benji hitched his mouth to a crooked smile and gave me a confused look. I grabbed Bonnie's hand. 'Mum, this is Benji.'

Bonnie turned away from Teddy's phone. 'Lovely to meet you, Benji, ' she said, raising her eyebrows at me. Teddy stuck out his hand: 'I'm Teddy. I didn't know Michelle had invited a friend.'

'Michelle?' Benji looked from Teddy to me, and laughed.

'Dad, it's Mickey.' I pulled at the hem of the dress again.

Helen gave me a small smile and Bryn pushed his glasses again.

'It's Michelle, that's what we named you, I'm pretty sure. Are you going to introduce us properly, Michelle?'

I gestured at Benji, and then at my father. 'Dad, this is Benji. Benji, this is Teddy, my father.'

Teddy nodded, a dreamy haze in his eyes, as though he was thinking about something else for a moment. 'So Benji, how do you know Michelle?'

Benji shuffled his feet. 'We're at school together,' he said. 'And athletics. We both run the 10,000 metres.'

Teddy's smile was toothy, quizzical. 'Athletics? Michelle doesn't do athletics.'

Bonnie put a hand on my shoulder. 'I'm sure it's fine, Ted,' she said softly.

'No, it's not fine.' He pointed a finger at Benji. 'What do you mean?'

'I meant what I said, man. She's at Birchfield with me. She's a bloody good runner. Our coach thinks she might podium at nationals this year.'

Teddy's face flushed red, his cheeks shiny and tight. He still held his phone, its screen showing Cleo's pudgy cheeks. Helen said, 'Benji, why don't I get you a drink?' She led him away from our parents to the bar. I wanted to follow them but Teddy's glare held me in place. Bryn gave me a quick shrug and followed my sister.

Bonnie brushed some hair from my face, and said, 'Is there something you want to tell us, Mickey?'

My first instinct was to lie, but deception was exhausting. It was time to confess. 'I joined the athletics club.'

'When? How?' Teddy's voice was loud and brassy. Other guests turned to watch. Bonnie let out a small sigh. It was the quietest, softest sigh, a mere exhale of air, and at the sound I felt ashamed of myself, of all the lies.

'In October,' I said. I pulled on the dress again. It was too short, too tight. 'I saved the money from my pamphlet delivery job.'

Teddy yelled 'Aha!' and stabbed his finger at me. 'You little sneak,' he said. 'You lying little rat.'

'Teddy,' Bonnie said. 'Don't be nasty.'

'She's been bloody lying to us, Bon,' Teddy said. He ran a hand quickly through his hair, and leaned over Bonnie to the bar. He snatched up a beer and sculled most of it in one gulp, the foam sticking to his upper lip. I started to walk away, and he pulled me back: 'Don't you walk away from me!'

'Or what?' I said. 'What are you going to do?'

He set down the beer glass and said, 'You're never going to get anywhere with that attitude. You're a bloody embarrassment.'

They both looked at me, their eyes hooded with disappointment. The whole room pixellated, colours and shapes fragmenting. I pushed away from Mum, away from Teddy. Benji and Zach and the others were there somewhere — I needed to find them. I circled the room. Where were they? Crowds of people and no one I knew. I found my way to the front door. Someone had smashed a bottle outside, and the shards of glass sparkled on the footpath like a night sky.

I don't know how long I sat out there. Long enough to wish I could start the night again and avoid that confrontation. The argument replayed in my mind, Bonnie's barely audible sigh of regret and disappointment growing louder in my memory. I didn't regret joining the club, not for a moment. In fact it was the only good thing that had happened to me in a long time. If only I could take back all the lies.

It was fully dark by the time Benji came looking for me.

'I thought you'd left me there to deal with your crazy family alone,' he said, sitting down beside me on the footpath. 'What're you doing out here?'

'Don't know,' I said, and gave a dry laugh. 'It's more fun out here.'

He smelled good — like leather and something sweet. I looked at him, careful not to stare. He was beautiful. Right then, all I wanted was for him to feel that way about me.

'You look good,' I said. 'You look better in your Birchfield kit though.'

He shrugged and shuffled his feet, kicking some of the glass. 'You look pretty good, too,' he said. 'You know, if your boobs were five times bigger, you'd actually have quite a nice figure.'

I put a hand on my chest, into the skin and bone of my body, and through the dress came the sickly, pulsating thud of my heart. He smiled. What he'd said was so cruel in its casualness that I wasn't sure he realised the impact of his words.

'Do you want to go back inside?' He gestured to the door of the bar.

'I'll be back soon,' I said. 'I'll meet you in there.' I left him sitting on the curb, streetlight pooling around his feet, music and laughter rising from the bar behind him.

I was wearing my school shoes, black Roman sandals. They weren't built for running, but they couldn't be any worse than the sneakers with the holes and the flapping sole. I started to run. First, I went towards home, then I changed my mind, turning up towards the hills. I ran until I was sweating, the dress material clinging to my skin. I wanted it to hurt, so I ran faster, faster. With no one there to see, I could almost convince myself that I wasn't crying.

THE RACE

THE BRISK CHILL OF THE early morning simmers off in the sunlight, though it's still crisp. Not a hint of wind and, above us, delicate wisps of thin silken clouds stream and converge on the horizon. Marathon weather. I glance up now and then, taking the land out of my line of sight, and for a second I can pretend I'm flying, revelling in that sense of unreality I always experience when the run feels this good.

I'm old enough now, and wise enough, to know it doesn't always feel good, yet you do it anyway. That's life, isn't it? What did Philippa say the other night? *Marathons are like life. A lot of it will be shit, more of it than you thought you could tolerate. But I bet you, when it's over, you'll say, 'Goddamn. Can I do that again?'*

We run as a pack along the bus lane, the Harbour Bridge in our sights. A drumming group has set up between the motorway and the ocean. The percussion bounces across glass-like water that mirrors the endless sky above, and then bounces back.

The group hasn't split much, with only a small gap between the front seven runners and the rest clinging on behind. I'm tucked in behind Marcus, Ruby and Dylan, who take turns in the lead. Two men I don't know sit right behind my shoulders, sometimes running close, too close. I imagine they want to intimidate me and assume this would be easy, given that their elbows are near my ears, and for every two of their steps I take four.

They know nothing about me. About what I can endure.

There's not another support station until the other side of the bridge, and it's a clear and smooth run now, no sharp turns, only the gentle incline of the bridge and the sloping downhill to the city side. The pace of the group picks up a notch. I don't need to check my watch to know. My body's attuned to the RPE. I detect the change, sensitive as a metronome.

Philippa told me she'd be at the support stations at 29 kilometres and across the road when I return at 33 kilometres. From here, I can almost see that point — how the bays hook around into the harbour. Bastion Point and Achilles Point jut out into the blue. Beyond that, Browns Island, and then Motuihe. The faint grey is Waiheke, and beyond that the cresting ridge of the Coromandel in faded blue. I admire the view for a second, the rising ridges of the land above water, and then my eyes are back on the road.

I feel obscenely perfect, as though I could run forever. What did Niall say to me the other day? *Everything was beautiful and nothing hurt.* That's Vonnegut, he said, and I told him my father would freak out if he knew his daughter was discussing Vonnegut with a poet. Right now, those words are exactly right. Everything is beautiful, nothing hurts.

The uphill takes us over the white roofs of the Northcote Point villas, and then higher, into the sky, into the sweet air close to the clouds. Here, this is it, the magic: legs strong and powerful, feet feeling light, torso soft, arms swinging with relaxed shoulders, running over the bridge, one of the leaders. Off to the side, the dark ridge of Rangitoto faces the glittering cityscape, glorious in pale pinks and blues and silver. A city built from broken shells. The sun hovers above the horizon, sending a channel of light down the harbour to the bridge, and I feel the light on my face. What a marvellous thing this is, being alive.

SEVEN

MUM DIDN'T YELL OR SCREAM, and she didn't give me a long lecture about trust and truth. I knew I'd damaged something between us — I saw it in the way she looked at me, her eyes glazed with a distress I didn't know how to fix. There was never a conversation about quitting, and she told me, in a hushed voice over breakfast the next morning, that if I told her the truth from here on in, I could continue training and competing.

'I love watching you run,' she said, fingering the rim of her coffee mug. 'It brings me a lot of joy.'

'Thank you,' I said. I stood to give her a hug, only she didn't hug me back — not the way she used to. She patted me like a stranger with an unpredictable dog, wary of how it might hurt you.

I ran as often as I could. Mornings, evenings, weekends. At training sessions no one was rude to me anymore, and Emma, her friend Georgia and others sometimes included me in their conversations. It made up for the fact that Benji was ignoring me. He was angry, I knew that. I'd left him at the party. He didn't seem to understand that I was angry, too.

After our last training session before Christmas, Daniel invited the group to his house for an end-of-year party. He lived in a white house that was all sharp angles and clean spaces. He told us to make ourselves at home, and set out pizzas on the glass-topped dining table.

The pizza smelled delicious, yeasty and warm. I slid four pieces to my plate and found a place to sit on the floor beside Georgia and Emma. Benji sat in a tight huddle with the other boys, and one by one they turned their heads, sending hot hard stares at Emma. She didn't seem to notice or care. Benji didn't look at me once.

'What are you up to for Christmas?' I asked Emma, desperate to break the awkward silence between us.

She took a tiny bite of her pizza, then wiped her lips with a paper towel. 'I'm going to Auckland to see my cousins.'

Auckland. It seemed so exotic the way she said it, but she was easy with it, too, like it was welcoming. To me, Auckland was the place my father had run away to, where Zach now lived, and Cleo. A city of longing.

'Cool,' said Georgia. 'I went to Auckland last year. We stayed in the Viaduct. It was so cool. When you're there, you should run along Tamaki Drive. I did that with Dad. We ran from the city around the waterfront to one of the beaches. Dad said it's part of the marathon course.'

'I'd like to run a marathon,' I said. The memory of the women in Sydney, their bodies finely tuned and strong, letting nobody stop them, was still bright in my mind.

'You'd probably win it,' Georgia said. 'You're a really good runner.' Those words were honey-sweet. Me, winning.

'I'll text you when I get back,' Emma said to her. 'We could go to the movies, or for a run before training starts again.'

I pushed the last crust to the side of the plate and licked cheese grease from my fingers. 'I'm stuffed,' Emma said. She set down her unfinished pizza. Georgia set her slice down, too, rubbing the crumbs from her hands. They'd not eaten one complete piece between them.

There was ice cream for dessert. Emma and Georgia stood, leaving their dirty plates on the floor and ignoring the tubs of ice cream on the table. They wandered off to talk with the boys. Then I saw Benji walking towards me, holding a bowl of chocolate ice cream. His hair looked longer, curling around the nape of his neck. He folded his long legs to fit in the space beside me. I could feel myself starting to breathe faster, as though I was running, and the pizza sat heavy in my stomach.

He didn't look at me when he spoke. 'What subjects are you taking next year?'

'History, statistics, PE. I have to repeat Level One English.' I paused, then said in a rush, 'I wish I could just run all day.'

He laughed. 'Me too. Fuck school. Let's just run and work out all day like they do in communist countries. Become super-athletes and win all the medals at the Olympics.'

If only I could forget what he'd said about my body. You need to change, he'd said, you aren't beautiful like this. I looked at his eyes, the long lashes, his body: there was nothing about him I would dare suggest be different.

Daniel knelt beside us. 'Everything all right here?'

'We're good,' I said. 'Is there any ice cream left?'

Daniel looked from me to the table and back again. 'Do you really need some?'

'I don't know,' I said. 'I want some.'

He returned and held out a large white bowl with a small scoop of ice cream sliding around, melting quickly. I scooped it up, and then it was gone. The top of my mouth stung with the cold. Daniel pursed his lips and let out a long exhale, as though I'd failed a test.

THERE WAS NO TRAINING FOR two weeks over the holidays. I didn't want to stop, so I ran every day, even on Christmas Day. The festive season calmed the world, and hushed its frenzy, and that day the streets were empty and clear. I ran in the middle of the road instead of the footpath, the tarmac bouncy and responsive under my feet. I thought I heard footsteps behind me, a soft echo of my steps, though there was never anyone there. At the walkway near the beach I paused to watch the surfers, the only other people spending their Christmas morning far from the unwrapping of presents and twinkling decorations and roasting turkey, and filled my lungs with the salty air. I ran faster, faster, faster, until my chest felt as though it would burst. Nothing could hurt me; nothing could catch me. I'd heard about a runner's high, the hormonal rush after prolonged, consistent exercise. This feeling wasn't quite like that. I felt high, as though I was floating above the ground, my mind clear and crisp as a diamond.

I QUALIFIED FOR THE NATIONALS at my first interclub meet in January, three days after my birthday. Daniel took me and two others to the event in Stratford in his Mitsubishi station wagon. I sat with him upfront, and he told us stories about competing internationally.

I made the qualifying time in the 10,000 metres. Went three seconds under, winning my age group. Some of the kids were slow, unfit sixteen- and seventeen-year-olds, faces glowing pink after half a lap. The faster ones were quick, their legs pumping strong and feet barely touching the ground. I followed them around the track for the first three laps, sitting in behind the whole group, and then moved up place by place every lap or two, until I was in the lead. Every time I overtook a competitor, I bumped up a gear, letting loose a burst of speed, and I felt their tension as I rushed by — their grimace, their clenched fists. My own body felt smooth and loose and light. In the final lap-and-a-half I pulled away, separating myself from the others.

Afterwards, I couldn't remember all the details of the run, but for years I could recall the colourful sneakers of the runners in front of me flicking up and down, up and down at the start of the race. When I was in the lead, there was nothing to see but the sweet curve of the orange track.

IT WAS THE ONLY INTERCLUB I'd been allowed to compete in. After the disaster at the twins' party, Mum insisted I earn the entry fee of any competitions I wanted to enter.

'If you want to make your own decisions,' she said, 'you can earn them. Wash the dishes, do some jobs for the neighbours.'

I did chores for Mum, and mowed the lawns of most houses on Rutherford Street. After each job I'd slide the precious ten- and twenty-dollar notes into my small orange wallet. Yet, despite all the work, I earned enough only for that one race at the end of January. Daniel assured me it would be enough to get me to nationals if I raced well. And when I did, he picked me up and spun me in an orbit of his golden head. It was set: I would race the 5,000 and the 10,000 metres at the national championships.

'I LEFT SCHOOL AT SIXTEEN,' Mum said, when I told her I wanted to go to the nationals in Palmerston North. 'I enrolled in nursing college, and I made uniforms for the local primary school to earn money on the side. The important things in life aren't just given to you, Mickey. You need to earn them.'

I wondered if it was Teddy, whispering to her down the phone that I shouldn't be allowed to go, and this was her way of placating him. She's doing it without us, Ted, she'd say. I hadn't spoken to him since the argument at the twins' birthday, and there didn't seem to be a way to navigate back to a more amicable relationship. It was as though he'd disowned me simply because I wanted to run.

Mum didn't just leave me to it, though. She helped me bake biscuits to sell, fifty cents a cookie. One weekend afternoon she organised for all the doctors and nurses from the hospital to bring their cars over to Rutherford Street. They parked on the verge and up our driveway, even along the street. Mum held out two buckets and a scabby sponge. 'Two hours,' she said, 'to clean them all for a hundred and fifty dollars.'

My arms and back ached at the end of the day. I tucked the three fifty-dollar notes into the orange wallet. Halfway there.

The final training session before the national championships was on a Tuesday evening in April. The leaves had started to turn, falling and carpeting the footpath in a spread of yellow and brown. Daniel called it 'marathon weather'. Crisp air, low chance of rain. We were tapering, he called it, easing off before our races. In a break from the usual quiet determination of our training, he let us joke around. I felt happy for the first time in months.

I knew I was more than ready to race again. There would be better runners than there had been at the interclub meet in Stratford — people from the South Island, and Auckland, where everyone knew the best runners lived, and the best coaches. But for now I wasn't intimidated.

When training ended, the other athletes drifted to the clubrooms. I wasn't ready to leave, so I stayed outside for a moment longer, taking in the stillness of the empty track. The sky was a purple-grey, the first star a faint silver dot. Whispering that rhyme about the first star I see at night, I made a wish: new shoes. I took a deep breath and kicked my ratty old sneakers off on the track.

I heard the thud of footsteps, and Daniel sat beside me. He wrapped his arm around my shoulders and squeezed. 'Be here at 4.30 on Thursday, okay? We leave at 4.45 on the dot.'

I nodded. He'd explained it all earlier: three-and-a-half hours to Palmerston North, with one stop in Whanganui to stretch our legs and find something for dinner. Competition would begin on the Friday. He'd pinned the programme up in the clubrooms, and I'd studied it all week, memorising my schedule. Ten thousand metres heat on Friday; final if I made it on Saturday morning. Five thousand on Sunday. Sitting beside Daniel, thinking about the races, I was swamped with a sudden anxiety. I'd only raced once, at a tiny meet. I didn't understand the nuance of racing. I only had those rubbish shoes, heavy and dirty. I was a rank amateur who had no business being there.

I lowered my head and said, 'Do you really think I might win a medal? Or am I dreaming?'

He shrugged. 'You've worked hard. It's your first nationals, Mickey. Those other girls will be fighting and race ready. They will have put in the hours on the road, on the track, in the gym. They'll not be carrying any extra weight. I think you should go out there and put it all on the line, and after that — it's out of our hands.'

I touched my hips, and felt around the bones, down over my butt, my legs. Was it softer there than it should be? If there was too much extra softness, would that hold me back? This was the first time I remember doubting my physical self, after everyone else had been doing so for years. I put my hand to my mouth and felt a slick of sick on my teeth.

His arm tightened around me, a mild constriction. 'Get changed, Mickey,' he said. 'Go home and get some rest.'

I picked up my sneakers and headed to the changing rooms. I needed a shower, the hot water on my skin. The feeling I'd had earlier, the lightness, the zing of electricity had gone, and in the heat of the shower cubicle my body felt large and heavy. I looked down. I couldn't expect to run on those short and dumpy legs.

The other girls were still getting changed when I came out of the shower. 'I can't even look at him,' Belinda was saying.

'I know,' Emma said. 'Daniel is like the sexiest man I know.'

'What about Benji?' Nerida said. 'He wants you bad, Emma.'

Everyone laughed.

My skin was sticky from the shower, and dressing felt like putting jeans on a seal. I wanted to leave, go home and sleep, but I couldn't help myself: I glanced up at Emma. Her hair was wet from the shower, and she'd braided it into two blonde plaits. Her body was long and curved and so beautiful it was insane. It made sense that Benji would like her.

Amy, a field athlete I didn't know well, leaned her head towards me and said, 'You're like a little doll.' She wrapped her arms around my chest and lifted me from the ground. She competed in the shot-put: her arms were hard and strong. I asked her to put me down, and she lifted me higher, carrying me around the changing rooms.

'She's not pretty enough to be a doll,' Nerida said.

'No, I just meant she's tiny. Like a doll!' Amy lowered me then, and I pulled on my tee-shirt, struggling to get my arms through the holes. Someone giggled, and I didn't want to look to see who it was.

Emma stared at me, her eyes grazing down my body. 'How do you run so fast with those short legs, Michelle? Is it steroids?'

I shoved my dirty athletics clothes into my bag. If Emma knew anything about steroids, she would know I wasn't taking them.

'Worst thing about being short,' Emma said, 'is how easy it is to get fat.'

'What do you mean?' Belinda asked, spraying herself with perfumed deodorant.

I picked up my sneakers and turned to leave.

Emma stood in my way. 'When you're tall, the fat is distributed on a longer limb. When you're short, it all sort of clumps together. Squishes up. You know what cellulite is, right?'

A few of the girls said yuck and laughed.

'The fatter you are, the heavier you are. And if you're heavier, you're going to run slower!'

She wandered to her bag, and as I walked down the corridor and onto the street, I looked down at my legs. I wanted to see the shapes they made, the way they looked to others who might be watching.

MUM WAS HOME THAT EVENING. We sat together on the couch in front of the television, although neither of us was watching. Mum had the newspaper spread out on her lap while she did the crossword, and I was staring at the ceiling, thinking about my races at the nationals.

'You know, Mum,' I said, 'women only started to race the 5,000 metres at the Olympics in 1996, but men have been running it since the modern Olympics began in 1912?'

Bonnie turned and gave me a twisted smile. 'Really? Where did you read that?'

I laughed. 'I didn't read it, Mum. You know I don't read. Daniel told me.'

Bonnie folded the paper and placed it near her feet. 'Good for him! What else do you know?'

We sat there for over an hour, and she listened to every little scrap of information I had in my brain about running. She held my hand and let me rave on and on. The blue and green light of the television screen flickered over our faces, and I grew warm from the nearness of her body. It had been a long time since I'd felt as close to her as this.

AFTER SCHOOL ON THE THURSDAY I went straight home to grab my bag that I had carefully packed the night before. Mum was at work, and there was a note on the kitchen table: *Have fun my Mickey! Left a little something in your room. Wish I could be there xxx*

On my bed was a box wrapped in brown paper, with a red bow, the way she wrapped all our birthday presents. I was confused. Bonnie rarely bought us presents outside of birthdays and Christmas — and without Helen, Kent and Zach around there seemed no need to make a gift a secret. I ripped the paper open. It was a neon-orange shoe box, with a pair of white racing flats inside. Each shoe was embellished with a bright red Nike swoosh and four spikes around the forefoot of the sole. I closed my eyes and inhaled deeply: the warm scent of leather and glue from the rubber. I could tell that these were light, much lighter than the shoes I'd been running in. The red swoosh was an exact match to the Birchfield Athletics red.

I slipped the shoes on my feet and walked around between the two single beds. The pins pricked into the carpet. The leather was soft on my skin, as though I were barefoot. I jumped up and down three times, feeling some bounce in the midsole, and the shoes crinkled and softened to the shape of my feet. I took them off and packed them into my bag.

I knew that I should eat before I left, but the conversation in the changing room was still on my mind. *Cellulite*. I swung my bag over my shoulder, locked the door and walked to the clubrooms.

THE RACE

THE INSTANT OUR FEET TOUCH ground on the city side of the bridge, the business part of the marathon begins. The course spins on itself up Sarsfield Street and then down Curran, around and under the bridge. Lofty renovated villas and established trees stand over us. There are dense crowds, cheering and clapping. Our pace doesn't slow on the uphill. Feet quick, knees high, and then we fly down, legs flashing until we are under the bridge, next to the water and fresh air of the sea. The next support station is there, a long table with a yellow cloth on it.

I spot my named bottle but none of my salted caramel carbohydrate gels. I've got one in the pocket of my shorts — it's my emergency spare, ready for later in the race when I'm feeling the pinch. The trouble is I need one now or I will regret it later.

Panic claws up my chest. Something's gone wrong in the plan — but there's no time to stop and figure it out. Shit. I take a drink and throw my bottle to the ground. Marcus is next to me, and close by are the other two women. We sweep away fast along Westhaven Drive, where the masts of moored boats hover like an enormous flock of birds. Our pace is quick, and we catch up to the leaders with ease. I can't panic about the gels. *Stay calm and problem solve.*

The hilliest part of the race is over: from here nothing is more than ten metres above sea level. It won't be as taxing as the Waiatarua, or doing Bullock Track in Western Springs eight times. I don't need to panic. I take the emergency gel from my pocket and squeeze it out. We've just passed 18 kilometres; there's still over 24 to go. Twenty-four thousand metres, each metre two steps. I can't do the maths right now: it's a long way, no matter how you slice it. I'll tell Philippa at 29 ks about the gels, and she can give me more. It'll be fine. I repeat this, It'll be fine, the words flipping in my mind like pancakes. Pancakes, cream and bacon. I'll have that when I'm finished. Queenies is not too far from the finish line. Just a hobble up the hill, past the New World. Niall can take me.

Niall's along the course somewhere. *You'll see me when you see me.* He's made a sign, I know that much. A surprise, he said. As long as it doesn't say Mickey Mouse, I'll be happy.

Dylan and Marcus and the four other men are pulling away. I'm right beside Ruby and one other man. He's straining forward, as though he's not quite ready to admit he's dropped from the front pack, that he's stuck with the ladies and the race has taken off and left him behind. I ignore him and keep looking straight ahead. I can't worry about anyone else right now: my race isn't really against Ruby, or Dylan. This race is against myself. Philippa's said it so many times: Don't let the other stuff distract you. *The battle is inside your mind. You have to be stronger than anything the world can throw at you.*

EIGHT

THE MOUNTAIN WAS SHROUDED IN thick, low-lying cloud as we drove through Inglewood and Stratford. I sat in the back of the van with my eyes closed; other kids listened to music through their headphones. Nobody spoke. In the rumbling quiet I thought about my races. My fingers felt cold and tingly. Nerves or hunger? A mix of both, maybe. I was forty-one kilograms, my body slick as water. I was ready. I was ready.

The motel Daniel had booked was on one of the main avenues. It looked cheap. The rooms had doors that split in half like horse stables and were decorated in various shades of brown: beige walls, khaki curtains, ochre bedspreads. Emma and I were assigned to share a room, and I suspected she wasn't as delighted about this as I was. We stood inside the door, surveying the two single beds and the dusty television. Through a door next to one of the beds was a grimy, windowless bathroom.

'Gross,' Emma said. 'Looks like someone shat everywhere.'

She was right. I put my bag in the corner and sat on one of the beds. My stomach growled, the sound like a strangled animal. Emma peered at me with distaste before going into the bathroom, and I heard the snip of the lock.

Daniel appeared at the open door. 'Is it all right if I come in?'

I shrugged. 'Sure.'

'Are you feeling okay, Mickey?' He sat on Emma's bed, facing me. 'You were really quiet on the drive and you didn't eat any dinner.'

'I'm fine. Just a bit nervous, I guess.'

'You'll be great. Just focus on tomorrow's heat, the rest you worry about later. Go easy on yourself. You know how to do this.'

Did I? I was seventeen, inexperienced, and I felt so alone. I'd be running against the best in the country — and some Australians too. The yawping hunger to run was tainted with worry that I was out of my depth. Other times I'd been in the spotlight, like reading aloud in English, had been a disaster. Why would this be any different?

'I believe in you, Mickey.' He reached across and touched my knee. The bathroom door opened, and his hand snapped back to his lap. He stood and said, 'Breakfast at six-thirty, don't forget.'

'What was that all about?' Emma asked when he'd gone.

'Nothing.' But I wasn't sure, and wished my mum was there. This was growing up: I was on my own.

I WON THE HEAT OF my 10,000-metre race in the fastest time of the day, 35 minutes and two seconds, and didn't even push to my limit. The race was pure fun, all my worries nothing but the big shadow of a small thing. The conditions were just right — no wind, clear sky, not too hot. The first few seconds after the starter's gun was the weakest part of my race. I slipped into the midst of the bunch, keeping my elbows pressed into my waist. Hunting. On the tenth lap I made my move from fourth place, slipping between the leading pair, pulling through as though I were on fire, my stride rate almost double theirs, moving into the lead. My ponytail whipped my back and my chest took in so much air with each inhale it felt as though I was breathing in the whole universe.

I HADN'T KNOWN WHAT AN event like this would be like: hundreds of competitors and supporters and coaches everywhere, the stadium buzzing and frothing with energy. It was incredible to be a part of it. While my teammates competed in the hurdles and sprints, long jump and shot-put, I sat in the stands behind the Birchfield banner, cheering and shouting along with everyone else but never venturing far from my team. Some of the others seemed to know kids from other clubs, and I watched enviously as Emma moved from group to group and sat with one girl for most of the day.

I asked her about it that evening.

'We've both been doing this since we were seven,' she said. 'Birchfield did a trip to their club and I was billeted out to stay with her family. She's really cool.'

Ten years. They all had a ten-year head start. Again came the niggling sense that I was a rookie, a newbie who didn't know what she was doing. Then I remembered that sometimes rookies won.

THE DAY OF THE 10,000 METRES final dawned chilly and damp. A thick autumnal murk sat over the town. Driving to the stadium, Daniel glanced at me several times in the rearview mirror, raising a thumbs-up and singing, 'Cheer up, Mickey Mouse, cheer up.' All the kids joined in, out of key and loud. I covered my ears with my hands and told them to stop, stop! but they didn't, so I laughed, and hoped the nickname might bring me good luck.

My spirits lifted as teams poured into the grounds. I dropped my bag in the seats by our club flag, then changed into my clothes for a warm-up. My body felt fresh, with no hint that I'd run a quick 10 kilometres the day before. It felt like a good omen.

I recognised several of the girls in my final, some from my heat. I joined them in the pre-race routine, twisting my legs into warm-up hurdle steps, lifting my knee and then turning it out to the side to tap my toe, swinging my arms, getting my body ready for the run. Then three slow, slow loops of the outside lane of the track. All of us were watchful, eyeing each other, gauging the competition.

An older man in a polo shirt stood near the changing rooms, and a group of runners had gathered around him. His chest was barrel-thick and his thinning hair was long around his ears.

'He's that coach from Auckland,' Emma said when I asked if she knew him. 'He used to run with Lydiard back in the day. He's coached Olympians.'

The man stopped speaking and pointed at one of the girls in the group. She took off on a jerky run, knees high, heels flicking up to touch her bottom. Her body was all limbs, like a stick insect, and she wore her hair cropped short. He folded his arms and stood watching her, and she ran back and forth in front of him, over and over again. He was clearly the most powerful man in the stadium, and I felt both repulsed and compelled by him. I wanted to meet him. I wanted to impress him.

I SAT IN THE STANDS and kept my breathing steady. An hour to go. Supporters filled up the nearby seats. Then someone was shouting my name from below.

'Mickey! Mickey Bloom!'

It was my sister, Helen. I leaned over the railing and we reached for each other. My whole body relaxed.

'Good luck for your run,' she said. 'I got one of my uni friends to drive me up. Bryn's here, too.' She pointed up to the higher seats behind me, and I spotted his ashy hair cut short, dark glasses hiding his eyes.

'I'm so glad you're here,' I said. 'You know Mum couldn't come.'

'I know,' Helen said. 'Sucks. I'm here though! Let's meet up after your race — I'll be up there.' She pointed again to where Bryn was sitting and squeezed my fingers one last time, her grip reassuring and firm. 'You'll be great, Mickey.'

I put on a Birchfield sweatshirt that Daniel had given to me and unlaced my new shoes. They were so beautiful, almost unreal in their whiteness. I knew Bonnie would be thinking about me. She wouldn't forget I was racing.

The crowd cheered as a limber teenager sprinted, turned, and threw his body over the high-jump bar with an unexpected grace.

Daniel sat behind me and massaged my shoulders. 'You feeling good?' he said quietly. 'Remember, go fast, turn left.'

I was feeling good. No, I was feeling great.

I TIED AND RETIED MY laces, fixing them in a double knot. Not even fear could undo them as I took my place at the starting line. A thin prickle of sweat ran down my back. Next to me, a tall girl with cherry-red nail polish exhaled noisily and shook her head so that her long plaits whipped past my face. I pulled my ponytail tighter and glanced up at the stands. Helen was there, even if I couldn't see her.

The final. This was the final. I let loose my breath in a low whistle.

The crowd grew quiet. The starter's gun snapped in the air. The race was on.

As I'd done in the heats, I didn't head straight to the front of the pack. Two girls in matching green racing kit pushed out ahead. They'd slow soon, I knew it. I could see in the shapes their bodies made that they'd flag sooner rather than later. I folded in behind them, just behind the shoulder of the girl on the outside. Heavy breathing all around, the slapping of shoes on track. My legs felt strong, my heartbeat calm. I breathed through my nose: inhale for four, exhale for four. Waiting to make my move.

One lap, five, ten. The leaders fell behind me and others took their place. Still I waited. When I made my break I would be all in; I couldn't afford to make a mistake.

The girl next to me on the inside stumbled and fell, crying out in pain. I didn't turn to see if she was okay. All I did was dig deeper and pick up the pace.

Thirteen laps. Fatigue started to settle in my legs, tendrils of lactic acid tickling my thighs, my calves. It was increasingly difficult to keep my chest lifted, my shoulders down. Go fast, turn left. A tall red-haired girl in black and gold kit was in the lead, pumping her arms. The girl with the red nail polish was right in beside me, and at the halfway mark of the fourteenth lap she pulled ahead, with me in her slipstream. The red-head seemed to deflate in the same instant, dropping behind where I could no longer see or feel her.

I stayed within the pull of the leading girl. The finish line felt closer now, tantalising, as we came through the eighteenth lap. At the next bend I swerved right, pulling alongside. The girl's plaits danced around her shoulders; I was so close I could see the intricate detail of the braid. She didn't flinch or look at me. We ran shoulder to shoulder, and when we rounded into the twentieth lap I knew it was now or never.

Lungs screaming. Blood pumping in my ears. An inch ahead, one step. The crowd was screaming like the crowd for Naoko Takahashi in Sydney — I remembered that sound. It made my scalp prickle. The world and the track started to blur and I leaned forward, forward. Ahead was the finish line, and I had no idea if I was in the lead or not.

Officials hovered, waiting for the photograph. It was close, too close. I sat on the side of the track, pulling air in, feeling my hands shaking. The other runners crossed, their cheeks flushed, hair unkempt. Some lay down on the track near me and gasped. Others went to their supporters for a hug. The tall girl with the red nail polish and the whipping braids was sitting on the other side of the track, her head between her bent knees. Her coach knelt beside her — the Auckland coach.

I felt Daniel beside me. He pulled me to stand and gave me a tight hug. When he let me go, the other coach was beside us.

'She's one of yours then, Merriweather?'

'Of course, Bruce,' Daniel said. 'I only work with the best.'

The man's chest heaved with a wheezing laugh and he rubbed his cheek. 'She's good all right. I think she got the better of Talia. Maybe even a record.'

I turned to Daniel. A record? His face was impassive, as though he too was taking his time to understand what Bruce had said.

The loudspeaker crackled into life: 'Results of the 10,000 metres under-19 girls' race.'

Most of the competitors were now huddled near the stands and off the tracks. Daniel took my hand and pulled me near them.

'A very close race indeed. In first place, only milliseconds away from breaking the record, in a time of 34 minutes, 04.75 seconds, is Michelle Bloom of Birchfield Athletics. Second place, Talia Meredith, North Lynn Track and Field.'

Daniel's mouth hung open, and he ran his hand through his hair. 'You did it!' he shouted. He grabbed me again and lifted me from the ground and spun me around.

'I won?' I couldn't grasp what it meant.

'You won, baby!' Daniel let me drop to the ground. Everyone gathered around us. It was like being seven again, winning the relay on the spiky grass, Zach lifting me to the clouds.

Bruce raised his eyebrows. 'She's quite something. Might be above your pay grade, Merriweather.'

'I can handle it,' Daniel said. 'There's more to come from this pocket rocket.'

'Pocket rocket all right,' Bruce said, looking straight at me. 'If you ever decide to take this seriously, kid, there's a place for you on my team.'

I WASN'T TAKAHASHI, I HADN'T won gold at the Olympics, but the euphoria of having that medal bordered on delirium. I even wore it to the team dinner. Everyone whooped and whistled when I came in and took my seat at the trestle table. 'Mickey's our champion,' Daniel called. 'Our golden girl.' The chant went up: *Mickey Mouse, Mickey Mouse, Mickey Mouse.*

After we finished our meal of lasagne and overly soft peas, Daniel announced that he would shout us dessert. 'My favourite, of course,' he said. 'Ice cream!' He shook his car keys to get my attention, the silver bright in the dull light of the room. 'Mickey. You come with me.'

Light rain had started to fall, and the van was covered in a fine dust of raindrops. He drove away from the motel, through the busy Saturday-night streets of Palmerston North. The rain grew heavier. Daniel flicked the windscreen wipers on and turned the heater up. Dry hot air blew over my face and bare legs. My medal lay heavy on my chest; I didn't know if I would ever take it off. I inspected the detail, the colour. I hadn't had time to talk to Bonnie yet, to tell her about the medal and the record. My phone was at the motel, probably out of battery. I would call her later. I knew she'd be waiting to hear from me — it wasn't a mystery what she'd say, yet I wanted to hear the words. *I'm proud of you.*

The car stopped with a lurch — I looked up — there was an intersection ahead, and we'd stopped suddenly at the lights. The rain had eased slightly; Daniel turned off the wipers with a gentle flick of his wrist. Long winding tears of water snaked down the window, and the neon lights of McDonald's and Wendy's and Burger King refracted in their trails. The car was stuffy and warm, the aroma of Pine Fresh air freshener clagging in my nose.

'You were favouring that right leg when you ran the last lap,' he said, glancing at me. 'Is it bothering you?'

'A bit,' I said.

'Get a massage,' he said. 'Did you see those tents at the far end of the track?'

'I can't afford a massage. They're way too expensive.'

He shifted his grip on the steering wheel. 'I'll shout you one,' he said, and smiled. 'Where does it hurt exactly? Here?'

Everything seemed to slow down then, as though time became sticky and didn't flow. His hand moved from the wheel, and I saw it like a stop-motion film, each split second so important, milliseconds taking on new meaning, as the hand moved, incrementally, from one place to another. When it stopped it was on my thigh, inches above my knee. He'd touched me before, helping me stretch after training, sometimes a hug or a high-five. He'd even attempted to plait my hair after training one day. He touched the other girls too, in ordinary ways like that. I sensed that this was different. It was late, and dark inside the car. We were alone. He wouldn't look at me, kept eyes focused on the traffic lights ahead. With gentle pressure, his thumb began to draw circles on my thigh. His hand shifted up my leg, constantly massaging, moving, massaging, until his fingers were under my shorts and rubbing against the elastic of my knickers. I prayed silently for the lights to change to green. Nobody heard me; the blood-red light blazed.

I pressed my back against the car seat, trying to lift my body away from him. As if that would stop him. He took my movement to mean something else, an invitation maybe, and he slid his fingers into my knickers. I couldn't breathe, I couldn't speak.

'God,' he said, followed by a shuddering sigh. 'You look like a kid, Mickey Mouse, but you feel all woman.'

I couldn't move. I felt his fingers as though there were in my throat, and I gasped.

'It's okay,' he said. 'You want this.'

'I don't,' I said in a voice so small I wasn't sure he would hear.

The red light vanished — the green blinked on.

'I won't tell anyone you liked it,' he said, and pulled his hand out of my shorts.

The cars in front started to move. He pressed his foot on the accelerator and the muscles in his leg tensed. I watched the hand that had touched me drift away from the steering wheel again, and my chest felt hollow. He didn't touch me; he merely turned the radio on. The hand swivelled the volume louder, and he started to sing along to Usher's 'U Remind Me'. When he asked what flavour ice cream he should buy, I told him I didn't care.

THE RACE

WE WEAVE THROUGH THE STREETS near Silo Park. After all the nice long stretches of road, these winding turns seem to jolt Ruby from a daze, and she takes the pace nuclear. We drop the other two women and I see the sign marking the distance: 21 kilometres.

We're about halfway. There's a serious certainty in the halfway point of anything. You consider the energy and time you've already put into the race and balance it against the importance of maintaining that for the next half. People still die on the way down Everest, even though they survived the long and torturous ascent.

Halsey onto Viaduct Harbour Ave, curving around to Customs Street West. I lean into the corners, left, right, around the small flat roundabout. The restaurants here are eerily empty. For a while it's just us runners in the city.

Crowds gather along Quay Street, whistling and cheering to lift our spirits. Someone chases us for a while behind the railings, their body in sight and then not, a blinking figure at the side of my vision. They drop off once we reach the Ferry Building: I see their chest rise high, then drop, panting at the sudden exertion. Part of me has always loved this feeling, knowing that I can run further and faster than nearly everyone in the city, in the country. It's not just about pride. There's something safe in that knowledge. Something exciting. It's exactly what Bonnie wanted for me.

I feel it then, a discomfort tracing the outline of my body: lactic acid. Whispering, *Slow down, don't make me hurt you.* But Ruby isn't easing off. There will be no respite. I grit with all my worth to keep my pace with hers. Whatever happens, however this ends, it will be the result of my own power. The power of my own two feet.

NINE

I KEPT TRAINING THROUGH THE autumn and into the winter. Always alone. I stopped running with anyone else, stopped going to the clubrooms. I didn't want to see Daniel; I didn't want to see the red and grey of Birchfield.

On those cold mornings, my reward was the magnificent sunrise. It was a gift hidden from those who didn't seek it out. I felt a great release running alone, letting myself all hang out, the sweat dripping, my face contorted on the steep hills. No one could see the things I kept to myself. The road and the trees held my secrets.

Some days I was sure I heard footsteps behind me, a cadence not my own. I could swear I heard it, that it wasn't an audible mirage of some kind and yet—

There was never anyone there. I was unnerved and not blind to the dangers of running alone, especially in the hours of dusk and dawn, but I was never frightened enough to stop. I was young, bullish and angry, and part of me might have been looking for danger.

Daniel called me on my cellphone several times. I didn't pick up. He left long, pleading voicemail messages: 'Hey Mickey, it's me. Look,

I'm not sure what's going on, and I hope you're okay. It's coming closer to cross-country champs, and I need you to consider coming to run for us, for me. I need you, Mickey, I do. The club needs you. Call me back, please, or text me?'

I remembered the feeling of running the school cross country — the wind in my hair, the smell of the rain-soaked ground, the slippery grass underfoot — and I wanted to say yes. I wanted to test myself against other runners at the national champs, but no. I never wanted to see him again.

At school, my behaviour went from bad to worse. Concentration was elusive as an eel, sneaking from my grasp. Reading had been hard before, but words now became tangled and insoluble mysteries. I couldn't care less about the Irish Troubles or Cronbach's alpha coefficient. The school called Bonnie, concerned about my attitude and my marks. It's Mickey's last year at Mangorei College, they said, it's important she do well.

Mrs Badditch requested another interview. I refused to go. I was a punk, grossly out of line — but I was wretched. The sight of a red whiteboard marker in the classroom was enough to set me off: I'd be back at the red light, the red orb I stared at while he touched me. Why should I want to talk about my future with Mrs Badditch? I wanted to run, and I knew I could. I couldn't go back to Birchfield, though, and without the club what chance did I have?

A phone call in July changed everything.

'It was a man named Bruce Madden,' Mum told me when I got in. 'A coach from a club in Auckland? He wants you to move up there and train with him.'

At first I thought she was joking. North Lynn Track and Field. The mighty Bruce Madden.

'No, honey, I'm not joking. He wants you to join as soon as possible. Maybe you could join him after the Christmas holidays?'

'You want me to wait until next year?' I said. 'No way. I'm not waiting that long.'

But Bonnie wouldn't budge. She wouldn't change her mind, not for my pleading nor for my tears. And Teddy backed her up. He sounded smug when he told me he agreed with Bonnie, and I hung up while he was still talking and threw myself onto the couch.

'Bruce might change his mind!' I wailed. 'He might tell me I can't come anymore. I need to go *now*.'

She took me into her arms. 'Oh, honey. What about a compromise? Once you've finished all your assessments, everything you need for Year 13, you can go.'

I pressed my face into her shoulder, feeling my tears soak into her blouse. 'If that's the best you can offer,' I mumbled, 'then I suppose I'll have to accept.'

Bruce Madden wasn't pleased when I told him. He clicked his tongue and said, 'You'll be getting here late in the season.' Then he softened. 'Ah well, I guess I don't have much choice. You get here when you get here, and when you do, you'd better be fitter than the world's finest fiddle, my girl.'

THE FINAL FOUR MONTHS OF high school dragged out to feel like ten. I couldn't wait to leave Ngāmotu, to take my running seriously. Bruce had set out his expectations — fitter than a fiddle — and I wasn't going to disappoint him. Any moment I had spare, I was on my feet, getting in the miles. As I ran, I counted down the days. I listed all the things I had to sort out before I left. Somewhere to live, a job. I'd never had a proper job before, or lived with strangers — it was a whole other life, and I needed to prepare.

Early one October morning, I was out for my usual run. The road turned a tight corner, I took the inside curve — and came face to face with Daniel. Neither of us was able to stop in time; we collided, then sprang apart.

I'd never seen him red in the face before, sweaty and panting. He hadn't run far with us in the training sessions, certainly he'd never pushed himself too much in our presence. He seemed to glow in the dim morning air, his orange running shirt bright in the gloom. An Olympian. He looked down at my feet, at the new sneakers Bonnie had bought for me, a celebration gift for my invitation north. They were a light blue with yellow trim, cushioned. They were things of beauty. She told me that Teddy had paid for half, and insisted I call him to say thanks, though I suspected that wasn't true. Over the years there had been too many birthday presents 'from your father' that I knew my mother had wrapped herself. I was glad I had new shoes — I was different now, I wanted to say to him. You don't know me.

'Mickey,' Daniel said quietly.

I needed to get away from him. I stepped onto my right foot to go around him, but he moved quickly, only a small shift, back into my path.

'How are you? I've been trying to call.'

'I know.'

He nodded then, his lips in a thin line. 'I heard you're going to North Lynn.'

Step left; again, a microscopic movement to block me, as though he was merely shifting his weight from one foot to another.

'Coaching track is really just about the numbers, right?' Daniel said. 'I'm good at numbers. I'm good at maths. Anyone who's good at maths can be a good track coach. Plus — I'm a runner. Bruce isn't a runner, he's a thug. You don't need to go to Auckland. Stay here and let me help you.'

Let me help you. I wanted to list all the ways he'd already helped me: he'd helped me feel dirty, weak and cheap. He'd helped me understand that my body was never my own, that he wanted to use it: for status, for pleasure.

I didn't say any of it. I spun around and ran back the way I'd come.

His voice followed me down the road, around the corner, all the way home.

'ARE YOU SURE YOU'VE GOT everything?' Mum eased the car to a stop near the InterCity bus terminal and asked me again: 'Mickey, have you got everything?'

I shrugged. My backpack was in the boot, my racing flats and my running shoes stuffed right in the bottom, the first things to go in. There were some other essentials — a few clothes, some toiletries — and a new pair of running shorts and tops from Helen and Bryn. So you look the part, Helen told me.

'Zach will pick you up in Auckland,' Mum said.

'Is this a good idea, Mum?'

'Mickey, honey. It'll be okay! Zach's there, your father too. You know where you're going to be living, and you've got a job. You're going to be running again in a club. I thought this was what you wanted?'

'Why do I have to leave, Mum? Why can't I stay here with you?'

'Ask the bulb in winter and it will tell you the spring blossom is just a dream.' Bonnie looked me in the eye. 'If you want this, love, you've got to do it, no matter how hard it might be. If it means leaving me, no matter how much I might hate the idea of my baby leaving me alone, then that's what it means. I don't think you can achieve what you want by staying here and living with me forever. I don't want you to look back in twenty years and regret not going.'

I still didn't move. I wasn't ready.

'God, come on, honey. You're going to miss the bus!' She got out of the car and pulled my backpack from the boot. We hugged, and she kissed my cheek. The driver checked my ticket, pushed my bag into the luggage hold, and I took the three steps up into the bus, on my way to a new life.

ABOUT TWENTY OTHER ATHLETES WERE already at North Lynn Track and Field clubrooms when I arrived for my first training session. They sat around outside the building, their long lean legs stretched out on the footpath. They were even more intimidating than Emma and the girls at Birchfield — they all had glossy hair and warm skin, and they wore bright running clothes and expensive sneakers. Hoka One One and Atreyu and Nike and Adidas and Asics. Wrists laden with Garmin and Polar and Timex watches. No one said hello to me. I bit my nails, but there was nothing left. They were already bitten down to the quick.

A couple of girls tightened hair ties and adjusted their sports bras. Beside me, a tall man in a crimson running singlet stood up and started to shake out his legs. He jumped up and down, hitting only the balls of his feet before springing back into the air. He was long, like a bean, and a Māori tattoo curled around his forearm. When he stood still again, he looked at me, and, so slightly I wasn't sure I didn't imagine it, nodded his head.

A short, thick-set man with broad cheeks covered in white stubble came out of the clubrooms. It took me a second to recognise him: Bruce Madden. All the runners stood, and I could sense a prickling tension among them. He stood on the last step down to the footpath and looked us over.

'Good evening,' he said. 'Nice night for a 20k Fartlek. I'm looking for three kilometres at your moderate effort, about 70 percent of your 10-kilometre pace, and then every fourth kilometre closer to race pace. Maybe 85, 90 percent. There you should be looking for RPE of about an eight or a nine. Has everyone weighed in?'

A quiet murmuring filtered through the group. I set my thumbnail between my teeth, trying to find purchase. RPE? Weighing in? I turned to the girl next to me. She had thin pink lips and large moles on her shoulders. I whispered to her, 'What's weighing in?'

She looked at me from my head to my shoes, and gave a faint, almost breathless laugh. 'You must be new. You need to go inside and get weighed. We do it every Thursday before the run. Body fat the first Saturday of the month.'

No one had told me to go inside. No one had said I'd be weighed, like meat at the delicatessen. I raised my hand.

Bruce pointed at me. 'Who are you?'

I lowered my hand, and a cold cramping clenched in my stomach. I said, 'I'm Mickey Bloom.'

'Ah, right,' he said. 'Forgot you were coming today. Only a few things you need to know this minute, Mickey — that's Alain, my assistant coach.' He nodded towards a sharp-nosed man standing in the doorway. 'And this here is Yuri and Emily, the junior coaches. Everyone, this is Mickey Bloom. She's joining North Lynn with quite a reputation. Ten-thousand-metre and 5,000-metre champion for under-19s at last year's nationals. She might not look like much but she's got the makings of a superstar, so I want everyone to show her a warm North Lynn welcome.'

He spoke lower then, as though no one else was there. 'Now Mickey, stay around after the run so we can go through the training schedule for the rest of the season. I hope you're fit and raring to go. Yuri will keep an eye on you today and he can give me an assessment of your current fitness.'

'Okay,' I said. 'Should I go inside and weigh myself first?'

'No no no, not now,' he said. 'Too late for that. Get here earlier next Thursday so you have time to complete the pre-session checklist. Hilary here will show you what to do, won't you, Hilary?'

The girl beside me, the one with the thin lips, smiled. 'Of course. Welcome to "The Family".' She hunched her fingers for effect.

Yuri and Emily led us from the clubrooms. We followed the hill that rolled down Sunrise Avenue towards the Mairangi Bay shops. I sat in the group near the middle, finding my groove, assessing the other runners, watching their bodies, the beat of their shoes. It had been so long since I'd run in a pack. It took me a while to get into the rhythm of it, to find a comfortable space in the mass of moving bodies.

None of the roads looked familiar. My new flat was near the clubrooms, and I'd gone on a run a few days earlier, circling these same streets, assessing the difficulty of the hills and how tricky the wide intersections were to cross. From within the group, though, it was impossible to tell where I was — I recognised nothing. It didn't matter, anyway. What mattered was showing Yuri I could hold a good pace. I focused my eyes on the shoulders of the person in front of me and kept my legs ticking over.

We ran the 20k Fartlek at the alternating pace Bruce had determined. The three easier ks kept us running together smooth and two abreast, and then the fourth, faster kilometre splintered the group into three distinct parts. I was the only one without a watch, so I tried to figure out my pace by the feeling in my body, the way I'd always done it. I ran near the back of the leading group, caught up in the sweep of their momentum. Yuri stayed at the front, and after every quick kilometre he glanced over his shoulder as though to see if I'd fallen back. I hadn't — they couldn't shake me off that easily.

Afterwards, most of the runners disappeared into the clubrooms to cool down and stretch. Hilary rolled her head around her neck a few times and smiled when she caught my eye. 'How was that? You look strong out there.'

'Yeah,' I said, distracted. I was watching Yuri talk to Bruce. They were talking about me, I could feel it. Bruce stood quiet, nodding sometimes, and then he clapped the younger man on the arm and came over to me. The first thing he said: 'Get yourself a watch.'

'I will, of course.' My new job, washing dishes and cleaning at the local café, didn't pay much. I wasn't sure how I'd afford a watch, but I had the feeling that whatever Bruce told you to do, you did.

He leaned in close to my face. 'I'm sure you've heard this one before,

Michelle, bear with me. It's the same water that softens the potato and hardens the egg. Are you a potato or are you an egg?'

To me, there was no simple answer. Each had its advantages. I understood the necessity of softness. My mum was soft, she was kind, she was the potato — when things grew difficult, when I boiled the water around us, she never grew hard. Yet I knew, by a deep instinct, that Bruce didn't want me to say potato. His face was so close I could see everything about him in excruciating detail: the long hairs from his nose extending past the nostril, his thick skin dotted with dark pores. He wanted me to say the egg, so I did.

'We're going to toughen you up,' he said, turning his head to the side, as though inspecting a used vehicle. Looking for the damage. 'We'll make a runner out of you. Well done on today. Yuri said you exceeded all expectation. May you continue to do so.'

Exceeded all expectation. A man who'd coached Olympians thought he could *make a runner out of me.* I would prove I was worth all his time, all his effort. I would become the superstar he thought I could be.

THE RACE

PANCAKES. ALL I CAN THINK of is pancakes. Fluffy, doughy pancakes, with a generous drizzle of sweet, sweet syrup. I want a soft couch. I want to lie on a couch and never move again, never. I want a beer, cold fizz on my tongue.

They rotate like a playlist on repeat. Pancakes, syrup and bacon. Cream. A cold beer, the bubbles on my tongue. Luxurious things, things that aren't running. I want all the things that represent the conclusion of this pointless effort. I know I can have them when I finish, not because I earned them but simply because I'm alive.

Pancakes.

I REMEMBER WHEN I WAS training with North Lynn Track and Field, after a long run or a particularly taxing track session, I'd go back to Louis and Hilary's flat. We'd sit around in the lounge, our limbs heavy and brains tired to the point of incoherence. The feeling of what we'd achieved would resonate through our bones. There was something special about what we were doing, I believed: the early morning wake-ups; our pure dedication to the sport; our commitment to pushing ourselves to our limits and then beyond — all this set us apart and locked us together. I'd always found it difficult to explain to Mum or Helen or Zach why I was motivated to run and train like this. Why I would choose a run over other things. I could talk in circles, *go fast turn left,* and yet I felt they never truly understood.

There was no need to explain myself to these people. I knew they were chasing the same things. Miles. Success. Endorphins. Faster times. The win.

Sometimes, during (or after) a run that had taken us to the edge of our ability, straining for more — a little bit more! — I'd wonder whether there was something else I wanted: the beauty of running. The freedom. I wanted what I'd felt at seven on the rugby field, what I'd felt at sixteen, muddy and wet and ecstatic around the river. I wanted to do what those women I'd seen on the television with my father had done — they'd flown over 42 kilometres that day in Sydney. No one had stopped them, no one had cursed at them, insulted them. Everyone celebrated them. What they did wasn't brain surgery, I knew that. It wasn't groundbreaking or essential. And yet it was important, necessary. Oh, and it was beautiful.

UP AHEAD IS THE PORT. Ruby finesses the pace the way you tune an instrument, finding the right tension for the correct sound, and I feel the change zing through me. A man on the side of the road yells in a deep, hoarse voice: 'All the way, ladies! Take it all the way!'

ALL THE WAY, I THINK. All the way to the end. My legs gear up and I let it rip.

TEN

HOW ADAPTABLE THE BODY IS. Under the correct conditions, with the right amount of pressure, a resilient body and mind can withstand many new things. Flatting for the first time with strangers in a new city. A new job, the first real job I'd ever had, at a café called Ann's, where I washed dishes and made smoothies and learned to use the espresso machine and make fluffies for the kids. A training schedule so rigorous it made my previous training seem like child's play. Seven longer runs a week; three sessions on the track; two gym strength sessions, focusing on core and legs; an appointment with Bruce's appointed physiotherapist every fortnight; an hour-long foam-roller and stretching programme we must do *every night*. I was surprised how quickly I adapted to the heavy schedule, and how I adopted the philosophy of 'The Family' without question. My body changed as well as my mind — I became lean and sharp at the edges, with muscles distinct and firm.

That first summer in Auckland, humidity cloaked the city day and night. I'd never experienced that sort of wet heat before. Summer in Ngāmotu meant scorching sunny days on black sand before the heat dissipated into long, cool evenings. There was no such reprieve here.

I didn't go home for Christmas — I wanted to keep running and going to the gym, so I stayed behind in muggy Auckland. When I woke on Christmas morning, I regretted my decision. There were no gifts, no carols. I was alone in the flat and overcome with homesickness. Bonnie called, of course, and must have sensed my mood. She suggested I call Zach, who was spending Christmas with friends at his flat in Torbay. I turned it into a training session and ran all the way there. We ate dry turkey and drank Corona on the deck. 'Merry Christmas, Mick,' he said when he dropped me home later that night. 'Come over for New Year's if you want.'

One mid-January Thursday I arrived at the clubrooms sweating before the workout had begun. Most of the others were already sitting in a semi-circle around Bruce outside. His voice was faint through the glass, detailing the tempo run we would do that evening. Fifteen kilometres, after a dynamic warm-up of burpees, squat walks, arm swings. I heard him tell Erin she'd need to run an extra 5 ks when the rest of us were finished. It wasn't punishment — he was quick to point that out. It didn't matter what he said: we all knew the only people asked to do more were those who'd weighed in too high.

I couldn't join the warm-up until I'd weighed in, and I couldn't weigh in until Hilary had finished on the scales. She stood stock-still, not making any move to get off. Her red hands were balled into fists, and I saw the long strands of ribs curving around the sides of her torso.

Yuri bent down to examine the scales more closely. 'Fifty-five,' he said, and for a moment the only sound in the room was his pen scratching in his notebook. 'Hilary, tell me. Are you sexually active?'

The question rolled through Hilary and into my chest.

'What's that got to do with anything?' Hilary's voice was tight and choked. How old was Hilary, nineteen? Twenty, perhaps — a bit older than me. Nothing was private, nothing was personal, not in The Family.

Yuri shifted his legs. 'Have you recently started on a course of contraceptive pills?'

Hilary said nothing. I couldn't breathe in properly, the air suddenly too thin.

Yuri let out a soft grunt. 'Birth control,' he said. 'I don't know what you call it. The pill?'

Hilary stepped off the scales. 'I don't understand why whether or not I'm fucking someone has anything to do with you.'

'You've put on weight,' Yuri said. 'Also, the changes to your body shape. Your breasts are full now, and your hips, you see, they seem wider, like saddlebags.' He grabbed either side of her upper thighs, pinching her buttocks between his thumb and forefinger. 'Some of these changes can be explained by the hormones from medications like contraceptive pills. We highly recommend not taking these medications. A baby, of course, would mean the end of your running career, so it might be a good idea to investigate other ways to prevent unwanted pregnancy that won't have such an impact on your performance.'

Hilary's eyelids were red when she turned around to leave. I looked away from her, down at the floor, and when she was gone I took my turn on the scales. Thirty-nine. Lighter than I'd been in two years. A sadistic relief flooded through me.

Yuri wrote it in his notebook and gave me a smile.

'Amazing work, Mickey. We're yet to determine your peak racing weight, but I think we're on the right track. Down two hundred grams today.'

I went out to join the others in ten burpees. My heart was hammering with the thrill of Yuri's compliment, but also with a distinct twinge of disquiet. His hands on her thighs. Questions about her sex life.

What could I say about it? Bruce and Yuri and Alain, they were doing this to help us. They told us this all the time. They were helping us achieve our goals. They were the professionals. They had their methods, and results to prove their worth. Desperation can make even the most rebellious of us gullible.

We followed Yuri to the road to begin the tempo. The footpath was covered with the last of the jacaranda flowers and the tar on the road was soft. Hilary was beside me, and we didn't look at each other. Even though the air was soupy and hot, I was shivering, my arms pimpled as if it was winter.

THE NEXT DAY OUR WORKOUT at North Lynn was a training plan Bruce called his 'Special Session'. It was a killer, moving between the track and the road for quick repeats, with very little rest time. Afterwards, Louis lay down on the track and shouted out in a pained voice, 'It burns! The lactic acid's in my *eyeballs*!'

We laughed the hazy, exhausted laugh of people unsure they'll ever take another breath, let alone another step. I knew what he meant — it was as though the gritty residue of pain stormed through your entire body, and nothing felt clean or in its proper place. My eyes hurt too, my scalp, my feet. It was a good pain, though, the kind you want to feel. So bad you loved it.

We watched Erin still running around the track in the dying light of the day.

Verne stood up, a bit shaky on his feet. He wandered over to where I sat, then grabbed his crotch through his shorts and shook his penis up and down in front of my face. 'Fuck,' he cried out. 'The lactic acid's gonna make my balls drop off! The only thing to save me is a wet place to put my cock. Help me, Mickey, help me!'

Howls of laughter again, though I managed only a dry snort. A couple of the other boys started to do the same thing, cupping their balls and shouting out how they needed help, asking all the girls to sort them out. 'Help me, save my future children!'

Hilary leapt to her feet. 'Sort out your own bloody testicles, you arseholes.' She stalked back to the clubrooms, the boys hooting and the girls cheering.

I lay on the grass and felt my body piece itself back together.

THE PRESSURE WAS UNRELENTING. EACH month meant more running, more drills, less food, less rest. Endless competitions. During the day, working at Ann's, I would be dead on my feet. A zombie, Ann took to calling me. My feet ached when I stood at the sink rinsing a never-ending stream of dishes, and when I practised my flat white and latte milk on the frother my eyes would shut from exhaustion and I'd burn my wrist on the machine. Every night I fell asleep before I'd completed the full foam-rolling and stretching routine, though I did try. I always pushed myself in the training sessions, trying to find the boundaries of myself, the parts where I could push and create change. To go faster, longer. Bruce said he could make a runner out of me, so I followed his training to the fringes of obsession. I wasn't lazy, I discovered; my father had been wrong about that.

I grew stronger, my body tighter. At each weigh-in, Yuri would smile and compliment me on my hard work, on my smaller, lighter figure.

It was all to achieve one goal: to win my 10,000-metre race at that year's National Track and Field Championships. Bruce entered me in the open women's division, even though I was only eighteen. The best runners in the country would line up with me, our toes on the same starting line, our bodies working through the same air for the same victory. 'No point slogging it out with a bunch of kids,' Bruce said. 'If you win against these women, the world is your oyster.'

The way he saw it, there was no other option but winning. On some of the slower runs in the taper, I'd return to the clubrooms to see him standing outside, watching us, and I was certain he was watching me. I felt observed and monitored, my whole self reduced to numbers in a book: weight, body fat, personal best.

THE NATIONAL CHAMPIONSHIPS WERE IN Christchurch that year. North Lynn paid for my flights and my entry fees, and though I was grateful, it felt like more pressure to perform.

I'd never flown before. As the plane accelerated on the runway, my body pressed back into the seat and I wondered how the narrow little safety belt, pulled tight across my hips, would help me in an emergency. How small are the things we think will help us.

The plane roared higher into the pale-blue sky, and I looked out the window and was amazed. The world looked altered from up there, a Toyland. The city and the islands out in the Waitematā, everything green and brown and silver. The white strip of surf along the coastline, the rising mounds of the mountain, the tiny cars zipping along the motorway, all growing smaller and smaller as the plane's engines thundered and we lifted higher. I was flying, truly airborne for the first time. My stomach rose in my chest and dropped. The sky was the rawest blue and the clouds streaked off to the curve of the horizon.

As we passed over Mount Taranaki, I had to swallow down a hard lump in my throat. I was supposed to be down there for Zach's twenty-first, not up here in the sky.

Even when I'd discovered that the national champs fell on the same weekend as his birthday, there was no question about what I'd do. Of course I would race. Then Zach asked me to sort a playlist for the party. 'I trust your taste,' he said. I felt incredibly guilty. I couldn't admit that I wasn't going to be there. I ignored his texts and phone calls for weeks. How do you tell someone you love that you're choosing to run instead of celebrating the very fact of their existence?

A week out from the party, I knew I couldn't put it off any longer. My fingers twitched when I pushed the green button on my phone. He answered on the second ring, and I skipped the pleasantries and told him straight: I won't be at your twenty-first.

There was a leaden pause, then: 'What do you mean, you won't be there?' His voice cracked.

I didn't know how to say that I didn't want to miss the party and I didn't want to miss the race.

'I'm sorry,' I said. 'I wish I could do both.'

'Skip it,' he said, his voice tight down the line. 'It's just a running race. Run it another time. There'll be another competition. Come on, Mick, this is my twenty-first we're talking about.' He made a low grunting noise. 'Hang on. Did you even consider coming to my birthday?'

I couldn't tell him the truth. I'd worked too hard to miss the nationals. This was it, my big break. The world, my oyster.

'So?' He was impatient.

'I'm sorry,' I said. 'There's nothing I can do. Could you change the date of your party?'

'It's too late for that, Mickey! I've sent out invitations, booked the venue. Besides,' he said, 'it's my birthday. I can't change the date of my birthday to suit your hobby.'

I held the crook of my thumbnail in my teeth and closed my eyes. Hobby. 'I'm going to nationals. It's—' Words seemed to mean nothing at this point. 'Zach—'

There was the dry, crinkling emptiness of the open line, and then the call was dead.

From my seat on the plane, the white tip of Mount Taranaki was no bigger than my thumbnail. I was on my way to nationals, to win the biggest race of my life. And yet ... Zach had touched a nerve. Was this just a hobby, no more important than knitting or crosswords or making a gingerbread house? Or maybe those things were important, and I was thinking about it all backwards. The darker corners of my mind grabbed those thoughts and let them settle and flourish. Running was simply the act of moving my legs. Around a track, along the road. Always moving forward, circling endlessly, going nowhere but back from where I started. What was the point? I wasn't delivering a message to Athens, proclaiming the victory of Marathon. Nothing so dignified or important. The only point was to see if this was a race I could win. And for this I would miss his birthday. I pulled down the window shade and pretended to sleep.

WE LANDED TO THE CRISP air of Christchurch in early autumn. I told Alain I was heading out for a short, easy run to shake my legs after the flight.

'Just make sure you're back before six,' he said. 'We'll eat dinner and then do the evening visualisation of your race.'

'Aye aye, captain!' I headed out, down along the straight avenues of the city.

Maybe running was nothing but moving my body — but damn, it felt good. I felt the beat of my heart move into the back of my head, and blood flooded the ends of my body. My fingers, my toes, the backs of my knees, the curve of my thoracic and into my collarbone. It all came alive, and I wished I could've told Zach that this was what I was chasing: it was more than a sport, more than my ego. It was more than a hobby. It was like flying, I should have said, it was like floating up above it all.

In the distance I saw the headlights of cars at intersections, orange turning to red. I stopped and turned around, keeping all that at my back. I didn't want to see the colours, the intolerable wait until the flash of green. I rolled my shoulders and loosened my body, letting it drift into the shapes it needed to make. I wouldn't think about that, about Daniel and the way I felt burned and empty from the mistakes of a three-minute wait for the lights to change. I turned away and focused on the now. Nothing would stop me. I couldn't afford to lose.

ELEVEN

THE STARTING LINE FOR THE women's race was much more daunting than the under-19 line-up the year before. These women were athletes — strong, physically mature in ways I couldn't fathom. Rock-hard stomachs and a grit to their faces that showed all the experience I was yet to accumulate.

Alain had run through a visualisation with us the night before — I hoped it would be helpful now. He'd asked us to lie on the floor of the hotel's conference room. The carpet was rough and smelled of cigarette smoke. 'Close your eyes,' he said, 'and imagine the race from the starter's gun to the finish line. I'll set a timer, and when you finish raise your hand. You should finish around the time you would actually finish your race. Imagine each step. Imagine each breath. The sounds, what you see, how you feel. Ready, set, go—'

The call had been made: we were to move from the marshalling area to the starting line. My imaginary race flashed away. I needed to focus on the real thing. I bounced from foot to foot. The stadium filled with cheers from the crowd as a man leapt into the air, his legs and arms extended out in front of him, then landed in the pit, sand spraying out on impact.

On my feet were the white-and-red racing flats that Bonnie had given me. They were soft, comfortable, and I jumped again, keeping my energy high. I inhaled deeply through my nose, letting my breath loose between my lips. Bruce had told me to go out hard, to hold the lead early. *Take control*, he'd said to me that morning. *Show them you're the boss.*

I felt uneasy about that idea. Going out hard, holding the lead. That was unnatural to me. Could I properly gauge the speed to take the race out in the first few laps? Was it possible to take the lead early and hold it for twenty-five laps? It seemed foolish. Risky. Marleen Renders had done that, taken an early lead, and held it — but only for a while. Soon she faltered, and she was swept up in the mass of the group and her name forgotten, her glory of leading the pack across the bridge worth nothing.

Twenty runners stepped to the line. I wasn't surprised to be the shortest — only children were shorter than me, and a lot of kids were taller. Sita, another North Lynn runner, stood along the line closer to the outside lane. I was suddenly glad she was there, though we weren't close friends. I stared at the burnt-tangerine track: twenty-five laps to go. It felt as though my life was in the balance. If I didn't win, I would have missed Zach's party for nothing.

At that thought my hands began to shake. I gripped them into fists and hit my thighs a few times. My body zinged with nerves. A light wind, rushing from the east. The smell of hot chips, the salt and the oil, wafting from the stands. My ponytail so tight my scalp hurt. I knew then that I wouldn't do what Bruce suggested. I knew it in that moment when the starter asked us to take our marks. My shoe touched the white line, and I bent my knees slightly. There was a pause. I heard the breathy exhale of the runner next to me, and our elbows touched. I would run the race the way I always ran: sitting behind the leaders, biding my time, hunting them down.

Get set. Go!

The smack of the starting gun, and we were off.

THE WHOLE GROUP RUSHING, RACING away from the line. Adrenaline hitting like a high. Bodies in motion, moving quickly together, finding my space, high knees, fast cadence, catch the breath, keep it steady. Heart leaping into my head, beating, loud, louder. Stay calm. Settle into the pocket. The leading group a set of five runners, the rest of the pack trailing out behind us like a hungry tail. We all want it. Nobody can be ruled out now, it's anyone's game.

Four laps, six. Feet on track, the sound and the feeling over and over. Crowds cheering, wind on face, sweat beading on chest, in armpits, on brow. Thoughts of the party, the one I would miss, dancing at the corners of my mind. Push it away, let the desperation pull me forward.

On the eighteenth lap I pulled level with the two women leading the way. I was on the outside, running further than I should. I knew Bruce would be cursing my choices. Slapping his hand through the air as though he could shift me to the inside, to take the lead already, like I was a puppet awaiting his manipulation. I didn't, though. I remained on the outside. We stayed like this for another half lap before the woman in the middle could no longer maintain the pace. I felt her weakness and pressed harder. Took it up a gear. Pressured her to drop off. It worked, and she was gone. I moved inward, beside the other woman, who was still slightly ahead of me. I kept in her shadow, letting her do the hard work for another two laps. Her eyes cut to me from the side every now and then. She was assessing the situation, trying to see how I was feeling. Her face was red, her arms jerky. I knew I had her then. Lactic acid filtered in to my quadriceps like a rumour — I ignored it. I was almost there.

I took the win in 30 minutes, 30.26 seconds, a New Zealand record. More than three minutes faster than my run the previous year.

I was totally spent. My muscles seemed to shimmer with tension and exhaustion. I hobbled to Bruce and Alain, standing near the finish line. I cried out a honking, ecstatic laugh. Alain clapped his hands in a short applause and Bruce nodded his head slowly. He looked at me with an odd expression, as though he expected me to answer a question he hadn't yet asked. Then he said, 'Well done.'

THE RACE

TO MY LEFT IS THE red fence alongside the port, the piles of rusty red and blue shipping containers behind it. Coming up to Vector Arena I see a sign:

GO MICKEY

I LOVE YOU

I almost trip over my feet in shock. I read it again to be sure I've read it right. Yes: *Mickey*. It must be for me: surely there's no other Mickey running this race.

Niall's head pops out from behind the sign. 'Go, Mickey!' He's next to me for just a second as I run by — our hands touch — and then I'm away.

Not a whisker of movement from Ruby, stony-faced and grim, her cheeks set in a grimace of commitment. Then the man running with us jerks sideways into my space and pushes me. I nearly tumble to my knees. Cortisol flares up in a burning rage: 'Careful, you idiot!' I'm embarrassed the instant the words leave my lips. I take a breath, let the stress drift away and let out a whoop of joy — I want to savour every second of this. He loves me. The dip in morale is over. I'm in it to win it. Or, as Niall likes to say, *Sometimes you gotta risk it for the biscuit.*

I want to look back and see him one more time, but I resist. I add this feeling to the fire inside my chest. It's burning hot, this bonfire of desire and ambition. *Give it fuel,* Philippa would say. *Let your fire burn.*

We head along Quay Street, up the incline to the intersection with The Strand. Up, up, chest heaving. It hurts, I'm digging, digging the cave. Feet pound on the downhill, a sublime stream of skin through air. There's a bit of shade along here from the trees, and the seven of us in the chasing pack sneak into it as much as possible. Water on both sides of us now: Judges Bay on our left, Mechanics Bay on our right. Blue and green around me and above me, and he loves me. He loves me.

The full tide is on the turn. Everything's ebbing, flowing, shifting, changing. I thought I'd messed it up with Joel and that I'd never find love again, but I was wrong. I found something better. I look over the water, at the peak of Rangitoto. The water's flickering silver in the wind, a messy chop giving the surface the look of velvet. Above the water a gannet soars on the breeze, its whiteness stark against the black-green of the volcanic peak. I smile. We're both flying, at peace in the moment, born to move and be free.

TWELVE

IN SPITE OF MY SUCCESS at the nationals, or perhaps because of it, the next year didn't pan out the way I hoped it might. Zach didn't speak to me for two months. I texted him and phoned him, but he didn't reply. I stopped by his flat when out on a long run, and he either wasn't home or didn't want to see me. I spoke to Bonnie on the phone on Sundays, and she told me to wait it out, that in time he would move on. He's your brother, he'll forgive you. She said I should celebrate my success. I'd earned it.

Except the win felt tainted. The record was more than a time, it was a record of my failure as a sister. The medal hanging from the knob of my bedroom door reminded me in equal measure of the greatest thing I'd ever done and possibly the worst. After a while I moved the medal to the drawer of my bedside table, hiding it among silver sheets of Panadol and cellphone charger cords.

The track season ended after the nationals. Bruce told me to keep running — a group of us would represent North Lynn at the cross-country champs in June. 'Stay on your feet,' he said. 'It isn't time for a vacation.'

Alain met me twice a week to keep the momentum going. The rest of it was up to me, so I kept at it, running further, lifting heavier weights; more drills, less food.

April rolled into May, then the start of June brought with it a freezing, wintry blast. It felt as though I never ran in daylight. I was a beast of the night, pounding the streets, where leaves collected in damp and rotting piles in the gutters. Sometimes I thought I heard the faint sound of footsteps following me, the invisible runner haunting my miles, but there was no one there.

Temperatures kept dropping, and I knew I needed longer leggings, some merino long-sleeved tops, if I was to keep up the training. I had no idea how I could afford them. It was Bonnie who came to my rescue.

'I don't want you running again until you have something decent to wear,' she said when I told her I was training in shorts and tee-shirt on eight-degree mornings. 'I'll put some money into your account.'

I checked the balance the next morning. Two hundred dollars, enough for new leggings and a warm top, as well as a merino-lined headband I could wear to keep my ears warm when I first started out. Every week after that, she deposited fifty dollars into my account, never asking for acknowledgement. I wish I'd told her the money felt like a message: someone cared about me and wanted to be sure I was okay.

When I think of that winter I remember mostly numbers, the way the season passed in a haze of data and information: the number of kilometres run, my oxygen uptake threshold, pulse oximetry, my heart rate and recovery rate; cross training; tempo runs, long runs, easy runs. New shoes, new socks. Calories burned, calories eaten, carbohydrate gels, electrolyte drinks.

The weight continued to drop off — until it didn't. I couldn't understand why the numbers would no longer shift on the scales. Every second of the day I was calculating what I'd eaten, and what I would eat later, and how much exertion would be needed to burn off the calories I'd consumed. I forced myself to do twenty squats before and after going to the toilet, and at work I shuffled on my feet, never letting my body rest. I'd heard that people who 'fidgeted' were slimmer by virtue of burning calories through posture changes, random tensing of muscles, tiny movements of hands and feet, so I fidgeted. I replaced breakfast and lunch with café coffee, knowing my body would zing from the caffeine. Dinner was protein heavy, with a small amount of carbohydrates. Over the winter I slowly cut out more from my diet: fruit, gone; no more starchy vegetables, no more bread; legumes and most dairy gone too. The weight wouldn't drop, though soon my body felt hollowed out and empty. My hands and feet felt transparent, and they tingled as if sparks of electricity were jolting through them. My hair fell out in handfuls with each shampoo. My period grew irregular, and then, by September, I stopped menstruating altogether. At first I was concerned, and then I stopped thinking about it at all. I was like a male athlete now, unhampered by the inconvenience of tampons and blood and hormones.

I won the cross-country championships — though it was close, only by 1.3 seconds. Bruce gave me a North Lynn jacket to put on at the finish line, and grimaced. 'That wasn't quite the display of dominance I'd been expecting, Mickey.'

I shook my head. I was exhausted. No race had felt like that one — every step a grind, muscles aching, feet sore, body sucked into the pull of gravity. It hadn't felt like flying. Bruce said we would have to work on a few things before the next track season began and that I should watch my fitness over the next few months. He paused between instructions to run his tongue over his lips, and after a while his voice faded into the cheers of the crowd, the grumble of thunder crashing somewhere just over the horizon, until I no longer heard what he was saying. I zoned out. I wanted to lie down on the muddy grass, right there, and fall asleep.

THAT EXHAUSTION, THAT WHOLE-BODY FATIGUE, it followed me like a loyal dog into the next track season. In truth, other things haunted me that winter too. The national record and the gold medal hadn't changed much for me after all. A part of me still hoped Teddy might call and offer his congratulations. That didn't happen. And there was the ghost runner, the footsteps echoing behind me, a fear always too far away to be seen.

During our first official training session of the new season, Bruce told us to have a check in with Yuri. We all understood what that meant: weight and body condition. There were plenty of familiar faces from last season, but some absences, too — those who'd quit or moved on to another club. There were a few new people milling around in the clubrooms as well. I understood how they must be feeling — anxious in their very bones that this was a mistake, and that their big break to train with Bruce Madden would be taken away at any moment.

My turn came to stand on the scales. The red digits flashed up, and I kept my eyes on Yuri, as if by looking at the numbers they would somehow get bigger, and that it was better luck if he read them out to me.

'Thirty-nine point six.' He looked me in the eye. 'Well done, you've maintained your training weight all winter. When we start racing in four weeks Bruce will want you down to racing weight, so you should start working towards that now.'

Racing weight. I'd been 38.3 at the nationals last year. Bruce had seemed happy with that.

I sat outside on the steps to lace up my sneakers, and felt my hands shaking. I'd had an extra coffee, black — milk had too many calories, too much fat — to give me some energy for training. How was I going to lose over a kilogram? I set my teeth on my pinkie fingernail and took a bite, catching an edge of skin with it. Looking down, I saw how my thighs pressed out onto the concrete step. They looked too big. I held my hands on my stomach, and pressed down until it hurt.

On the first Saturday morning training of the season, I arrived late — everyone else was on the track doing drills. Yuri was inside. He didn't say anything when I came in. The calipers were on the table next to him, and he picked them up and pressed them first to my thigh. Then my hip, my arm. The metal was cold on my skin — I hadn't missed this at all.

He glanced at the calipers and then at the notes in his book. 'You're at 16 percent.' He made another note next to my name. 'Maybe spend some time considering what you can do to get it down to, what, 13 percent? Twelve?'

Red indentations remained on my skin where the calipers had pinched. I couldn't look at Yuri, at his smug face. Without wanting to, I sighed. 'Why, Yuri? Can't I just stay like this for a while? Please?'

He sniffed. 'You got a problem, Michelle? Take it up with Bruce.'

I didn't take it up with Bruce. I knew what he'd say: extend the gym session on Monday afternoon by half an hour. Do more active recovery — swimming, cycling. Increase your activity, inspect your diet. It was impossible to do more than I was doing, to eat less than I was eating. My body had entered survival mode.

It is surprising that so few people said anything about my appearance. I suppose they thought I was a dedicated athlete, with different nutritional needs, and my physique was perfectly normal for someone pushing their body to the limit. In fact, I was a shadow, a hollow wraith.

Only two people mentioned my weight over that summer. One was a friend of my flatmate Heather, who came to a party at our flat in the sticky holiday period around New Year. He must have thought I was out of earshot when he said, 'Why doesn't someone feed that girl? She's fucking anorexic!'

The other person was Bonnie. I went back to Ngāmotu for Christmas. The house on Rutherford Street was bursting with people and noise — Helen came home with Bryn, a small diamond ring on her finger; Kent, single and preparing to leave New Zealand in the new year for a job as an editor at a UK publisher. Zach was there too, with his latest girlfriend, a red-head named Callie, who had long feet and a micro-fringe that sat spiky over a pimpled forehead. At first it was awkward between Zach and me, our eyes cutting away if they dared meet. When he spoke to me, it was with the detached interest of an acquaintance. The change in the dynamic between us was painful, and I could see the others preferred to pretend there was nothing wrong.

After Christmas lunch Mum disappeared into the kitchen to wash the dishes, and I followed her to help. I filled the sink high with suds and dunked the plates and cutlery. 'You relax,' I insisted, snatching the tea towel from her. 'You did all the cooking.'

She eased herself onto a chair. 'I won't say no to an offer like that,' she said. 'It's nice to have you home, honey.'

My siblings were laughing and talking in the lounge, and I knew I'd excluded myself from them in some significant way. By choosing to miss Zach's party I'd made it plain that something else — my hobby, my ambition — was more important to me than they were, even if that had not been my intention. Helen had asked me over Christmas lunch what the long-term plan was with my running, and when I said I hoped to run at the Beijing Olympics in the 10,000, the look on her face reminded me of Mrs Badditch. A look of pity. So it was a relief to be alone with Mum in the kitchen, the lightbulb blown once again in the fitting above the sink. Surrounded by the mess of the cooking, it felt almost as though I'd never left, and I'd made no terrible choices, and nothing terrible had happened to me.

I looked at Mum, her hands clasped between her knees, her eyes weepy. I dried my hands on the tea towel and asked if she was okay. She seemed almost as tired as I was, but she flicked the question and turned it around to me.

'I'm fine. Just a bit run down. Are you sure *you're* okay, honey? You hardly ate any dinner. I'm worried about you.'

'I'm good,' I said, turning back to the sink, lowering my hands into the soapy water. 'I'm at racing weight.' That was a lie — I'd stood on Mum's scales that morning and the pointer swung around to 39.5. Well over. Yuri and Alain and Bruce would be furious. Too much rich food, Bruce would say, makes a poor runner.

There was a moment of silence before she said, 'You know, Mickey, that I would be proud of you even if you weren't a great runner? You know that, right?'

I scrubbed the brush over the roasting dish, lifting the baked-on potato and kūmara. The cloud that had been smothering the sun moved away, and outside the window, in the bright Christmas day sun, the cicadas' thick humming filled the air. The sound was frantic. Without turning to look at her, I said, 'I know that, Mum.' And I wasn't lying. I knew my mum loved me, even when I didn't understand why she did.

ON MY NINETEENTH BIRTHDAY, YURI led us on a 19k run, full of hills. 'In your honour,' he told me, with a mock bow. We alternated kilometres at our race pace and then a slightly slower pace. It was a humid afternoon, and the heat was oppressive. Even I couldn't appreciate the brilliance of the day — I felt awful, as though I was dragging my body over the hills like a sack of dead cats. Afterwards, we gathered in the shade under the jacaranda tree near the clubrooms. Some of the group were flat on their backs, others with their knees bent, heads hanging down, arms propped on their knees. Olive, one of the runners who'd joined us in October, was dry retching and spat yellow onto the grass. Louis didn't look as though he was breathing at all. I sat for five minutes, barely moving, and my breathing didn't slow. All the muscles in my legs throbbed, and not in a good way. A shrill twang rang in my ears. I wondered if there was something wrong with me.

Yuri stood up. 'It's clear you're in pain,' he said. 'I too have experienced this most exquisite suffering. It is our duty as runners to become intimate with this pain, and then find a way to the other side. This pain — she is a ghost. A phantom. If you are too scared to confront her, she will haunt you forever with the words, what if?'

Was he right? I certainly did feel haunted. I wanted to believe every word he said, despite a kernel of suspicion deep inside. I knew this couldn't be the only way to get faster. I knew this sort of punishment wasn't normal, and that it shouldn't be encouraged. It was masochistic, and egotistical, to suggest that what the coaches were asking of us was justified. Deep inside, I knew that what he'd said was ridiculous, that most of what Yuri said was ridiculous, and yet — there was another part of me that was seduced by it. The pain he talked about was real. We were all diving headfirst into that pain, and discovering who was strong enough to survive, who would come through it to return again the next day, and the next, to do it all again. A part of me loved the pain, I loved that I was one of those who kept coming back for more. Because on the other side of pain — or so I was told — was where the best runners lived.

THE RACE

PANCAKES ARE STILL ON MY mind when I feel a contraction in my stomach. It's powerful and sudden, and I press my lips together. I'm not sure what's wrong. The thought of pancakes now gives me a headache.

I focus on my breath, on the pace. I watch Ruby's plaits swinging. We cruise along, and I'm disoriented. Is that Kelly Tarlton's? I don't know where I am. The wretched pain returns, and I start heaving. My stomach lurches upward, out of control, and my mouth fills with vomit.

I hold the bitter taste of bile in my mouth for a few steps. My cheeks bulge with the pressure of it. My throat gags, a reflex I can't control. I have to hold it in — there's a man beside me, if I spit it out I'll cover his shoes with chunks of my spew, and I can't spit onto the road, I'm not as disgusting as that — there's no choice. I swallow down my vomit, and shudder at the rotten taste left in my mouth. I don't feel good. The body's working too hard. Letting me know how it stands.

There's a long way to go. My gut relaxes. I don't vomit again, but I feel as though I'm watching myself run from above, my legs flicking back and forth in a flash. I hear the soaring of a plane up high, and look up to see the three white prongs of the jet: tail and wings. I will never understand how something so heavy can fly. How does it escape gravity and all the other things conspiring to hold it down? I remember the first time I sat in a plane, on the way to the track and field champs in Christchurch, and feel my stomach clench. I'm not sure I can do this. Run a marathon. I'm not fast enough to escape the pull of Earth's gravity, the pull of all the things that conspire to keep me down.

THIRTEEN

PERHAPS IT WAS PRIDE THAT did me in. I was a fervent disciple of Yuri's philosophy — that the only way to avoid being haunted by the ghost of *what if?* was to keep pushing through the pain — so I didn't listen to my body when it was telling me to rest. I kept pushing, and pushing, and pushing—

And then—

Everything went from great to hard to horrible so fast, too fast. Life seemed to narrow, and there was nothing but fatigue, running, hunger, anger, sorrow. Nothing was beautiful, everything hurt. I was addicted to the pain, obsessed with becoming a great runner. It took me longer and longer to recover between training sessions. My muscle aches became permanent. I couldn't seem to find my way to the other side of the pain. At North Lynn training sessions, I was unable to chat and joke with the other athletes, and even Hilary eyed me warily. My brain felt full of fog, and at work I made lattes when I should have made flat whites: Ann said she was finding my inconsistency extremely frustrating. Worry about losing my job only added to the stress. My flatmates even held a house meeting. I needed to pull my weight with the cleaning, they said. If I couldn't be an adult about it, we'd have a cleaning roster so I wouldn't be able to say I didn't know it was my turn.

I was nineteen and I felt ninety. Running no longer felt like flying. It felt like bone-grinding work.

ONE CLEAR SUNDAY MORNING IN early March I woke before dawn and, as usual, went for a run. Bruce had insisted it should be a recovery day — we had a big competition in Papakura the next weekend — yet I couldn't help myself. The only way to the other side of pain was through it. I took off down Beach Road towards the Milford shops.

I was near the marina when it happened. I'd been running cautiously, my body rebelling with every step. My brain felt bruised. I didn't want to stop — that felt like giving up — so I kept pushing, trying to find some joy in the empty streets, the feel of the cool autumn air on my skin. Yet I kept hearing those steps, the ghost runner bouncing down the hill behind me, and I felt a tightness in my neck. I turned, several times, to see nothing but the empty grey tarmac, the power lines cutting black across the candy-pink sky. No runner. Nobody following me. And then, as I rounded the corner down to where the boats sat moored in the lagoon, it happened. The pain in my left leg that I'd been nursing for a few weeks grew unbearable, and I couldn't take a step without a lightning strike flashing up my shin, my knee, my thigh. I made a noise, a deep, deep cry, and a myna bird startled from its perch.

The pain radiated from a spot above my ankle bone, mid-calf, and I hobbled a step or two. The pain didn't lessen. I stopped, breathing rough and shallow, hoping that after a moment's rest the agony would subside and I'd be running again. I tried to jog, nice slow steps, but no — the sharp sting of pain was too much. I turned around and walked gingerly home, the injury shivering with every step.

I didn't tell anyone. At work, my hands trembled tamping down the coffee and I spilt the grounds all over the floor. 'Are you okay?' Ann asked. 'You seem to be limping.'

'Cramp,' I said, the lie too easy.

I skipped five training sessions and didn't return to North Lynn until four days later, when I realised I could no longer ignore the phone calls from Alain or Yuri.

THE OTHERS WERE ON THE track, preparing to do a series of 800 metres. I lay on the grass nearby, gazing up at the sky. No one came over to see me, to ask why I wasn't training — Alain would be the one to do that. The assistant coach always did the dirty work.

I heard the group as they lined up to begin the set, the shuffling of feet along the line. Alain would be with them, his fingers on his watch to start the timer. I heard their feet — the session had begun. They rounded the track past me, the thumping, whooshing noise of the bodies growing loud and then diminishing. I felt sick from both the pain in my leg and the guilt of missing the workout.

'You going to join us, Mickey?'

It was Alain, in his navy running shorts and white socks pulled up over his calves. He squinted down at me, flicking his wrist to check the time as the group curled around the track once more. I waited until they'd run by the stand of conifers at the far end before answering.

'I don't know, Alain. My leg hurts. Everything hurts.' I blinked away tears. Crying wouldn't help, and it would make Alain angry. Only soft people cried. I wasn't soft — I wasn't a potato! I was an egg.

'Don't give me that, Mickey. Get up and finish the workout, and then we'll have someone check you over.' He paused and bit his lip. 'Did you weigh in before training today?'

I nodded. I didn't want to think about it. Forty kilograms. The heaviest I'd been in eighteen months. Yuri had jotted it in his notebook. 'The only person you're hurting with this weight gain is you,' he'd said. 'You'll need to do an extra hour on the stationary bike after the training session this evening. And we'll do a body composition test today too, seeing as we're racing this weekend and your weight's way over.'

His hands were cold on my skin. First, the measurement at the tricep, my right arm. In the soft spot between shoulder and elbow, where Helen used to pinch me when we'd had an argument. His hands moved to my waist then, to measure the suprailiac, a diagonal fold in the space just above my hip. Finally my leg, midway between my knee and the top of my thigh.

The results weren't too different from last time. Fifteen percent. Yuri was sceptical about the accuracy of the test, calling it a blunt tool. 'You're carrying a lot more fat than 15 percent,' he said. He'd heard that American professional athletes took full body scans to measure fat, and also checked out the athlete's bone health. 'It would be great to get one of those. Get some real science. Anyway, Mickey. Disappointing numbers today. I think you need to assess what you can reasonably do to get that down to 12, even 11 percent. And the weight. What we're seeing today just isn't good enough.'

Lying at Alain's feet, I watched a seagull circling idly over the athletics club. Alain opened his mouth, as though to say something else, but he didn't speak. The seagull flew away. How lucky it was to fly anywhere it wanted. When I looked again, Alain was gone.

The runners were beginning the warm-down, five minutes easy, when I saw Bruce, wide, beefy, hands in his pockets, white stubble striping his chin, coming towards me. I sat up, bending my knees to my chest, and wiped my eyes.

He sat on the brown, prickly grass with a grunting sigh, and for a while he didn't say anything. We watched the group go around and around.

He spoke first. 'I'm not sure where we go from here, Mickey.'

I didn't say anything, so he looked at me with a stern eye and continued: 'When you came here two years ago, you were an exciting prospect. So young. Age-group champion. A hunger in you to compete that I'd not seen in a teenage athlete for a long time.' We watched the runners move past us again. 'You haven't fulfilled the potential we saw in you. Time, money, resources — what we had available, we have given to you. The best coaching in the country. A training philosophy second to none. And still you've let yourself down. You've let all of us down.' His voice dropped low when he said, 'You miss training. Your weight's out of control. Your attitude's starting to affect the other runners, and I can't have that.'

It was like being scolded by Teddy. I'd given my everything and now here we were, me with an attitude problem, my presence no longer tolerated. In a small voice I asked what I should do now. He shook his head, and said he didn't know. 'Get your leg checked out by a doctor,' he said, 'and don't bother coming back here until you're ready to be a professional.'

I MISSED THE COMPETITION THAT weekend in Papakura. I wanted to call Zach and spend the time with him, but I didn't think he'd want to see me. I took Monday off work and went to a radiologist clinic for an x-ray. The next Thursday, instead of standing on the scales at North Lynn Track and Field, I stood on the scales in my GP's office. The numbers were still important even here — 39.8. In spite of everything, I felt a thrill: I'd dropped two hundred grams without even trying. The doctor, Harim, asked me to stand under a pull-down measuring tool, and took down my height, tapping the result into his computer. I sat while he took a moment to read the report from the radiologist about my femur x-ray.

'I'm inclined to think this stress fracture isn't an isolated incident,' he said at last. 'When I look at your BMI, there are a few red flags, and I'm worried this is symptomatic of a much larger issue.' He scrolled his mouse, rolling down the radiologist's report again. 'It's a significant stress fracture, and I suspect one of many.'

I thought of the feeling through my legs during my last run, the agony of my hips, my lower back. I imagined my whole skeleton as an x-ray, spectral white on black, insubstantial.

'Tell me about how things have been going lately. What was it again? Sprinting?'

Longer distance, I told him. Ten thousand metres.

'That's a long way,' he said. 'And how's that going? Are you finding the training more or less difficult than you previously have? How's your mood?'

I looked down at my feet and gave him the bare details of how things had been since I'd won the national title last April. The slower times, my lack of motivation. Training sessions that were once easy now felt insurmountable.

His face softened. 'And your eating habits? Could you describe what you'd normally consume in a day?'

The question sat in the air for a moment.

'I guess I don't eat much,' I said, and let out a shaky breath. 'I think I've got a problem.' I'd said it now. *A problem.*

'What sort of problem?'

'It's probably obvious,' I said, looking at the floor. 'I think I've got an eating disorder.'

He sat back in his chair and held his hands in his lap. 'I think, Michelle, that you're suffering from anorexia nervosa, a psychological condition that can be treated with some cognitive therapy, perhaps some medication. I'm going to refer you to a psychologist, as well as ask you to have some blood tests and an MRI. Right now, I'm going to listen to your chest and your heart.'

He leaned forward and lifted his stethoscope to his ears. I pulled my tee-shirt up and he pressed the chestpiece onto my sternum. He looked up to the ceiling, avoiding my gaze. Every few seconds he shifted the chestpiece, pressing it down elsewhere, moving around my ribs, onto the skin near my collarbone. I turned around, and he lifted my top higher, placing the stethoscope onto my back. He asked me to inhale and exhale, and didn't mention the soft hair along my upper spine.

'Your heart sounds okay,' he said, taking the headset from his ears. 'Although I might have an ECG arranged, just to be certain.'

He typed on his keyboard and I sat waiting for him to speak again. The office walls seemed to flare and move in and out, and I thought I might faint. When he finally spoke, he didn't look away from the computer screen.

'And your periods? Are they regular or irregular?'

I put my hand over my mouth, and said, 'I haven't had a period in seven months.' I bit my thumbnail, clipping at the hard edge. How ironic, I thought then, that I'd always hated feeling invisible and now I craved it.

He stopped typing for a second. 'That's a real concern, Michelle. Amenorrhoea is a sign of hormonal dysfunction, and potentially can impact on fertility and bone health. I'll also need to refer you to a sports medicine specialist.'

He typed for a moment, then rubbed his chin. 'I'm aware this is all quite a lot to take in. I'm hoping we've caught the warning signs early enough and that you'll be able to return to your sport in the near future.'

Return to your sport in the near future. I felt as though I'd been electrocuted. I couldn't listen to what he was saying, his voice droning on and on. I interrupted — 'Do I need to take time off?'

'I think it's advisable,' he said, 'on the strength of this one x-ray, that you take at least six weeks off running, and find yourself a good physiotherapist. Once we have the results of the MRI, we'll know a bit more about where we stand and how to proceed. I'll have the results sent here and also to the sports specialist, and you'll be in his care from now on.'

He gave me a stack of paperwork when I left — MRI form, more x-rays, blood tests. He'd email the others to the specialists, he told me, before ushering me out of his office. I held the forms tight as I walked slowly home, afraid they'd blow away in the wind — though a part of me hoped they'd float away over the glittering green water to Rangitoto as if they'd never existed, as if there was no problem worth investigating.

Only there was no wind that day. March was warm, and my scalp grew sticky with sweat. I was bone tired. The pain in my leg was sharp, like needles, but still the thought came to me that this would be a perfect afternoon for a run. As I crested the hill, the Hauraki Gulf spread out ahead, sparkling in the sunshine. The beauty of the world continued just the same, unconcerned with me.

IT WAS COLD INSIDE THE MRI. I didn't understand how it worked. The tunnel seemed inert, yet it was gathering information from inside my body, releasing the secrets held inside, the ones I'd thought would remain hidden.

The hem of the thick grey gown the nurse had given me tickled my leg, and I breathed deep, filling my lungs, letting the exhale release slowly, trying to resist the urge to move my hand and scratch. My body felt hollow, as empty as the machine itself. Lying flat on the bed of the MRI, the shape of my hips and legs was being imaged — the size of them, the heft of them. I couldn't imagine what I looked like, I'd lost the sense of where my body ended. I was uncertain about the space I took up in the world. I inhaled again: there was a lingering smell of peppermint in the air, perhaps from the previous person. It was comforting, as if someone was close by, and I was not all alone, inside a machine that threatened to end it all.

It couldn't be the end. It couldn't be as bad as what the doctor had said: no more running. It would be one small fracture, six weeks' rehabilitation, then back to the grind. That would be it; I held that hope in my mind and spun it around. All the painful thoughts slipped away like fish from a fist.

A beeping noise woke me up. I was still in the chamber. What the hell was happening? *You're possibly suffering from something known as RED-S*, Harim had said. I'd googled it: Relative Energy Deficiency in Sport. I needed to get out of this machine. I knew the interminable length of a second, and each one in here felt as long as an eternity.

When at last I was free of the MRI I found it hard to walk. My body was stiff and inflexible, and there was a flickering in my feet as the blood rushed back.

THE SPORTS EXERCISE SPECIALIST WAS a short man with a thick dark beard that covered most of his cheeks. He spoke too quickly, trying to explain what he'd seen in my MRI results with medical jargon that went over my head. The verdict seemed to be that I had multiple stress fractures. Later, I understood why they called them that: nothing can withstand constant stress without cracking.

'Will I be able to start running again soon?' I asked.

'Of course not,' he said. 'You have a significant crack in your right fibula, two in your femur. A series of tiny fractures down your leg, a series of fine breaks in your pelvis. Think of it like your body is falling apart.'

I laughed, but he didn't seem to see the joke.

'No running. Absolutely not,' he went on. 'You need physical therapy, a nutritionist, too. I'd estimate a minimum of six months' rehab, no less. If you're not careful, you might not run ever again.'

A week passed before I felt ready to tell anyone at North Lynn.

Hilary was the only one who seemed to care. She placed her hand on my shoulder and said, 'I'm sorry, Mickey. Are you okay?' A few of the other runners told me I'd been an inspiration. Yuri and Alain expressed a modicum of sadness; Bruce, unmoved, only nodded his head at the news.

'Some of us are thoroughbreds,' he told me, 'and some of us are workhorses. There might be less beauty in watching a workhorse do the job, but a thoroughbred's delicacy and unreliability mean it doesn't often last the distance.'

It wasn't clear whether this was a compliment or an insult. It seemed a fitting end to a relationship that had promised much and delivered little.

I left that afternoon. I wouldn't be an Olympian. All the sacrifice had been for nothing. I called Bonnie, and she told me to come home.

PART
TWO

FOURTEEN

BLACK NOTHINGNESS. A SHIMMERING grey-and-white skeleton, my bones ghostly lines. The pen of the sports specialist dancing along my tibia, my femur. Shattering: here, here, here. Some of the dark lines are fractures as fine as the strands of my hair. His toothy face and black eyes, my heart and stomach dropping away from my body to the floor.

This dream haunted me for years, at first almost weekly, then every few months. Each time I would wake in a fright, my heart racing. It was a dream, of course, so it wasn't the same as the reality. The reality was crisper, less dramatic — and happened only once. The dream came twenty, maybe thirty times, and my memory was shaded and altered by its impression.

AFTER MY DIAGNOSIS, I MOVED home with Mum. It was like travelling back in time: the same sheets on the bed, the same flickering lightbulb in the kitchen. She paid for me to see a nutritionist and a physiotherapist, never once asking me to pay her back. I ended up staying a year.

The rehabilitation was intense. I went from running 10 kilometres on the track in half an hour to three minutes on the stationary bike: no more than that, said the physio, a spry woman with salt-and-pepper hair. 'It will take some time to get you back on your feet.'

It did. A full year after my MRI, she said she had some good news. I could slowly ease back into running. 'Start small,' she said. 'Jog for a minute, walk for a minute. Jog, walk, jog, walk. Do that ten times, have a day of rest, and try again. Over time your body will adapt and you'll be back where you were.'

I didn't want to run and end up back where I was. I felt humiliated, and I was furious with Daniel, Bruce and Yuri — though mostly I was angry with myself. I'd failed. Everything Teddy had said about me was true — I was lazy. Lazy people don't run, so I wouldn't. I put my sneakers away, said goodbye to Bonnie once again, and moved back to Auckland.

I found a room in a dingy house in Henderson with three random flatmates, and accepted a job as a barista at a café in Titirangi called Four Loaves, next door to a garden centre. My weight crept up, 42, 43, and settled around 45 kilograms. Part of me knew this was a healthy weight, a perfectly ordinary weight for someone of my height, but the devil inside me taunted: *you're too fat, you should lose weight.*

I sank into a darkness like the black-green river, but now Kent wasn't there to pull me up the way he had that day I'd plunged in to the depths before I'd learned to swim. There was too much to hold inside — I wanted to split myself open and let it all out. With a pair of scissors I cut open the disposable razor I'd been using to shave my legs. The thin blade fell from the plastic handle, and I held it in my fingers. Then I pressed it against the skin on my thighs and my stomach. I held my breath and began to cut, tiny slices at first, then larger and deeper, down my thighs and on my stomach. Bloody tracks marking my skin, scabs that took a long time to heal.

What I was doing was foul — and it was simultaneously delicious, a release from all the self-loathing. Cutting myself was disgusting — but I was disgusting too. My body had betrayed me. It had let me down in so many ways — too big, too small, too touched, too imperfect, too fractured. The red lines on my skin felt like a message to others: it's okay, the message said, to find me repulsive, because I do too.

Alone in Auckland, I could hide the damage. I wore long sleeves. No one saw me naked. It was a private, lonely hell, kept secret from everyone until I visited Bonnie for Christmas. The weather was mint — cloudless skies and no wind. She suggested we walk down to the river for a swim, and when I reluctantly stripped down to my togs there was no hiding the scars in all their pitiful glory. Bonnie didn't speak when she saw the rippled skin, the lumpy scabs. She pulled me to her and held me close, arms tight around me. Her heartbeat was loud in my ear. I blinked, surprised to find I was crying. After a moment she murmured, 'Oh my darling.'

She helped me find a counsellor in Auckland and paid for twelve appointments. The counsellor was dull and patronising. It was obvious what she wanted me to say, the feelings she wanted me to explore, only I couldn't tell her everything. Was it even helping? I wasn't sure. A failure even at this. I felt guilty about the wasted money, all the money she'd wasted on me — until she told me I was being silly. She wanted a different life for me, she said. 'It's only money. You're more important to me than money. Keep going to the counsellor, please. It might not seem like it but it will help you, if you let it.'

She called me every day, without exception, and sent me packages in the mail: magazines, chocolate, hand cream. When she could take time off work, she drove up to Auckland and booked a room with two single beds in a run-down motel in Te Atatu. 'We can have a sleepover,' she said to me on the first visit. We ate fish and chips on the floor, and she taught me how to knit. 'If your hands are busy, there's less chance you'll get into mischief.' She placed her hands on mine as she showed me how to unravel a mistake in the stitching.

With time, Bonnie's love and patience, as well as the practical advice from my counsellor, I did stop cutting myself. By the time I was twenty-five, almost six years after I'd stopped running, I'd found a way to live in some version of happiness, despite the nagging urges that stalked me. The cuts healed and the message faded, though in the right light the silver lines still glittered.

AT A RAUCOUS PARTY FOR a flatmate's birthday, I met Joel. I was twenty-seven. I liked the way he wore a tee-shirt, his close-cropped hair, the baggy jeans with steel-capped boots. He told me he was an electrician, even though I didn't ask, and there was something in the way he kept his dark eyes on mine that I liked. He saw me, and wasn't cruel about what he observed. We started dating, and after two years moved in together to a unit in Oratia. We kept chickens in the small patch of grass outside our bedroom window; we played backgammon and drank cider. We went to the movies and Super Rugby matches. Neither of us read books. I thought I'd found my soulmate.

Our lives were simple: I drove my '96 Corolla to Titirangi each day for work; Joel drove his smoky ute to whichever house had called him out. We stayed home watching Netflix, and sometimes we'd go into the city and have a big night drinking and dancing. It was a life, unambitious and untroubled. We talked about marriage, kids, and although I'd never thought I wanted children there seemed little reason to say so. My life was empty and open, like Joel said: what else was there to do? We were born to procreate, he said. I'll work while you raise the sprogs. And because I'd made bad choices before while thinking I understood what was best for me, I let Joel take the lead, mapping out the future for both of us.

Days, months, years passed. Grinding beans and dumping used grounds into the knock box, backgammon and Netflix, Christmas in Ngāmotu or in Te Awamutu with Joel's parents. A vague general remorse hung over me, a bodily malaise. Maybe my life wasn't what I'd dreamed of, but there was companionship in it, and something a little bit like love.

By the time I'd turned thirty-one, I'd learned how to avoid thinking of the what if, the haunting ghost of my other life, although sometimes the thoughts came unbidden, particularly when I saw someone running. The first time a jogger ignited the sparks of a fiery panic attack in my chest, I called Bonnie. She was never too busy to talk, and we fell into the habit of speaking or messaging most days. My siblings and I had grown apart. We shared news and photographs on our WhatsApp group chat: Helen sent pictures of her newborn daughter and Bryn on the Wellington waterfront; Kent offered pictures of his Norwegian Forest cat Knausgaard sitting on the windowsill in his London flat. Beyond the cat I could see bare-branched elms in front of brick terraced houses, and felt a yearning to travel the world, though Joel wasn't interested. 'Everything we need is right here,' he'd say. 'Nothing better than old En Zed.'

Zach sent only emoji messages. Never photos. He still lived in Torbay, closer to me than any of the others, and yet I heard from him the least. He had been robotic and rude the one time he'd met Joel, who nicknamed him the 'Weird Bloom'. I never found the courage to explain to him why Zach acted as he did — that it was my fault. I didn't tell him that if anyone was the 'weird' Bloom, it was me.

Over that time, I saw Teddy four times. Three times at Christmas: stilted, distressing reunions over glazed ham and incessant Michael Bublé. The fourth time I saw him was by accident, a strange coincidence of time and place. It was November, a few months before I turned thirty. Joel and I were walking along Dominion Road on our way out to dinner. It was cool for late spring, and a brief rain shower had left the road slick with wet. Joel walked a half step ahead of me, his head swivelling to look inside every shop window, then turning to gaze at every car that drove past. There was a man walking ahead of us who

I thought looked like Teddy, nothing more, but when we drew near he reached out a hand. His face lifted, eyes wide with a happiness I couldn't remember seeing before: 'Helen!'

'Mickey,' I said, then I walked away. Joel didn't notice — he was watching a red Tesla Roadster, whistling at the car's sleek form as it drove by. I didn't turn back.

ONE MIDWINTER NIGHT NEARLY TWO years later, I was on the couch with Joel, as usual. An episode of *Stranger Things* rolled through the credits and Netflix threatened to begin the next episode in three, two, one — Joel turned it off and picked up his phone. The light hit his face in a rectangular yellow glow.

'We're going out for dinner this weekend with the boys,' he said. His finger flicked on the screen, scrolling, scrolling. 'Been far too fucking long between drinks.'

The boys were Joel's friends from school. They were a tight and loyal group — most of them still lived locally and they kept in touch daily, texting almost as often as I texted my mum.

'Saturday?' I lifted my head. Joel nodded, and said yeah, Saturday. Why, was there something else on that night? I shook my head and said no, there was nothing on that night. But I was lying. There was something on, and I didn't want to talk about it: the Opening Ceremony of the Rio Olympics.

JOEL LEFT BEFORE LUNCH TO repair a switchboard in Grey Lynn. 'Be ready for dinner when I get back,' he said. I nodded, distracted by the time: the ceremony would begin at midday. As soon as I was alone, I set my phone to silent, turned on the TV, and sat on the corner of the couch, picking at the loose skin around my cuticles.

When the teams began to enter the stadium with their flags, I muted the sound, overwhelmed by the noise of the crowd, exactly the same as when Naoko Takahashi had entered the stadium in Sydney to the thunder of voices. A part of me was still grieving the fact my teenage dream had come to nothing. I didn't even run anymore. It was too much in the end. I switched the TV off before New Zealand entered the stadium, and went outside. It was freezing, the wind howling and lashing the trees, but it was better than being indoors.

I was there still when Joel returned home. Our two chickens pecked at the grass by my feet. I wondered if they ever wanted to fly away, take off into the air with their glossy feathers and glide free. I knew they couldn't. Joel had clipped their wings.

'What are you doing?' He stood at the back door, looking down at me and the hens.

I shrugged. 'Nothing.' It was too difficult to explain, and the words I tried to piece together in my mind sounded ridiculous, insulting. This isn't the life I wanted! It was more complex than that, though. People I trusted had hurt me. I'd been assaulted. I'd been led to believe I wasn't enough, that I needed to change. Nobody liked me unless I was winning. I wanted to scream these things, hurl them from my body into the air between us. I couldn't say any of it to Joel. He wouldn't understand — he knew almost nothing about my running and what had happened before we met. He didn't live in emotions and regret, didn't stew in the past. He lived in the present moment — and in the present I didn't run.

'We need to leave in fifteen minutes,' he said. I stared at him and he jerked his head and said, 'Dinner with the boys, remember?'

I hadn't forgotten about the boys and their precious dinner — I just didn't want to go. Dinner with the boys always involved too much to drink. Someone would swear at the wait staff before the food was served. But Joel hated cancelling plans, so I said nothing.

He followed me back into the house. 'Are you going in that?' he said.

I was wearing jeans, a white tee-shirt and a red-and-white striped cardigan that Bonnie had found at an op-shop near the hospital. It was soft and smelled of Mum's detergent. Joel let out a throaty moan, opened our wardrobe, yanked his clothes aside, and started rifling through my jackets. 'Don't you own any dresses?'

'I don't think so,' I said. 'Those black pants are quite dressy.'

He took them out. In the afternoon light they looked drab and faded. They were missing a button at the waist. He threw the trousers on the floor and unhooked another coat hanger.

'What about this?' He held out a dull-violet minidress I'd bought from SaveMart for a party a few years earlier. The polyester fabric had pilled with white lumps.

'Not that dress,' I said. 'What about those pants and my red top?'

His mouth curled into a fox's grin. 'Just try it on,' he said. 'Come on.'

I took off the jeans and cardigan and pulled the dress over my head. Joel whistled.

'That's what I'm saying. This is how you should dress all the time. Turn around.'

I turned around. The dress covered more than my old racing kit had, but I felt almost naked. The silver scars peeked out from under the hem. I pulled it down, only the material had no give. The dress was too tight around my hips, too loose around my chest. Joel stared at me, and I wanted to vanish.

'If you were taller, babe, with pins like that. Shit,' he said, shaking his head, 'you'd be hot.'

I pressed down on the neckline. The material felt plastic and flammable, prickly on my skin.

'Have you got a padded bra?' he said. 'That might work. Or you could get a boob job.'

'What?' I held my hands over my chest. 'Are you kidding? You think I should get breast implants?'

'Of course not,' he said. 'There's no way you could get a boob job before we're supposed to meet the boys.'

The restaurant was newly opened and heaved with diners. It was like a cave, with black walls, and green and pink neon light displays above a wall covered in ferns and monstera. The music was too loud. Joel pulled the chair out for me and glanced around, as though checking to see if anyone had noticed his chivalry. I tongued my fingernail, wondering if it was him, or if it was me, because everything he did irritated me. I bit the nail and rolled it in my mouth. Remain calm, I thought. It's me, it isn't him.

The food was spicy and the cocktails expensive. The boys ordered a lot of both. Plates of beef and noodles, calamari deep-fried with aioli. Joel kept squeezing my hand or running his fingers up the inside of my thigh. The glass of wine I'd ordered went straight to my head, and I felt queasy. As expected, Henrik and Reed were soon drunk and swearing. Other diners looked over their shoulders at us and the waitress avoided coming to our table. Joel stood up and yelled at her — he wanted another beer.

'Fuck,' said Henrik in a loud voice, a half-eaten dumpling visible in his mouth. 'I saw some of the fucking Olympic ceremony today.'

'Waste of money,' George said, flicking his long hair out his eyes.

I snapped. 'It's not a waste of money.'

'Oh, she says it's not a waste of money, George,' Henrik said. 'So don't worry, we're all wrong.'

I ignored him and focused on my plate.

'You don't know what you're talking about, Michelle,' Tom said.

His girlfriend Holly was beside him, ignoring the conversation, talking instead about handbags with George's girlfriend Rebecca. These boys, I thought, they just wanted us to talk about handbags and makeup, high heels and baking — they hated a woman to have an opinion about anything that mattered. Tom lifted his beer, and the glass hovered near his mouth for a moment before he slammed it down on the table. Foam spilled over the lip of the glass onto Holly's leg, and she brushed it off. He was drunk, I could see that, and he stared at me as he spoke.

'For New Zealand there's very little benefit in the Olympics. It's not like rugby, say. I mean, the Rugby World Cup is in a league of its own, really. Brings the whole country together. Especially when we win the thing.'

Henrik and Reed gave a short cheer. I snorted. 'And when we lose,' I said, 'all the men beat up their wives.'

'Come on, Mickey,' Joel said. 'It's not that bad.'

'Isn't it?'

Joel paused. 'But you like rugby.'

I laughed. 'You like rugby. In my opinion there are better sports.'

'What's so good about the Olympics?' Henrik poked a fork in my direction. 'It's a political fuckfest. Between the deaths at the '72 Olympics and the endless boycotting through the Cold War, it's a political power play. There's nothing sporting about it, in my opinion.'

My face felt hot and my voice was loud. 'There's problems with it, I agree with you about that. But I don't think it's all bad. The marathon, for example. It's a dream and it's beautiful.'

'Typically feminine response,' Tom said, his lips quirking up in a sly smile.

Joel stared at me. 'You think running's better than rugby?'

'I didn't say that.' I felt cold then, his hand on my leg like ice.

'You know, guys, Mickey holds the New Zealand record for the 10,000 metres,' Joel said, and he lifted his eyebrows. 'Pretty fucking cool, eh?'

'How do you know about that?' I'd told him nothing about my running, no details of successes or failures, only sketched in the general idea of it.

His cheeks flushed. 'You mentioned it once,' he said, looking away from me. 'I googled it. Thirteen years and it still hasn't been beat.'

'A runner, hey,' Henrik said. 'Do you think you could beat me in a race?'

I didn't hesitate this time. 'I fucking hope so.'

Holly set down her cutlery and asked in a cool voice, 'Why did you stop running, Mickey?'

'I got injured,' I said quickly. It was the truth, though only part of it — I hoped it would be enough to satisfy her. I returned to my meal, eyes on my plate.

'Did you ever want to go to the Olympics?' she said.

A piece of eggplant caught in my throat, and I coughed. 'I did,' I said. 'But I think I probably wasn't good enough.'

Joel put his hand down, knocking his fork on his beer glass, silencing the table for a moment. Everyone glanced up at him, and then shot their eyes to me. The neon lights of the restaurant glittered on Joel's ring as he rubbed his hand on the tablecloth several times, back and forth, back and forth. He kept his eyes on the corner of the room and said, 'If you'd really wanted to go, you would've gone.'

I took a drink of water and didn't respond. I didn't know which was worse — if what he said wasn't true, or if it was.

THE FOLLOWING DAY I WOKE late, my mouth dry and rank from a hangover. Our bedroom reeked of stale beer and sweat. I showered and left Joel sleeping. I wasn't ready to talk to him.

My phone was in the lounge, flashing: three missed calls from Mum. I swiped on the green phone icon, and she picked up on the second ring.

'Mum? Is everything okay?'

She sniffed, and laughed, but there was something hollow in the tone of it. When she spoke, her voice was thin and soft. 'I'm sick, honey. I'm going to need you to come home.'

THE RACE

TWENTY-FIVE KILOMETRES IN AND I'M still digging. The man running with Ruby and me is wheezing, his cadence uneven. We keep on the pressure, and for the first time I see sweat on Ruby's sports bra, a grey stain spreading across the white.

I'm feeling the miles in every muscle. Especially one — my brain. I repeat lyrics from songs to distract myself from the moment, to let my body just continue moving. It's doing everything without my brain — legs keep pumping, an autonomous action, like breathing.

Sunlight filters down through the pōhutukawa on both sides of the road. The water looks almost silver in the glare, and I'm mesmerised by the ocean for a moment, dreaming of dipping my searing-hot body into its coolness. I don't notice the man trip, only feel his foot underneath mine — and I'm down on the road.

Ruby doesn't turn to see how I am. I know what I would do if I was her: I would dig deeper and pick up the pace.

Blood oozes from my right knee, and the exposed skin smarts. The man's beside me, his mouth hanging open. 'Are you all right? Shit, I'm so sorry, I just didn't see you there and next minute—'

I brush gravel from my knee. I give him a curt nod and set about hunting Ruby down once more. The knee feels tender, but I know it's nothing structural. It's all in your mind, I think, and your mind is a muscle. I work it until it's strong enough to handle the toughest of hurdles.

FIFTEEN

GINNY SAID, 'TAKE AS LONG as you need, Mickey, your job will be here when you get back.' Joel wasn't as considerate. He seemed almost reluctant to let me go, and we parted without a goodbye kiss.

I stopped once on the drive down, for a coffee in Te Kūiti, rushing into a café and ordering a flat white to go. It was bitter and over-extracted, the milk slightly burnt. The sky was clear as I swung around the coast, hurtling the Corolla along the roads at 120, refusing to brake going into the bends. I was over the speed limit through Awakino and the dark hills of Mount Messenger, slowing only when I nearly hit a car coming through the one-lane tunnel. And then, finally, I was driving through Urenui, Waitara, Bell Block, the mountain beside me all the way home. I pulled off into Fitzroy, and I was home, tyres crunching on the gravelled driveway, parking behind Mum's car. The yellow door opened a crack, and my heart did too, at the sight of Bonnie rushing out to meet me in her slippers. Her face was pale and lined, her eyes wet and wide. We stood beside my car and hugged. It seemed impossible in that moment that it could be true: in my arms, her body felt warm and alive, no different from how it had always been.

I WAS WRONG, OF COURSE. There's a lot you can learn in two weeks about a human body. How a body can look one way, and yet still be ripe with cancer. You can understand bodies and their weaknesses in a new way in only two weeks, by comprehending for the first time how the disease can live inside us and grow for months — for years! — undetected, giving no clue. And then … it's undeniable, and irreversible. It's terminal.

There were tests and more tests, scans. Blood taken and analysed, more blood than I thought should be outside of her body. I held Mum's hand and watched needles pierce her skin. Appointments at the hospital, a telephone call with an oncologist in Palmerston North. There were long hugs, tear-stained shoulders. The aching agony of powerlessness. Long phone calls with Kent in London, an anxious evening waiting for Helen to drive up with Wilma, the baby now one-and-a-half. She could only stay for a few days, she said, but she'd be back, alone next time, if Bryn could take a few days off work to care for Wilma.

'See you next week,' she said to Mum before she left. They were both crying.

Her silver hatchback headed down Rutherford Street to the main highway south. It seemed to me then she was always leaving me, was no longer around when I needed her. I remembered how her hand would reach across the space between our beds at night. *It's just a nightmare, Mickey. Everything's going to be okay.*

The doctors had said we should be ready for the worst but also hope for the best. Even I could see it was fruitless to hope. Bonnie was too weak for chemo, so we hung around the house, waiting on a miracle.

Mum was exhausted, and we couldn't halt her weight loss. I swore I could see the shape of her change in front of me, the softness of her flesh slipping away and the truth of her bones stretching her skin. I looked at her and saw my own skeleton, the pale shimmering bones of my dream, and I felt the same ghastly rage at what I was losing burning inside me.

The changes continued through the second week: her voice, her skin, her hair. She couldn't get out of bed without help. I showered her and changed her, turned her in the bed to ease her sores, and I thought that it was right and fair that I should do this: she'd raised me alone, and then brought me up a second time, when I'd returned home at nineteen. She slept a lot during the day, when the pain medication kicked in, and I sat in the lounge, on that same old couch

One Sunday night, two weeks after I'd arrived, she woke in pain, and I carried her out to the lounge room. There were several channels of Olympics on TV and I scrolled through them. The women's marathon was about to begin.

'Let's watch this, honey,' said Bonnie. She leaned her head back onto the cushions and sighed.

I wasn't sure I wanted to watch the marathon. It seemed like an exquisite form of torture when I was already suffering. But I made myself do it, and sat on the floor in front of the couch, in almost the same place I'd sat sixteen years ago with my father. The house was in darkness and Mum and I watched the runners lining up, our own bodies bathed in the glow of the screen, together in our private cocoon.

For a long time Bonnie was silent and still. I thought she'd fallen asleep. I glanced at her a few times, and in the flickering light I couldn't be sure if her eyes were open or closed. She seemed at peace. I hadn't seen her rest like this for days, and I relaxed into the moment of calm.

Christ the Redeemer stood tall on the peak of Mount Corcovado, towering over the silver-silk ocean and the white strips of Copacabana and Ipanema. The runners, in highlighter-yellow and pink shoes, were bright against the dark-grey roads. There was Jemima Sumgong from Kenya, who won the London marathon in April, even after falling on the seat of her pants, and there, at the front of the line-up, Mare Dibaba from Ethiopia, the 2015 world champion. She looked so short on the screen I turned on my phone and searched her height online. One centimetre taller than me: 151 centimetres. And she was four years younger than me. She wasn't too short, too fat, too female. She was perfect.

Sometimes the footage flipped from live action to slow-motion replay of their bodies in flight: feet flicking, arms bent. Other footage was taken by a drone, capturing the one hundred and fifty women stretched out like a long colourful tail. My heart was in my throat watching them, and then I heard the commentator say there were several forty-four-year-olds in the race. I wiped my eyes. Why hadn't I been one of those people who could push through the pain and make it to the other side? Watching this was watching my *what if?* I glanced up at my mum, and knew I needed to get a grip. I was exactly where I needed to be.

When the runners rounded 37 kilometres, Eunice Kirwa and Dibaba and Sumgong were in the lead, hunting for the medals. I heard Bonnie shift a little on the couch behind me. 'Tell me what it feels like to run the way they run,' she said, 'so I can imagine it.'

I watched the women on the screen, and I thought about all the miles I'd run. What could I say? What words did I have that would do justice to the glory of an empty road, the long, winding, black bitumen snaking away into the densely forested hills beyond the house? How to describe the beauty of the teal-blue ocean peeking out between the curves of the land as you round each corner? What way to express the feeling of your heart thundering, your mind blown open, as you breach the top of a steep hill and soar forward along the flat? How to tell her about the way the air changed colour in the trails because the sun was guarded from the depths by a thick canopy, how the colours of the furry ponga trunks and the scrubby ochre trails tinged the air brown? How would I tell my mother that running made my mind feel as open and spacious as the wide sky above, as endless and mysterious as the universe beyond? How to explain the thudding in my chest, similar to sex? Better, sometimes, than sex?

I said none of this. Bonnie's breath shifted to sharp shallow gasps, and I took her papery hand, and said, 'It feels like freedom, Mum. It feels like the most beautiful thing in the world.'

She squeezed my fingers. 'You're beautiful, honey. I can't believe I won't get to see you run again.'

I turned to the screen, my grip on her hand tight. The commentator's voice: *Has she perhaps left some of her best running back on the road somewhere behind her?* He was talking about Sumgong; he was talking about me.

'You have to start running again,' Bonnie said. She was smiling, though it was more like a grimace.

'But it feels so ... It feels so pointless.'

'It's not pointless, honey. Look at those women — that's not pointless. Even if you're just jogging around the block it's not pointless. I'd give anything to jump up right now and run until my heart gives out, just to feel alive. Look at them, so healthy and strong. I can't do it. Look at me! But, Mickey, darling, you can do it. Do it for me.'

I started to cry.

She leaned forward from the cushions and said with a firm voice, 'I want to know when I'm gone you're out living your life. I want to remember you running. I want you to be fast like them, so that nobody, not anyone, can get you. So that nothing can hurt you again.'

I watched Dibaba's cadence as she ran around the course alongside the ocean, a thin bridge in the distance, no clouds marking the brilliant blue sky. If you concentrated on her bright-yellow sneakers, you could see the moment when both feet were off the ground, and she was flying forward.

'I remember the last time I went for a run,' Mum said. Her hand slipped from mine and her voice went dull. I turned off the television. It was very quiet in the house. 'This was before I fell pregnant with Zach. I ran a lot then, did you know that? When I was at nursing college. Not as far as you run, or as fast, but I liked it. At first I just wanted to lose weight, but then I grew to like other things about it. I felt capable

— that no matter what happened, I could get myself somewhere else. Sometimes that's important. Knowing you can change your situation.'

'I don't want you to go, Mum.'

Bonnie looked up at the ceiling for a moment and then back at me. I turned to kneel and lean into her, my arms around her body, my face in her chest. Her pyjama top was smooth on my cheek, and I breathed her in. She smelled of honey and death, and I let another wave of tears plunge me down.

'Neither do I, my darling. But sometimes you can't change your situation no matter what you do, and you have to be able to sit with that discomfort and ride it out.'

We stayed together, holding each other, for what felt like hours. My knees grew sore on the carpet. My arms twisted around her, her arms around me. I listened to her unsteady breathing for a while, until finally it eased into the more regular airy breath of slumber. Still I held her, unwilling to let go, to ever let her go.

JOEL CALLED ME THE NEXT day. I was at the supermarket. We'd talked a few times since I'd been away, but never at any length. When are you coming home, he'd ask, and I'd say *When my mother dies,* expecting at least some sympathy. It seemed to have the opposite effect.

I juggled the phone between my ear and shoulder, placing a carton of custard into the trolley, a tub of yoghurt, some cheese.

'What about your job?' he asked. I told him again — Ginny had given me the time off, there was no problem. 'What about Helen? Why can't she be there?'

I sighed. Helen had been up and down three times, sometimes with Wilma, sometimes alone. 'She is here,' I said to Joel. 'She has a job and a child.'

'You have a job.'

'I'm a barista, Joel. She's a senior associate in an architect firm, and she's got Wilma. She can't give Mum all the time in world. I can.'

I pushed the trolley to the checkout. Broccoli, crackers, muesli. Most of the food was for me, and I felt sick looking at it all. The custard, that was for Mum. I remembered her at the stove when we were growing up, wooden spoon stirring in the saucepan. Custard powder, sugar, milk, bring it to the boil, and how I'd drag a chair from the dining table and stand on it to watch the magical moment when the watery yellow would quicken, thicken, and Mum would douse the gas and say it was ready. I didn't think I could make custard, not as well as she could, so the bought stuff was a last hope. She'd not eaten for two days, and I needed her to keep eating. The importance of this hit me then: I should have got two cartons. I glanced back at the aisles, considered leaving the checkout and running for more.

'Are you even listening to me? Mickey?'

'Sorry,' I said. 'What did you say?' I gestured to the checkout operator that I would be back, and she nodded without smiling.

'I asked if you even thought about me in all of this. I'm here all alone. I need you, too.'

'Joel, that's not fair. I'm not on some sort of jaunt. I'm basically—'

There was a strange noise on the line, so I checked the screen. We'd been disconnected, or he'd hung up, or I'd accidentally cut him off — whatever it was, I knew he'd be upset. I would deal with it later. I took another carton from the fridge shelf and hurried back to the till.

BONNIE WAS IN BED, THE duvet pulled flat to her chin.

'What's the time?' she asked, and coughed. I held a cup of water with a straw close to her mouth and told her it was the afternoon, around four.

'Where have you been?'

'I went to the supermarket while you slept. I got you custard.'

She smiled. 'You should make the custard, Mickey.'

There was a knock on the front door then, followed quickly by another.

Mum twisted her head to look toward the hallway. Another sharp knock, and I called out, 'I'm coming!'

It was Teddy. His hair was mussed and his glasses were smudged with fingerprints. There was an air of neglect about him and he seemed strangely vulnerable.

I held the door half-shut, keeping him outside. 'What do you want?'

He pushed his hands into his pockets. 'I need to see your mum,' he said. 'I need to say goodbye.'

'She's not dying today.'

Teddy's voice softened. 'They told me it could be any day now, Michelle.'

He was right, I knew that — Claire and Ingrid from the hospice came by in the mornings and evenings to adjust her medication, to get her comfortable, and they'd told me that once Bonnie stopped eating and drinking ... well, I should know what that would mean. Still — I didn't want him there. I didn't want him in the house.

'Let me in, Mickey,' he said, looking me at me directly. 'Come on.'

Mickey. I leaned away, letting the door swing open.

He stepped inside and followed me down the hall to Bonnie's room. 'Mum? Dad's here.'

She didn't move. In her small, rasping voice she said, 'Hello, Teddy.'

I switched on the bedside lamp and a mellow light settled over my parents. Teddy sat on the bed next to Bonnie, the mattress creaking under his weight. He didn't say anything, only groaned a bit, and Bonnie laughed, though it turned into a rough cough. Teddy shushed her and gently brushed the hair from her face. I stood by the door. I felt like an intruder. I saw then that I'd always ignored the connection between them, preferring to think of them as as two separate entities: Mum and Dad, apart and discrete. But here they were together, and I was witnessing one of the worst moments of their long and private history. I knew I should leave, yet I couldn't move.

'Teddy,' Bonnie said. 'You came.'

'Of course I came,' he said. 'Couldn't let you leave us here without saying goodbye.'

'That would've been karma, Ted.'

Teddy let out a strained laugh. 'It might have served me right,' he said. 'I guess I asked for that.'

I couldn't hear what Bonnie said next. Teddy leaned down, his ear near her mouth. Seeing their faces so close together — a shiver chased something down my spine. My parents. I couldn't remember seeing them touch each other, or hug. Now, Teddy's hand was on Mum's hand, his face so close his breath would soon become her breath.

I went to my bedroom and shut the door. Bonnie's death was closer than I could admit to myself. That was the only explanation for why she and Teddy would be like that: because there was no time left and bygones must be bygones. My mouth filled with a tangy fear and I got into bed. I heard their voices through the wall, soft unintelligible murmurings. This is what it might have been like before he left, I thought. This might be what Kent, Helen and Zach remember. The music of their voices, playing late into the night. Zach had said they'd never yelled, that he didn't realise they were even arguing. To me, their conversation sounded like the quiet cooing of birds, and if I hadn't known better, I might have said it sounded like two people in love.

AFTER HE'D GONE, BONNIE SPOKE less and refused to drink. Three days later, Claire from the hospice told me I needed to say goodbye.

'Tell your family to come. It won't be long now.' She put a hand on my shoulder. 'I'm sorry, Mickey. Your mum's not in pain, so take some comfort from that.'

It was little comfort for me. I rang Helen, who said she'd leave

Wellington as soon as she could though it might not be till later. She said she'd call Kent. I took a deep breath and agreed to call Zach.

When was the last time he'd answered when I'd called? 2003? Thirteen years ago, before his twenty-first birthday. Well, I needed him now. Mum needed him.

He took the call on the fifteenth ring. 'Mickey,' he said.

'Hi. It's Mum.'

He said nothing, just let out a mournful howl. I started crying then too, and told him he needed to come home.

'Oh shit, Mick. Oh shit. I'm coming, I'm leaving now. Just tell her to hang on, I'm coming.'

IT WAS DARK WHEN SHE died, and it seemed as though the night had swallowed up everything outside her room. I knew that beyond the house the world still existed — that off to the west the hills sat surrounding the town, and that only a few minutes away the waves moved ceaselessly to the shore. I knew that somewhere on the road between Wellington and Ngāmotu, Helen was on her way, beetling along in her silver hatchback. Still, it seemed as though there was nothing else: just this room.

Zach and I sat with Mum in the darkness. She was peaceful, her face undisturbed by pain, though her breathing was irregular, and often we worried that this was it — until she took another inhale and we'd relax, content to have another moment more.

Around eight, a light rain started to fall. The sound on the roof was the music of sorrow, and Zach and I told Bonnie and each other our favourite memories of childhood: Mum watching every cricket game Zach ever played; the scones she baked; the way she wrapped the birthday and Christmas presents in the same brown paper with ribbons for all of us, every year. I talked about her incredible patience — I'd been hard work as a kid, I couldn't deny it, and despite it all she never stopped loving me. I told Mum how I'd never forget watching her wade into the river with us, feet unsteady on the rocks, her smile as she dipped under the cool water, her eyes closed when she floated on her back, pulled downstream by the current.

Not quite an hour later, she stopped breathing. Her body was still warm, and I smoothed her hair, the silver strands that she never dyed mixed in with her sandy brown. Zach put his hand to his mouth and sobbed, and I was glad I wasn't alone. My phone buzzed: a text from Helen. She was half an hour away.

SIXTEEN

TEDDY SENT ME AN EMAIL the week after she died. I read it several times to try to understand: he was selling the house, and we had five weeks to clear it out. A real-estate agent would come the next day to do a valuation. *If you aren't there, Michelle, that doesn't matter, the agent has a key and will be entering the premises regardless.*

Impossible. Could he sell the house? I called the number for the lawyer who was executing Bonnie's estate.

'That's correct,' he said. 'The house was owned partly by your mother and partly by your father, so it reverts back to him.'

'What do you mean? It was her house, not his. Doesn't the house just to go her kids?'

'Not in this instance, no.' The lawyer's voice sounded far away.

My head felt light, and I ran my teeth along the rough ridge of my nail but didn't bite. It took everything to resist. I wouldn't hurt myself anymore. I sat down and listened carefully to what the lawyer was saying, knowing that each word would cost a hundred dollars. He explained that the paperwork clearly stated that Theodore, my father, was co-owner of the house, and that in the circumstances of my mother's passing, the house was now his.

I forwarded the email to Helen, Kent and Zach, with an attached note: *If there's anything you want, you have five weeks to get it.*

BACK IN THE DREARY ORATIA flat with Joel, I thought about Rutherford Street. The old house contained my whole life in its foundations, and very soon I'd have no connection with it. Joel was no comfort. He didn't seem to understand, or care, that I was grieving, and even expected me to go out drinking the night before the funeral because Richard was up from Wellington for the weekend.

'Go by yourself,' I said. 'I have to get up at four in the morning and drive five hours to my mother's funeral.' I took a breath and started to scream. 'In fact, maybe you shouldn't go drinking. Maybe you could come with me?'

He slammed his hand on the wall, leaving a slight impression in the plasterboard.

I slept on the couch that night. I didn't say goodbye when I left the next morning.

MY BOSS GINNY HAD BEEN considerate, letting me take more time off to arrange the funeral and travel down to Ngāmotu once again, but I needed more than that. There was too much to bear; I didn't know what to do. The loss of my mother, the growing knowlege that my relationship with Joel was over — how could I make it through? All my old coping mechanisms beckoned: stringent control over what I ate, the violent chaos of cutting. I wouldn't let myself succumb. For Mum's sake I had to be strong. I remembered then what Bonnie had wanted me to do. Run. I already knew how to make it through. I needed to control the only thing I could control: the next step. I just needed to put one foot in front of the other, and move forward.

I found my old running shoes in the cupboard. They were grey and stiff with age, and the sole of the right shoe was beginning to lift away at the heel. They might do more harm than good. I thought about the sneakers I'd had as a teenager, the sole worn right through. I'd run in those; I could run in these. I couldn't wait. Not one more day. It had been twelve years since I'd last laced up sneakers and set my body to a pace quicker than a walk. It was time.

The evening was cool. Clouds hovered low, and any vestige of early spring warmth was gone. A sudden downpour had doused the streets, leaving them slick and wet, and the smell of the warm asphalt filled the air. I pulled the laces extra-tight, leaving no room for doubt. The shoes felt comfortable and easy on my feet, as though I'd been wearing them only yesterday. I hopped on each foot a couple of times. Keep it light to start with. Back into it slowly.

The first steps were glorious. They felt natural and true. Running was a movement I remembered how to do in mechanical terms. Arms bent at the elbows, landing on the forefoot, tight through my core. I was away.

After a few minutes, it didn't feel so good. I was out of breath. My chest tightened and my speeding heartbeat boomed in my temples. My hands felt clammy. In the reflection of a parked car's window I saw my face was already flushed a deep red.

It was as though I'd never run before. There was no lightness to the movement. With each downstep I felt the softer parts of my body shake with the pull of gravity. My breath came heavy and noisy. There didn't seem to be a way to fill my lungs with enough air, and I coughed. My stomach cramped and the urge to vomit pushed into my throat. I heard a thudding set of steps behind me and I looked over my shoulder, ready to move aside to let a fitter, stronger runner go by. There was no one there.

I stopped and kicked my foot against a concrete power pole. That felt good — so I kicked it again, harder. The nausea and the rage faded away, and I ran again, nothing more than a plodding jog this time, my flat feet slamming on the footpath. It didn't matter what I looked like, I told myself. It didn't matter what anyone driving past might think when they saw me stumbling along in my junk shoes. It didn't matter that I was 10 kilograms heavier than the last time I ran. It didn't matter at all. The only thing that mattered was that I didn't give up.

Two more minutes, three. My body was tense and tight, my hair sweaty. Was this what I'd missed? This was more of a sorry mess of flailing limbs than a glorious sprint. My lungs were lined with fire, and I stopped once more. Two kilometres: it was something. Further than I'd run in years. A leaping excitement made me catch my breath, and I coughed and then began laughing. My legs hurt but it was good pain. I knew how bad pain felt, and this time the only bad pain was in my heart. I turned around and started again, alternating between jogging and walking, sucking air in thick gasps and grimacing all the way back to the flat.

I lay on the grass outside our bedroom window for a while. The chickens were nonplussed, fussing around a sparrow caught in their feeding box. I could hear the low thrum of evening rush hour now that I was still, and my heartbeat joined in with the rhythm. The clouds were pillow-soft, drifting in and out of my vision. I let my mind float to them. I didn't spend enough time noticing the beauty in the world. Lactic acid made my body tingle, and there was something else too, as though I was waking up from a long sleep. I felt the edges of myself on the ground, the nerves in my fingertips buzzing. It had been years since I'd felt like this.

I let the feeling fade, sat up and went inside to shower. I towelled my wet hair, and realised it was the first time in months I'd gone longer than thirty minutes without thinking about Bonnie. I missed her terribly, but having a moment to breathe, to not feel myself defined by grief, felt good.

So I ran again the next day. And the next. Every day after that. I knew I looked bizarre — an out-of-shape thirty-something running at a pace that looked more like a wacky walk. I wasn't embarrassed, though. Running felt personal and private, as if the reality of the moment was only in my mind.

I kept doing it. Sometimes I heard the footsteps behind me, but not once was anyone there. There was just the hint of a person, the sound a mere trace. I remembered this from before, the spectre of a runner behind me in the hills in Ngāmotu, and the sound stalking me along Beach Road from Takapuna to Long Bay. It had always scared me, and it still did. The whisper of someone on the road behind me, the shadowy nature of the sound and the emptiness of the road whenever I turned to look.

Each day I ran further. The muscles on my legs grew stronger, and the tingling pain of the fractures was buried too deep to hold me back. Sometimes I felt guilty at the joy I felt in such movement. I'd think of my mother's body in the bed, Zach and I beside her, not quite able to admit she was gone. Then I told myself I was making Bonnie proud, and kept going.

The miles clocked up. I drove the Corolla to Piha after work one day to try a new route. I didn't tell Joel where I was going, and ran along the beach, and up around the tracks of the Waitākeres. Run fast and turn left. I didn't go near a running track. I kept my feet on the road, the footpath, the trail. Further and further I explored, not quickly, though my speed increased as my fitness grew. I came home pink and sweaty. It didn't matter how hard it was. I kept going in case the next run felt amazing.

THREE WEEKS OF RUNNING, NO days off. I still didn't run far, or fast, but the consistency was the point. I wore the dirty old shoes and whatever tee-shirt and shorts I could find. At work all I could think of was the next run, even if the last one had been misery — in rain and icy-cold wind, legs like stones, soupy blood and low motivation. It didn't matter about the run itself, not all the time, because if it was terrible the feeling afterwards was even sweeter.

On a Thursday in early October, I arrived home from a four-kilometre slog, dog-tired and craving a beer. Joel was sitting in the kitchen. 'Where have you been?' he said.

I took a beer from the fridge, sat next to him, and only then saw his arm extended across the dining table, bloodied in parts, with eight stitches tacked along a deep cut. 'Oh my god, Joel. What happened?'

'Cut it at work.' He looked down at his forearm. 'Bloody Nigel. I tried to call you but you didn't pick up. Had to get Henrik to collect me from the hospital.'

'I was running,' I said. I never took my phone with me. No music, no podcasts. I preferred to run to the beat of my heart, the sounds of the world, the thoughts that spun in my head.

'Why have you started doing that all of a sudden?' he said. 'You're never home, I never see you.'

I touched his arm, and he flinched. 'You see me all the time,' I said. 'We live together. We sleep in the same bed every night.'

'Sleeping, yes,' he said. 'Bit of an understatement. Every time I come to bed, the room's pitch black and you're dead to the world. Christ, when was the last time we fucked?'

He stood up in a rush, the chair tottering behind him. I followed him into the lounge, where he sat heavily on the couch and ran his hands through his hair. The movement of his body unleashed something, and I smelled the tang of him, the day's work and the blood made into scent. I'd always liked the smell of him. People said that was a sign of chemistry. Soulmates, they said, whatever that meant. In this moment his smell was offensive. It made my gut twist.

'Joel, I don't want to fight,' I said, backing up to the door, away from further conflict. I set the beer on the TV cabinet. I no longer felt like drinking. 'I'm going to have a shower, and maybe we should talk after dinner.'

The low light from the sun was blinding when I turned to leave the room, so I couldn't see him when he said, 'What is it that you're running away from, anyway?'

'I've never been running away,' I said. 'The real question is: what am I chasing?'

WHEN THE HOUSE SOLD, TEDDY split the proceeds five ways. I used my share to buy a one-bedroom unit in Titirangi, only two minutes' walk from Four Loaves. Joel didn't help me move, and the last time I saw him he flipped me the bird and said, 'Sayonara, Mickey.'

The first person I invited to see my new place was Zach. We ordered pad thai and drank a couple of beers, talked about Mum, his job, Teddy. I was awkward, twitching and nervous. There was so much to say and there were no words. 'I'm sorry—' I began, but it was like reading Cordelia's speech, the right words fumbling on my tongue.

'It's okay, Mickey,' he said. 'I understand.'

He told me he was using his money from the house sale to move to Invercargill. He could afford something decent there, and Southlanders needed plumbers as much as Aucklanders. 'Everyone's shit blocks up the loo at some point,' he said. 'Besides, I want to meet someone and settle down. Have some kids.'

'You'll be a great dad, Zach.'

We hugged before he left that night. I didn't hear from him again for a few months, apart from emoji messages on the group chat every now and then. After Christmas, he sent a photo of a white weatherboard house with a red roof, along with the caption: **Come visit, Mick. Any time you like.**

THE RACE

WHEN I'M IN RUBY'S SLIPSTREAM once more, I swear I won't lose her again. A gentle ache settles into my quads and my hip flexors, and my knee stings. There's a tightness on my shin where the blood has dried, too. Nothing I can't handle.

We run around Okahu Bay and to the point, water in front and behind us, the sound of the splash against the rock, the blue on blue of horizon. We skate past the kayak-rental place, and up ahead I see the golden strip of Mission Bay. The shouts of the supporters along the path lift my spirits. In my stomach, a rumble sets in, and I'm reminded I'm in energy debt. I need the gel I missed earlier. Thank god Philippa will be at the next support station. My saviour with the gel.

I know my face is flushed an unflattering magenta-pink, that my sweat smells funky as all hell. My leg is bloodied, and my mouth feels as though something crawled in there and died. I still love it, though: I love the power running gives me to believe in myself. Believe in my body and the space it takes up in the world. Each step is more than a movement forward, it's a mark on the earth to say, *I am here. I am loved. I am enough.*

SEVENTEEN

CHRISTMAS WITHOUT MUM WAS A quiet devastation. To get through the days, I ran every morning, the sunrise my reward. I went to work if the café was open. The steps stayed with me, the phantom runner, the haunting *what if?*

On New Year's Eve, Ginny gave us all a bottle of Lindauer and a fifty-dollar note and told us to enjoy the coming days off. The first of January was a drenching hot day, no wind, scorching sun. I drove to Bethells for a swim. The beach was packed, but I didn't mind the crowds. It was so much like home out there, the black sand and wildness of the west coast. The Tasman Sea, rough and untamed, stretched out as though to the end of the world.

I set down my towel near some children who were digging a deep hole with plastic spades. I lay on my stomach, hiding my face from the glare. Over the children's voices I could hear cicadas trilling up on the dunes, the slamming boom of waves. A new year without Bonnie. I cried into my towel for a minute, then turned onto my back, letting the sun dry my tears.

A shadow fell over me. A tall man in green board shorts was

standing beside me

'Hello, Mickey.'

It took me a moment to recognise him. The long legs, the curly hair. Benji. Older now, and thicker through the face and body, his chin bristled with a day's growth. He was no longer the boyish wisp I'd chased along the trail beside the river.

'I saw you arrive,' he said, 'and I thought, there's only person in the world who walks like that. Legs like twigs, almost a bloody dwarf. Mickey fucking Bloom!'

'Benji — hi! Wow, how are you?'

'I'm good, I'm good,' he said. 'I heard you'd quit running. Not surprised, to be honest. Very few people can handle the pressure.'

'What about you?'

He shook his head. 'Not running anymore either. I trialled for the Commonwealth Games a couple of times, didn't quite make it.'

He told me he was working at KPMG — an accountant on their corporate team, or something like that. I couldn't follow the jargon, but nodded and made noises when he seemed to expect it. 'Sounds great,' I said.

There was a break in the conversation then, filled with the thumping slam of the west-coast waves.

'Anyway, good to see you, Mickey,' he said. 'I always wondered where you ended up.'

'I ended up right here,' I said. 'As you can see.'

He wandered back to a large group just down the beach, but his words sat with me. Had that been my problem? An inability to handle the pressure? The pressure to be thinner, to be faster, to run more, to be stronger, to not complain, not be lazy, let anything happen and just grin and bear it. Was that what it meant to compete? All the women out there racing and winning and losing, all of them taking the same shit I couldn't take for one more second. Then I remembered what I was doing now: I was running. Every day. And the road held no judgement. It didn't care less whether I'd failed or I'd succeeded, only whether I kept taking another step.

The sun lifted higher in the sky. A helicopter hovered overhead. The tide swept too far, filling the children's hole completely; I heard them scream in frustration. I dived under the waves and considered where I would run the next morning, which roads to take, which hills to climb.

WHEN I RAN, THOUGHTS SPUN like clothes in the tumble dryer, a record skipping to replay the same snatch of song over and over again. Breathing, lifting feet, trying to keep going without stopping — the rhythm seemed perfectly designed to encourage rumination. I thought sometimes of English class, the way the teacher repeatedly singled me out to read aloud. Was it to torment me, or did she not understand the scale of difficulty for me? I thought about work, and whether making coffee was what I wanted to do for the rest of my life. Of course I thought about Bonnie, and Teddy. Kent and Zach. I thought about Hilary from North Lynn, the only real friend I'd had. We'd lost touch, but I knew she'd gone to London in 2012. The jealousy had made me nightmarish for a month or two. Joel had put it down to 'women's troubles', and I didn't try to explain the real reason. Hilary had run in the 5,000 metres and finished in twentieth place. The camera didn't linger on her for long, and I felt torn between relief at her disappointing result and pride at her having done it at all.

Sometimes I thought about Helen, a mother herself now to Wilma and another babe on the way. This led always to thoughts of Joel, and the niggling worry that I'd given up on my chance of love. Of making a family of my own, however that might look. He hadn't called or even texted since I left. It was as though the five years we'd spent together never happened. On bad days, it was easy to spiral into sodden self-pity. I'd never find someone else, I'd never have a family, I'd be alone forever. I would fail, like I always had, again and again. There was only one way out: I would run up the steepest hill I could find, over and over until I could barely breathe, until my mind was clear.

The best runs were when no thoughts came — when I thought of simple things, like the colour of the sky, the feeling of the sun on my face. They could come at any time, these good runs, in the morning before work, or on a Friday night when others were at bars or restaurants. I kept going until exhaustion and elation hit, and I was high on the bliss of moving through the world at speed. Sometimes the footsteps I heard behind me were perfectly matched to the beat of my heart, as though they were nothing but the glimmer of my soul bouncing out into the world.

THE MORNINGS GREW DARKER, THE evenings cooler. One Monday afternoon in March I was out on a 5k run when a white Subaru station wagon drove past, then immediately slowed. I was used to occasional drivers roaring up from behind, driving as close as possible as if to knock me over. The Subaru driver was careful, even drifting over the centre line to avoid hitting me, then pulling over to the shoulder up ahead. I kept running towards it, cautious but determined not to be intimidated.

I had drawn level with the passenger window when the driver leaned over and yelled, 'Hey there!'

It was an older woman with thick auburn hair swilling out from her head like a mane, a square jaw and bright eyes. I put my hands on my hips. I was sweaty and tired, and if this woman was going to yell at me about the perils of running on the open road I was ready to tell her to go fuck herself.

'Don't clench your fists like that,' the woman said. 'Loosen your arms up a bit. You're holding your upper body tense as a sphincter. Relax. At least pretend to enjoy it.'

I bent over to get a better look at her. She wore a faded black tee-shirt with orange bleach stains, and her skin was tanned and lined, striped as though she were a rare tiger. She grinned at me.

'Okay,' I said. 'Thanks.'

'No worries,' the woman said, shifting the car into gear. 'See you round.'

The car eased back into the road. I watched it disappear around the corner, then started running again. I kept my shoulders down, away from my ears, and relaxed my hands, holding them in loose curves. It felt better. The lady was right.

ABOUT THREE WEEKS LATER, RUNNING along the road that curves past Oratia District School, I saw the white Subaru again. I was certain it was the same one. Same ding in the rear bumper, the same 95bFM sticker peeling from the rear windscreen. It was parked off the road this time, shaded by a large rhododendron. Beside the car was a latched white gate and a letterbox shaped like an enormous orange cat.

It was a windy morning, and the scattered bite of raindrops came on the gusts. I was almost at the ginger-cat letterbox when the woman came out from the gate. She turned and raised a hand. 'I thought I'd see you again,' she called. 'You didn't look like a fair-weather sort of runner to me.'

I stopped beside her, and she looked down at my feet. I knew what was there — my socked toes visible through a hole in the front of my right shoe, both sneakers brown with mud. 'Probably about time to retire those old girls,' she said. 'You don't want to mess up your training for want of some proper shoes. '

'I'm not training,' I said. 'I'm just running.'

'Could've fooled me. Still, even if you're just running, those things will give you an injury.'

I shrugged. 'They're just shoes.'

The woman considered me for a moment. A rhododendron bloom, enormous and almost lasciviously pink, fell onto the roof of the Subaru, and she picked it up and held it close, inspecting it. Without looking at me, she said, 'That's one way to think about it. But next time I see you, I don't want to see those things on your feet.'

I laughed and said I'd try my best to make that happen.

'Your best is all I ask.' Her lips curled in a smirk — a kind one, though, not nasty. I took off again and heard the car door slam shut. I inhaled through my nose, counting my steps to four before letting the exhale out through mouth. One, two, three, four—

The station wagon drove past, tooting two short blasts.

HER NAME WAS PHILIPPA ANDERSEN. She turned up at Four Loaves the following week, with an enormous German Shepherd. She greeted Ginny like an old friend, though I didn't remember seeing her at the café before. 'Cappucino, if you don't mind, Ginny, and one of those date scones.' When she saw me behind the espresso machine, she tipped her head and gave me a strange look, as if I were a puzzle and she was trying to figure out how to fit the pieces together.

She sat at a table near the window, and the dog lay with its head on her foot. 'Do I know you?' she asked when I took over her order. I was nervous, shaking slightly, though I couldn't understand why. A small amount of coffee spilled over the edge of the cup and pooled on the saucer.

'Not really,' I said. 'We've talked a couple of times when I've been out running.'

'Of course! Now I recognise you.' She looked down at my feet. 'Not wearing those death-trap runners, I see.'

I felt myself flushing. 'I don't wear them to work.'

'Ginny's a good woman.' She looked over at my boss. 'How long've you been working here?'

'Nearly eleven years,' I said. 'I'm Mickey Bloom.' I held out my hand, ready for her to make a joke about my name.

She didn't react to my name. She just shook my hand and nodded. 'I'm Philippa Andersen, and this is Titus.' She nodded at the dog, who was peering up from under long eyelashes. 'What is it you're training for then? Why do I see you out on the roads every hour of the day?'

'I'm not training for anything,' I said. 'I just want to run.'

'That's right. You mentioned you weren't in training. Run where, though? Run fast? Run far? Take a seat.' She pulled out a chair beside her.

'I just want to run,' I said, and then, without thinking, just to fill the silence: 'When I was younger I wanted to run at the Olympics. Crazy, eh?'

Philippa paused before replying. 'I wouldn't say that was crazy. Dreams are the building blocks of life, in my opinion. Why do you run now if you think running to go to the Olympics is madness?'

'I run so I can feel something good, I suppose.'

Philippa smiled. 'Don't you feel good anyway?'

I fingered the edge of my apron hem. 'Not really,' I said.

'We can fix that,' she said, leaning forward a fraction of an inch. 'It's not just the running that can help you feel good, I see that. But it's a start. I'm no expert on anything else that's getting you down, just the running, so I'll help with that. Did you get the new shoes like I said?'

I nodded. They were still in the box, a week after I'd bought them. Something about them reminded me of the shoes Bonnie had given me years ago, that first pair of racing flats. They were red and white, bright and clean. They looked like the running shoes of someone else, someone more likely to achieve their dreams. Someone younger, a person expected to have ambitions. The idea of ambition at my age felt humiliating. So the shoes had stayed in the box.

'Good.' Philippa tapped on the table. Titus lifted his head and gazed up at her. 'We start today then. What time do you finish work?'

'Four-thirty,' I said. 'Why?'

'I'll meet you back here at six. Be ready for a run.'

'Are you going to be my coach or something?'

Philippa lifted an eyebrow. 'I prefer *or something,* but if you need to label it, then coach sounds about right.'

'I don't know if I can afford a coach right now.'

'Don't worry about that. The greatest coach this country's ever seen didn't take money from his runners, and I don't either. Right now I have the time and, if I'm not wrong, you have the talent. That's all we need, really. But be warned: it won't be easy. I won't ever promise you easy. I'm inviting you to a world of pain. Come with me and you'll discover things inside yourself you only imagined you might find.'

Ginny walked to the table and stood beside me. 'How's Ana doing, Philippa?'

'She's doing well, thanks, Ginny. At home again, healing nicely. I'm on my daily break from duty. Her sister's come to stay.'

'Say hi from Trevor and me,' Ginny said, heading back behind the counter.

'I should get back to work too,' I said. 'I guess I'll see you back here at six?'

Philippa took a sip of her coffee and watched me for a moment, then nodded. 'I'll see you at six.'

I CHANGED INTO A BLUE running top and black shorts. My new shoes: so clean they seemed to glow. I put on the proper running socks the salesperson at the shoe store had talked me into buying — extra padding in the high rub spots on your foot, she'd said — and I ran back to Four Loaves. Philippa's Subaru was parked on the street, and two glossy black hens scavenged in the thick weeds on the verge beside it. Philippa was sitting on the doorstep of the closed café. She stood when she saw me and called out, 'You ready to go?'

We jogged together, away from the café and through the high street. Philippa wore new running shoes too, shining clean but more worn than mine, and she had on long white socks that stopped halfway up her calves. I hadn't seen her in anything other than jeans, and I was surprised at her muscular legs; under the soft, sun-spotted skin, they were lean and defined. 'We'll do a 10k loop,' she said. 'Not too fast, mind, I'm old and you've got new shoes. And while we're about it you can tell me what you know about a good training programme.'

'Not much,' I said. 'Keep my weight low; run fast, turn left.' I laughed, a gawky honk. I sensed that I'd said the wrong thing, but I didn't know what else she might want me to say.

Philippa was taller than me but slightly slower, and together our pace seemed to fit. We ran at what I'd found was my perfect speed — quick enough to warm up, slow enough to talk. The evening air was blue, almost the hue of a peacock feather. It was peculiar to run with someone else — it had been months of running solo, only my own thoughts and breath for company. I liked it, for a change, the feeling of another body moving in sync with my own. There was another change, too: the ghost runner was gone. No sound but our breathing, our four feet clipping along the footpath. I almost missed the yearning mystery of the runner behind me.

I thought Philippa must have forgotten her question, and my reply, but suddenly she said, 'I would disagree that those make up a good training programme. And that's no slight on you. I'm imagining the voices of many coaches in what you say. The rules for training, in my opinion, are similar to the ones I believe everyone should live their lives by: eat well, move enough, sleep all night.'

'Right,' I said cautiously. Her words felt like a trick. I hated myself for feeling cynical, but what she said didn't marry up to anything I'd experienced before.

Our footsteps echoed along the road. We crept up a hill, and the air was suddenly tinged with the smell of the sea.

'I want you to look after yourself,' Philippa said. 'That's my number one rule.'

We rounded back down into Titirangi, easing up on the speed down the hill and around the leafy streets to Four Loaves. Philippa loosened her hair tie and the auburn waves fell around her face.

'So,' she said. 'You go home. Have a good dinner. Sleep. I'll call you tomorrow.'

I nodded. I could do that. Maybe she did mean what she said. We swapped phone numbers, and Philippa drove off, tooting her signature two sharp beeps. I waved and looked at my new shoes. They were still white, glaring and bright, only now they were splattered with bits of dirt and leaves. They looked like someone had run in them. They looked splendid, like the shoes of someone ready to want something.

THE RACE

THE SUPPORT STATION FOR 29 kilometres is close. I see the table and the sign up ahead. Philippa will be there, somewhere, waiting for me. With an extra gel. My brain froths at the thought of glucose. I haven't needed something so desperately in a long time. But there's a fuss ahead, people gathered around the sideline, officials in high-vis vests. There's a worried buzz to their movements, and spectators are craning their necks to perve.

I see it now, what they're doing. It's Marcus. He's sitting on the curb, his face contorted in devastation. He drops his head as we run by, catching it in his hands, and I don't know why he's there but I know it's over for him. The goal he'd set for himself is shattered, along with his self-belief. I know the feeling.

I know that all he has to do is get up tomorrow, and put one foot in front of the other and try again. If we persevere, we can do anything. Nothing worth having ever comes easy, I would say to him, but he's no beginner. He already knows all this.

My heart's in my mouth. I see the veins in his calves, his forearms. There's an eerie feeling that I'm seeing my future, that soon it could be me in the gutter, head hanging low, the dream over—

'Mickey!' There's Philippa, wild hair frizzy in the sun. She's reaching out to me with a drink bottle of electrolytes and water. I take it, and she runs alongside me, easily keeping pace.

'Keep with her,' she tells me. 'Don't let her shake you off. Stay in her step and you'll get there in a good time. Don't worry about passing her or trying to take the lead. No need for heroics.'

I'm taking in her words and the drink, trying to keep my body soft and strong at the same time. I hand her the bottle. When I flick my wrist to check my watch she reaches out and swats at my hand.

'Don't look at that thing! Listen to your body. It already knows what to do. Trust yourself. Enjoy it.'

She pulls up then, leaving me alone. People throng along the streets of Mission Bay, come to gawk before they head off to brunch. I send a check through my body: feet, ankles, Achilles, calves, knees, hips, back, shoulders, neck. Unclench my jaw. I'm feeling good again. My body is ready for greatness, ready to take on the rest of this race.

Of course there's a part of me that's wary too. I might have studied the course map, run sections of it over and over to understand its nuances, where to take the turns, how to tackle the hills. But in reality I don't know what's ahead of me.

Then I remember I forgot the gel, and feel a jolt of panic.

EIGHTEEN

PHILIPPA DIDN'T WASTE ANY TIME: she called me at seven o'clock the next morning.

'Mōrena,' she said. 'I hope I haven't caught you at a bad time.'

'Not at all. I'm eating breakfast.'

I heard Titus bark, a woman's voice in the background, and Philippa saying, 'You don't have to do that, Ana, you go lie down and I'll bring it in to you in ten minutes.' Then, back to me: 'So, are we going to do this or what?'

I swallowed my toast. 'I don't know. It depends on what this is.'

'I told you already,' Philippa said, and she laughed. 'You're a bit old for this hard-to-get shenanigans, Mickey. I'll help you train, you prove me right.'

'Right about what?'

'Right in my prediction. And before you start asking me *what prediction,* let me tell it to you straight: I think you've got what it takes to run the majors, and run them well. I haven't got a crystal ball but I've got instincts and I trust them.'

'You don't think I'm too old?'

'Only too old if you think you're too old.'

'But why do you think I can do this?"

'Now, I'm not a dunce,' she said. 'I know who you are. Aren't too many runners go by the name Mickey. I remember watching you win the 10,000 metres. Your record still stands.'

I set down the last of my toast. 'So you probably know why I stopped running.'

'I know a bit,' Philippa said. 'I know Bruce Madden and his bunch of clowns up at North Lynn. You aren't the only one.'

I thought of Hilary on the scales. Yuri's hands on her thighs. Each of us standing, calipers pinching flesh, bodies reduced to data. The residual damage on my skin, the silver lines of hatred. The thought of others suffering like I had, like I was … I felt ill.

'It's not just who you *were*, mind,' Philippa said. 'You could've set the record for heading across the Sahara unsupported for all I care. Nah, it's more to do with what I see today. The way you run, it's gorgeous. The way you run with a lift and not a push. The look on your face.' She sighed. 'I see something in you, and crikey, it's something.'

I didn't say anything, but I felt it, in my chest, that same hopeful dream I'd had when Marleen Renders led the field over the Sydney Harbour Bridge, what I'd felt when I saw Mare Dibaba, the same height as me, take the bronze in Rio.

'Yes,' I said. Then again, more emphatically: 'Yes, let's do it.'

'You set the goals,' Philippa said. 'I provide the opportunities and information to make it happen. You have problems? I can help you get a psychologist. You have issues maintaining proper eating habits, fuelling right? I can get you a nutritionist. The one thing I cannot do is read your mind. So if there's a problem—' She paused before carrying on quietly, almost tenderly — 'if there's a problem, you need to tell me. Nothing will faze me. Believe me, I've seen it all.'

She came to the café the next day around closing time, and we walked back to my unit. She looked around it without talking, as though cataloging my living space, taking it all in. We sat on the couch and I handed her a beer, which she took with a sharp 'Ta!' It was 5.30, and outside was the murky blue of early dusk.

'You live alone, then? No kids?'

'No.'

'That makes things a bit simpler.' She laid out her ideas: lots of long runs, hills, rest, food, sleep. Like Lydiard, she explained, but modern — and for a woman. 'I want you to work around your period, understand your hormones. When to push it and when to pull back. Does that make sense?'

'I suppose,' I said. 'I am a lot heavier than when I last ran. How much do you think I need to lose?'

'This is what I'm talking about.' She put her empty beer bottle on the windowsill behind us. 'You don't want to be getting into that territory. I don't want to hear anything about weight, race weight or otherwise. I want you feeling good. Eat good foods. If the weight comes off, fine. If you put some on, I don't give a shit. Work hard on the miles, take care of your joints. The rest is irrelevant.' There'd be tempo runs, and Fartlek. Drills to warm up, lots of stretching. Swimming, she said, was particularly good for active recovery. 'Gentle on the body,' she told me. 'Can you swim?'

She made me promise to buy a notebook, and list the distance and age of my sneakers. 'Ideally you want to rotate two pairs. Keep a log, replace them every four to five hundred miles.'

'What's that in kilometres?' I asked, teasing.

'I'll keep in touch,' she said as she stood up. 'Let you know the week's plan on a Sunday, and you follow it. Let me know how you're feeling, what you're doing. I suspect you haven't got a running watch. Don't bother. You just listen to me, listen to your body, and you'll be right.'

I WOKE EARLY THE NEXT day. This was to be my first run under Philippa's guidance: 22 kilometres before work, the longest run in what I'd started thinking of as 'my comeback'. It was still dark when I changed into my running clothes, including the warm long-sleeved top I'd bought with the money Bonnie had sent me the winter I'd run in the cross-country champs. Touching it somehow felt like touching her again, and I pulled it on with hope that it might bring me luck.

The course took me out of the village and up into the hills that curved and rose gently before the first steep incline. I kept my pace slower to start with, placing one foot, then the next, each movement another inch closer to the flat.

For a time it seemed like the uphill slog would last forever. My heart started to thump in that brutally brilliant way it did when I was working hard. I knew that if I didn't give up, if I just continued to push on, I could make it, just as I could make it through other, much tougher runs. I kept my knees in line with my hips, lifted my chin to look ahead, neck long.

And with that thought came the downhill. A soaring, sweeping descent. The delight of speed, the release of worry.

I KEPT RUNNING INTO MAY. The distances grew longer, the routes more gruelling, but I ate it up. I loved every aspect of it, how when my energy started to flag my mouth became dry and gritty, like it does when you eat candyfloss. I loved when it hurt. I'd forgotten that capacity I had for craving sweat and terror, and how good the pain could feel — the good pain. I leaned into it, like Yuri had said, followed the pain to the other side, determined now to outrun the *what if?* I was older now, and I hoped wiser, though I knew the difference this time might be Philippa.

She listened when I spoke. She explained things clearly and as many times as I needed to understand. A lot of what she said I already knew, but some of it I'd never imagined might come from the mouth of a coach.

'Take it easy today,' she said to me before a 28-kilometre long run. 'I give you permission to go as slow as you need to. Shit, give yourself permission. Miles are miles, ain't nobody gonna accuse you of being lazy if you don't do them all at race pace.'

When she came on runs with me, our pace matched, she'd tell me about some of the training runs she'd done in the late seventies, in Flagstaff, Bozeman, Albuquerque, Boulder. The long roads, the mountains, the thin air, the best runners in the world on the path beside you. Other times, she would ride on her bike beside me, no helmet, her long hair streaming out in the breeze. This was when she'd push my pace, direct my form. 'Don't lean too far forward,' she'd say. 'You're robbing yourself of the chance to lift your knee. The knee lift is *everything*. It's your stride length and your power.'

It was camaraderie that bred trust. She was easy to talk to, and though she was nothing like my mum — Bonnie was soft, where Philippa was prickly — I felt safe in her company.

One evening in June, the day before what would've been Bonnie's sixty-third birthday, we sat together on the lawn outside my unit. It was unseasonably warm, and crickets were buzzing around us, even this late in the evening. I kicked my shoes and socks off, feeling the grass between my toes. The big toenail on my left foot was purple.

'That looks ripe,' Philippa said. 'How are you feeling?'

The session had been a tempo run. Philippa had kept her bike just beside me when she could, pulling me fast through the kilometres and slowing me down when I should ease off. I felt tired, more than I should feel after that distance, and the purple toenail throbbed. A sudden burst of grief for my mother surged through me. Every atom of my body wanted to be with her one last time, to touch her, hear her voice. I couldn't share that with Philippa — it was too much.

'I've been better.' I lay back on the grass, the soft, damp green cold on my body.

'Something you want to talk about?'

A plane was flying overhead, the lights on the wing and the tail bright, slowly advancing then vanishing behind wisps of cloud. I started to cry, swiping away the tears with a vicious hand. A morepork called then, its cry haunting in the growing darkness.

'Just let it out,' Philippa said softly. 'Just let it all out.'

We stayed without speaking for a while, and I stopped crying. Philippa tapped me with her foot and said, 'I'm going to take a wild guess and say you were the baby of the family.'

'How did you know?' I propped myself up. I hadn't told Philippa anything about my family, my childhood — we talked about Nike sneakers versus Asics, and Lydiard's principles of general conditioning: feeling-based training, response-regulated training, sequential development and peaking. We talked about A-skips and hamstring stretches; the most personal thing we discussed was Titus.

'I could tell,' she said, laughing. 'There's a competitive fire in you that I believe is unique to the youngest child. Let me guess — two older brothers?'

It was my turn to laugh. 'And an older sister.'

'Four of you! Bless your poor mother's heart.' She stood then, and told me to go inside, have a shower and sleep. 'Tomorrow you should go to the pools and swim, or go do a yoga class. Friday I'll meet you after work for a run. It's supposed to be wet, so prepare yourself.'

I DIDN'T GO TO THE pools the next day. Helen called, and we spoke for an hour about Mum and Wilma, and the new child on the way. Helen mourned for the little person who wouldn't have the chance to meet their grandma, a woman of patience and quiet love, and I mourned with her. I doubted I could ever be as loving a mother as Bonnie. Maybe I was more like Teddy than I wanted to believe.

Kent called, too — he was in Italy with his new girlfriend, Indira. 'I hear you're running again,' he said. 'That's great. Let's make sure we catch up when I'm home for Christmas. Can't wait to see you.'

Same, I told him, and I meant it, even though it had been so long since we'd been together. I felt a sense of inexplicable remoteness from him — was he the same person who'd saved me from the river, the person I'd been so comfortable with? I'd climbed on his back, my head next to his head, while he carried me through the water. I couldn't understand how siblings — once so close, almost like one person — could grow apart the way they did, almost as though they were strangers.

Zach sent a message on the group chat: a photograph of a candle burning. For Mum, the message said. I didn't hear from Teddy, and I tried to convince myself that I didn't need my father, his love or his approval. I was kidding myself, though. I'll never stop wanting that.

FRIDAY AFTERNOON WAS WET, AS Philippa had predicted. Thick cloud hung low over Titirangi, and a drizzle set the bush electric green in the low grey light. The Subaru wasn't parked at Four Loaves, but there was a blue Rav 4 outside, and a man sheltering from the rain on the café steps. He was tall — I thought everyone was tall — with dark hair, wide shoulders and a purple tee-shirt. I didn't go too close, wary of talking to a stranger in the early darkness.

'You're Philippa's girl?' He stood and gave a wave. 'I'm Ryan.'

I walked closer. His calves were lean yet thick; he wore pale-blue Hoka sneakers. He had to be a runner.

'I'm Mickey.'

'Like the mouse?'

'More like a cheetah.'

He gave a bright, musical laugh. 'We'll see about that,' he said.

'Philippa asked me to come and pace you for this run. I hope that's okay. Ana needed her at home. Her instructions were pretty fluid but I got the impression we're going to dig ten miles tonight. You good to go?'

We started out slow but steady, and without prompting he told me about himself. He lived in Devonport with his fiancée, he worked as a software engineer in the city and he ran ultramarathons. 'I prefer 80 to 100 kilometres,' he said. 'Anything over that feels too much like hard work.'

'How do you know Philippa?' I asked.

'I think Philippa knows just about every runner in the city. I met her when I was much younger, maybe at the Rotorua marathon. How did you meet her?'

'She pulled over on the road and corrected my running form.'

He chuckled and shook his head, flicking his long brown hair from his eyes. 'Sounds like her.'

He told me about the Tarawera Ultra that he'd run in February, 102k with over 3,000 metres of elevation. Muddy, he said, but beautiful — the lakes, the redwoods, the forest. 'I qualified for the Western States, but I won't be going, not this year. Hils is due around that time, so I'll be here waiting for baby.'

It was strange, running beside a man. Ryan was in his late thirties, I guessed, and quite unlike the guys I'd run with at Birchfield and North Lynn, who were scrappy and twig-like, still teenagers in many ways. Ryan was solid, strong. His body floated in a manner I liked, his arms suspended by his sides. He kept the pace steady so that we could talk, though I felt the push through my legs as we worked up and down the inclines around Glen Eden and along narrow footpaths, dodging dog shit on the verge.

He looked down at my feet as we ran and said, 'The Pegasus?'

'My sneakers?'

'Yeah, of course. They look like the 33. Comfortable upper, smooth ride, versatile. Bit heavier than the 32. Can handle a high daily mileage. A good choice for this sort of running. You might want to consider something else for your tempo runs, and you wouldn't wear those on a track.'

'Okay,' I said. 'Thanks Mr Sneaker Head.'

'I admit it. Could talk sneakers all day. You know most athletic shoes are designed for men and then shrunk down for women? Which is —' he took a moment to run around a rubbish bin set out on the curb — 'which is ridiculous when you consider the structural differences. Your ankle, for instance, sits at an angle quite different from mine.'

'Philippa's got a bit to say about my shoes as well. She makes me fill in a diary and log the ks and everything.'

'Philippa knows a thing or two,' he said.

I was beside him, our bodies in rhythm.

'What's your next race?' he asked as we came up past the Glen Eden RSA.

'I'm not racing,' I told him.

A car drove past then, slowing down to a crawl, and a man leaned out the passenger window: 'Take her home, Daddy, it's not safe out here for little girls!'

'Fucking hell,' Ryan said under his breath. 'You should race something, Mickey. Be a waste if you don't.'

'I don't know,' I said. Racing: the thought of it made me feel both giddy and petrified. I was thirty-two years old, out of shape and out of practice. I liked to win — but what were the chances of winning now? Slim to none. There would be professional runners there. Yet Philippa was right. I did have a fire inside me. I heard the commentator of the Rio marathon again: *Several of the women running today are over forty.*

'You could do the Auckland marathon,' he said. 'I'm thinking about doing it for a bit of fun.'

'Maybe,' I said. 'I'll think about it. '

That was as much as I could promise. But as we looped around, my feet skipping along four for his every two, I turned the idea over. A marathon: even the word sounded magical. I knew what a marathon looked like, the hours of working and sweating and grinding. Did I have the intensity of spirit to run that far, that fast? I wasn't sure.

We turned off Glendale Road and headed right along West Coast Road, through the commercial part of town. The lights at the Glen Eden train station lit up the darkness. Ryan said, 'You look like you're favouring your right leg a bit, Mickey.'

'It's okay,' I said. 'My IT band's a bit tight.' I moved away from him slightly. I'd heard those words before. I knew what could come next.

'You should see a physio about that before it gets any worse. Our bodies need all the loving they can get. My physio has saved me from complete ruin several times.' Ryan didn't stop running. He didn't offer to help; his hands didn't touch me. We turned down Pleasant Road, heading back to Titirangi.

When we got back to Four Loaves, it was nearly 7.30. The streets were quiet. The drizzle had stopped and some of the cloud had parted. I saw a thin sliver of moon hanging low in the sky.

'We should do the Waiatarua on Sunday mornings,' Ryan said. 'Be like the OGs. It's different now. Some of the roads have changed but it's almost the same.'

'Run the what?' I said.

He laughed. 'Mickey, you're a crack-up. Tell me you know who Arthur Lydiard is.'

'I know who he is.' Philippa had told me how all the Auckland clubs had said no to his training style so he'd started his own club. She just hadn't mentioned the Waiatarua.

'Let's do it soon. We'll pop your Waiatarua cherry.'

'Sounds romantic,' I said, and he laughed again. He took out his phone and let me tap in my number.

'Let me know when it suits you to run,' he said. 'I'm also happy to provide sneaker advice should you ever need it.'

I waved goodbye, and a warmth spread from my stomach to the ends of my limbs. I shook my head. *I think I've made a friend.* I jogged home, and there it was again: the echoing steps of the ghost runner, the tension of an invisible soul right behind me. And suddenly it occurred to me that maybe the sound was my own footsteps, that I was both running away from and chasing myself.

THE RACE

WATCHING A MARATHON RUNNER, OR any sportsperson, you can see how they've taken adversity and made it great. They've been under pressure and they've transformed, like sand into pearls. There's always the odd armchair expert, disgruntled and unfit, ready to downplay their performance, to remark on how easy it is — but it isn't. What you see is only the race, the match, the competition. You don't see the hours of training, the years of their life. All the sacrifice, for this performance.

And it is a performance. Performance art, in my opinion. I think of the runners around me, in front and behind, creating a story with their bodies, a dramatic visual spectacular. After two hours and 30 minutes, or four hours and 50 minutes, most of the runners will have collapsed at the finish line, crying with jubilation or devastation. Everything they've worked for, and now — it's over.

The slogan of the marathon is RUN THE CITY. I have run the city. I know Auckland now in a way not many do. You learn things about the places you run that you can never understand from the comfort of your car. I've had my feet on the footpaths of its suburbs. I know its state houses with wide open lawns. I know its leafy streets with pruned hedges and maintained services. I know Auckland's building sites, its renovations, the houses and shops in a state of constant renewal. A city shifting, drawing people in. I know its maunga, the trails winding up the grassy slopes. I know its harbours, the Waitematā, the Manukau, the golden sheltered bays of the North Shore, the unrestrained ferocity of the West Coast beaches. I know its roads over motorways, its public toilets, its broken footpaths. The pockets of bush, the playgrounds, the strips of shops in Ponsonby, Onehunga, Browns Bay, Howick, Māngere Bridge. I know its limits, I know its expanse. Now it is my home.

NINETEEN

PHILIPPA WAS HESITANT WHEN I told her I wanted to run the Auckland marathon. She was at her favourite spot by the café window, Titus under the table.

'The one in four months? That Auckland marathon?'

'Yes,' I said. 'That one.'

'Goddamn, Mickey, that's not a lot of time to prepare.'

'Come on,' I said. 'Let's go crazy. I can do it.'

She shook her head and sipped the coffee I'd made her. 'It's not that I don't think you can do it. I know you can. You just have to be sure you can put in the work. You can't just wake up one day and expect to be able to race a marathon. Sure, you've got talent, but that's only going to get you so far. Even the best put in the work, day after day, year after year. It takes patience as well as miles. You were born human, but were you born patient? You need to work on this muscle up here.' Philippa tapped her head. 'And marathon training? You're heading into a dark old tunnel, my girl. You're gonna be in there for a few months. You'll need patience, because they'll feel like the longest damned months of your life. You won't know if you're coming or going. Though I promise you, when you get to the other side, that light you'll see at the end of the tunnel? It will be the sweetest light you ever saw.'

Maybe it's like grief, I thought. Maybe I'm in the tunnel and if I just keep going I might find some sweet light.

'I want to do it,' I said, slapping my hands on my apron. 'I'm going to bloody well do it.'

Ginny called out and told me to get back where I belonged.

'Get in there,' Philippa said. 'We can't afford to have you fired. Call me when you're finished work.'

TRAINING FOR A RACE REQUIRED a more structured plan. 'We'll follow the same general principles,' Philippa said. 'We need some big kilometres now, then later a bit of speed work, hills, track, fun stuff like that, and then a taper. You ready?'

I WASN'T READY, AND YET I was. I had always been ready.

BIG KILOMETRES: WE AMPED UP to 120 ks a week. When Philippa found out I was running in the mornings on an empty stomach, she let me know it had to change.

'You wouldn't do that to your car, would you? So stop doing it to your body.'

'I like running this way,' I told her. 'It feels good to run like that.'

'You like it? Or you like what you think it might do for your weight? What are you using for fuel? There isn't a pinch of fat on you. You're going to use what? Your muscles? Your bones? Your heart? Your brain?'

She was right. A part of me still thought if I lost weight I'd run faster.

'It's dangerous,' Philippa said. 'And it would be irresponsible of me to let it continue. Food is fuel, Mickey. It will keep you strong, and it will keep you going.'

I nodded.

'In evolutionary terms, we're all runners.' She was really letting me have it now. 'Stop thinking about it as a method to lose weight and all that jazz. Start believing in yourself. Start thinking about it as a movement towards wisdom, self-awareness, knowledge. The difficulty of it, the marvel of it, is the point. Adversity, my girl, is possibility.'

She made it clear: wake up two hours before my morning runs, eat something, a banana or some peanut-butter toast, a Milo maybe, then go back to bed. It wasn't just in the running that I was learning how to challenge myself: every day was another chance to love myself.

MARATHON TRAINING WAS JUST WHAT Philippa said it would be. I felt as though I ran all the time. When I wasn't running I was working or sleeping. My favourite runs were the twilight miles. The hour or two when the world fell into the deepening hollow of dusk. The noises of the day — the traffic buzz, the music, the industry, the hustle — it would all seep away, leaving the calm of night to settle into the creases of the maunga. Sometimes I would drive to Remuera for my run, telling Philippa I needed a change of scene. I'd park the Corolla on Shore Road, then, on my own power, wind up Arney Road, along Remuera, to hurtle down Portland, a short zip to Victoria Avenue, and my legs would have to push hard to reach the top once again.

I'd rein in the pace for the steep uphills and try to enjoy the ride. Say hello to aloof Persian cats perched on stone fences and the snouts of dogs peeking out from under electric gates. Another run along Remuera Road, through the shopping bustle of evening, before easing back into the hush of the residential streets when I turned down Orakei Road. The sun would shimmer over the world, the last rays casting a spell before vanishing completely. Car headlights would come on, and streetlights flicker to life, casting unreal puddles on the pavement. Curtainless houses stood open for viewing: I could peek in without worrying, because seconds later I'd be gone. These houses were mansions, with swimming pools and tennis courts and the protection and opportunity I assumed came with money and privilege.

It didn't make me angry. I thought it was obvious that I'd struck the better end of the bargain. Look at me: the night air fresh on my face. My legs short but strong. I might not have had money growing up — shit, I still had no money. But I had the freedom to do as I wished. I had a dream to fly, when others chose to stay earthbound.

I ran in almost all weather. Only on the days when rain fell in heavy silver sheets, torrents racing down the curb and flooding the stormwater drains, would I drive to the gym and run on the treadmill. It wasn't the same, but the work still needed to be done. If it rained when I was already out, I'd feel the skin on my feet grow soft, blister and peel away where it rubbed on the sneakers. I'd slow down then, or sometimes stop altogether, cursing myself for being so ill-prepared. But most changes couldn't be seen: it was in my heart, its efficacy at delivering oxygen to my muscles; the mental stamina to continue even when it hurt, even when it was agony, when all I wanted to do was sleep in, instead of pounding the streets at four in the morning so I could make it to work on time.

THAT WAS HOW I SPENT the rest of June: miles in the rain, in the whipping cold wind. I'd arrive at work like a zombie. I spoke to Philippa every day. I ate more too, fighting the revulsion that came with feeling too big to run. It never left me, the desire for a thinner body, only now I understood the waste of that old compulsion. The time and energy I'd spent obsessing about food and size and speed: there were other things I could've done instead, that I should have done. Being lighter hadn't helped me; it had done nothing but weaken my bones. Now, when my period came, the bloom of crimson was a sign that all was working as it should, that I was strong and capable of absolutely anything.

Ryan and I kept in touch. He texted me about new running shoe releases and I quizzed him on the intricacies of ultramarathons. One night he texted: **It's almost obligatory to do this route if you want to call yourself a runner**, followed by **LOL**. So I agreed to meet him on the first Sunday of July, on the corner of Wainwright and O'Donnell, at 5.30 a.m.

It was dark and cold. I was shivering and my stomach was churning with nerves. I'd heard the Waiatarua was tough.

'You good to go?' Ryan was wearing a white cotton tee-shirt and he'd tied his hair in a knot on the top of his head.

'I'm as good as I'll ever be.'

And we were off. I lifted my knees in an exaggerated kick to spread the blood, knowing it would take me a minute or two to warm up.

O'Donnell Avenue had overgrown grass verges and modest houses. A dog sat outside on a weedy lawn and barked at us with a growly, vicious undertone. We passed a square brick house with a gravel driveway and a yellow door, and for a moment I thought it was my house, the one on Rutherford Street. We turned right onto Richards, the four lanes empty on a Sunday morning, a great swathe of road all our own. The echo of our steps bounced back to us and I remembered the ghost runner. Where was she now?

Left onto Hendon Avenue, the bare trees pruned to divide around the power lines. We curved past an orange dairy and then straight until New North Road. The big intersection was deserted. We cruised along, up the incline to St Jude Street. From the top of the hill we saw the crest of the Waitākere Ranges in the distance.

'That's where we're headed?' I asked.

Ryan nodded. 'Following the footsteps of legends.'

After 5 ks we hit New Lynn, going through in around 23 minutes. We talked a bit while we ran, though mostly we were quiet, concentrating. Left at West Coast Road, cars already at the McDonald's drive-thru for breakfast. More houses, Countdown, Subway. A tūī sliced through the sky with its distinctive wingbeat: one two three, glide. Fences green and brown. I kept my breath under control and smiled. Out on the road before most people woke: it always made me feel like I knew something other people didn't.

Ten kilometres at Parrs Park. We veered left, heading to Oratia, into roads I knew well. The house I'd lived in with Joel was down that road there — I didn't know where he was now. Past the big red church that looked like a barn, and then Ryan told me we were hitting it, the start of the beast section.

'The climb begins here and won't finish for quite some time. Let's start digging.'

There were no footpaths on this part of the road. I kept my steps strong, inhaling the dank scent of the bush that loomed on either side. Upward, ever upward, the road snaking in loose curves. A footpath again and we skipped onto it just in time — a red ute came tearing down the hill towards us, then passed in a cloud of exhaust fumes. It was punishing, that hill — kilometre after kilometre of black tarmac and no relief. I told Ryan I usually ran West Coast Road in the other direction. He grinned and said I wouldn't be choosing the easy option any longer.

'You want to mix it with the big guns in this marathon?' he said. 'You need to do the hardest, the longest, the most punishing. Your body will adapt, as long as you treat it right. Not too far now and we'll reach Waiatarua and the peak.'

At Bush Road, my knee started to niggle and my hip felt achey and tight. My IT band was straining and overworked. I gritted my teeth and kept going, the twanging hip refusing to let up. A goat tied up at a gate bleated and lunged on its rope, and I startled, tripping but not quite falling. My lungs were screaming. It's never going to end, I thought, never, ever going to end. Higher and higher. Hamstrings pumping calves burning whole body wants to stop, please, to stop. My world shrank to the space around me. All that mattered was the next step.

I couldn't get enough air, I wanted air. One step, then the next, minute after minute feeling like hour after hour until finally—

We were there at Waiatarua. We stopped at the corner and looked back, a tiny peek at the land stretching out below us between ponga fronds. I rubbed my hip and shook my knee.

Ryan asked, 'You feeling all right?'

I tipped my head from side to side.

'IT band again?'

I nodded. It hurt and I didn't want him to know how bad.

As we turned to continue up West Coast Road, I groaned. 'More hill? How is this possible?'

'Buck up, Mickey. Show me what you're made of!'

'Easy for you to say. I'm working twice as hard as you on these short-arse legs.'

'Well, you're carrying about 30 kilograms less than me. So I guess we're even.'

Once we turned onto Scenic Drive, it was pretty much downhill from there. I stretched out my stride, cutting loose and following Ryan down the winding road. It was incredible, thinking about all the runners who had peeled out these roads before me, their feet on the same ground, years of runners separated by only the mysteries of time.

When we drew near Titirangi I knew it, the slight rise in the road, the scattering of houses. We were coming through 25 kilometres in 1:45. We were making good time, considering the hills and my knee. We strode past Lopdell House, then past Village Kebab and the Gull. Ginny was outside the pharmacy and called out, 'Run, Mickey!'

It was eight o'clock when we returned to the corner of O'Donnell and Wainwright Avenue. Thirty-five kilometres of unrelenting road: I wasn't sure I could walk to my car.

'I'm impressed, Mickey. That's a good time, especially for your first bite at the apple. Two-and-a-half hours. Jeff Julian did it in 1:55, so you have a way to go to beat that record.'

'I'm wasted,' I said. 'That was a workout.'

'See you here next Sunday?'

I nodded, my chest still heaving as I cooled down. 'Same time, same place.'

A FEW DAYS LATER I was out in the cool drizzle of evening, running from Mount Eden to Cornwall Park. I looped around the roads to One Tree Hill, over the cattle grates before scrambling up the steep road to the very top, pausing for only a moment to appreciate the view over the isthmus, sparkling grey from both harbours almost touching. In the pause I heard the ghost runner, creeping up behind me, the sound followed by the melancholy call of a sheep. When I made it back to the Corolla, there were two messages on my phone. One was from Ryan, inviting me to dinner at his house the next night to meet his fiancée and, as he liked to call her, his 'baby mumma'.

The other was from Sera, Teddy's wife: **Gold Card Party for Teddy, Saturday 15 July, Duck & Monkey Bar**

My phone buzzed again. It was Helen: **I'll see you on the 15th!**

I replied: **I don't think I'll go**

You have to come, Bryn and Wilma will be there too

I wanted to see them. I loved my sister and my niece. I would have to go.

TRAFFIC WAS CLOGGED UP, AND I was twenty minutes late for dinner with Ryan and Hilary. I pulled up flustered and red in the face, my hands shaky with hunger and exhaustion — I'd woken at 4.30 that morning to complete a 24k tempo run before work. I'd had too many coffees and not enough food. Philippa would be furious. I almost turned around and drove home, but already Ryan was opening the bright-red front door of a small bungalow and waving, his long body almost filling the door frame.

'You're here!'

'Sorry I'm late.'

'No sorrys allowed.' He took the bottle of red wine I'd brought with me, and said I shouldn't have bothered. 'Unless you're going to have a glass with me, Mickey?'

He led me inside. It was warm, filled with the golden glow of lamplight. A fire was burning in the hearth. It felt homely, like Rutherford Street. There was a feel of nesting. Piles of perfectly folded baby clothes, a brand new pushchair parked up beside the door, ready for its first outing.

'Hilary,' he called. 'Mickey's here.'

From the door at the end of the hall came a woman I recognised immediately — Hilary from North Lynn Track and Field. Her long hair was braided over her head and down her back, and her pregnant belly stuck out curved and round.

'Far out! If it isn't the one and only Mickey Bloom in my house. Long time no see, my friend.' She hugged me, her arms light.

'Hilary?' I couldn't believe it. 'I watched the Olympics ... You were amazing.'

She smiled and patted her stomach. 'Ah, that was a long time ago now! Look at me, barefoot and pregnant. Be a while before I'm out chasing the miles again.'

We sat at their small table in the kitchen, and ate a lamb tagine with apricots and couscous. It was spicy and sweet and I felt better, the unease in my stomach vanishing with food. I told Ryan to pour me a wine — 'Are you sure?' he said. 'I don't want Philippa roasting my arse tomorrow over a pinot noir' — and listened to Hilary talk about her Olympic experience, and how she met Ryan at a trail-running event in the Hunuas four years ago. The rest, she said, rubbing her stomach again, the rest is history.

'Baby's due any day,' Ryan said. 'I should be in California doing my run but instead I'm here, with my love, waiting for my new little love.'

I looked down at my plate and swallowed. The room was full of the gorgeous anticipation of a newborn, the smells of the meal, their love. Ryan was going to be a great father. I wiped my mouth, giving myself a moment to find some composure.

'I'm so glad you're running again, Mickey,' Hilary said. 'How any of us survived that hellscape of North Lynn is beyond me.'

'I didn't survive,' I said. 'Not really.'

'You're right,' she said. 'It doesn't really go away does it, even when it's over. What made you start running again?'

'My mum,' I said. 'She died last year, and she told me how much she loved watching me run.'

'That's so sad, Mickey, but inspiring too.' She stood up and leaned back, easing her muscles. 'It's been hard in this last trimester. I can't wait to get back into it.'

'I don't know if I could stop,' Ryan said. 'Running's done something to my brain. It gets into your soul, like right down deep, doesn't it? I guess there are other things that give you that same buzz — change-your-life type stuff. Like mountain climbing. Surfing. Maybe yoga? I don't know, the sort of stuff that gets people outside their comfort zone and sees them pushing against their limits. Just to see what's beyond, you know what I mean? I suppose that's why I'm going to Melbourne in November, just to keep sharing that with as many people as I can.'

'Yes, he's leaving me here with the baby to run the Melbourne marathon with Keegan,' Hilary said, sitting again and taking a sip of her juice. 'You know he's a guide runner, as well as being a fabulous boyfriend and father.'

'A guide runner? What, for someone blind?'

'Yeah, I do it through Achilles New Zealand. Keegan's a real good dude. I'm hoping Hils and the babe will come with me, but we'll see how it pans out.'

We were interrupted by a rap on the door.

'Stay where you are,' Ryan said. 'I'll see who it is.'

Hilary shrugged when I glanced at her. I took another sip of wine, savouring the taste. I was enjoying myself — it wasn't like dinner with Joel and his boys. No one was drunk or crass. There was only good food, nice wine, intelligent questions. I didn't want to leave.

Ryan returned with a man in a long-sleeved tee-shirt with Peninsula Physiotherapy embroidered on the chest. He was shorter than Ryan, with a body as slight as a paperclip and a head covered in a flop of sandy curls.

'Thanks for the K-tape, mate,' Ryan was saying, tossing a roll of purple kinesiology tape from one hand to the other. 'You want to stay for a drink?'

'Ah, go on then,' the other man said in a thick Irish accent. 'Hello, Hilary, looking beautiful as usual.' He looked at me and nodded.

'Niall, this is Mickey,' Ryan said as he poured another glass of red wine. Hilary half-stood to hug Niall, and when he sat down our legs were close under the table. I pressed myself into the wall to give him space. 'Mickey, this is Niall, the world's greatest physio. Maybe he could take a look at your IT band?'

Niall let out a whistled breath. 'IT band? You're a runner too then, I take it.'

'How did you know?'

'That's a classic running injury. Would you like me to take a look?'

'It's fine,' I said. 'Really, it's fine.' It sounded rude, but the thought of a strange man's hands on my hip, my glutes, my leg made me bristle in alarm.

'You're sure? I don't mind.'

'Completely sure. I've got an appointment with a physio tomorrow.' That was a lie, though it wouldn't take much to turn it into truth: Philippa would know a physio. Someone good; someone safe.

A sliver of tension sat in the air — for a moment I worried he'd ask who I was seeing, or feel slighted I'd rejected his offer — though it was possible I imagined it, because he simply nodded and drank his wine.

The four of us sat late into the night, talking about running, TV shows, travel, upcoming races, the baby. Niall asked a few questions about my training, and when I mentioned that Philippa was my coach, he said, 'You must be quite a runner, then. Philippa doesn't coach just anybody.'

Hilary gasped at a series of Braxton-Hicks, pretending the labour was starting in earnest and clutching at the table in mock-agony. She was funny, with a true sense of comedic timing. Why hadn't we been closer when we'd run together at North Lynn? I wondered if it was because I'd been so blinkered, so consumed by the data and the urgency of it all. Obsessed with my weight, my VO2 max, my splits. I'd been starved, run down, belittled, with nothing left to give. It was a shame it had been like that. If I'd had a friend, someone to talk to when it was all so bleak, maybe it would've been different.

I wouldn't make the same mistake again. Running might be an individual sport, but I didn't have to do it alone.

NIALL AND I LEFT AT the same time. We said goodbye to Hilary and Ryan in the warmth of the hallway and walked through the gate to the street. Night had closed in, and I could see across the harbour to the skyline of the city, the lights of the Sky Tower and the other tall buildings glittering against an asphalt sky. It was so different from the Auckland I'd run in only a few days earlier with Ryan: Tāmaki Makaurau, such a multifarious city.

'It was a pleasure to meet you, Mickey,' Niall said as he walked away. 'Hope you get some relief from that inflamed iliotibial band.'

'Thanks,' I said. 'It was nice to meet you too.' I unlocked my car and suddenly did not want to be alone again. 'Do you want a ride?'

He swung around, the silver glow of the streetlight dancing along the line of his jaw, his neck. 'Oh no, it's fine, I'm only a fifteen-minute walk away.'

'Are you sure? I don't mind dropping you home.' I nodded toward the car, and he hesitated.

'Only if it's not out of your way.'

The streets were quiet, only cats lurking, their eyes shining in the car's headlights. He lived in Cheltenham, he told me, closer toward Narrow Neck. I took a wrong turn and he had to direct me back on course.

'You're running the Auckland marathon?' he said. 'Turn left here, then go straight.'

'That's the plan. Not sure if it's a good decision or a bad one.'

'Ah,' he said. 'Every time we make a scary decision, I think it's a sign we've made the right choice. Can't be sitting around stale for the rest of our lives.'

'You like to take risks?'

'You bet,' he said. 'Moving to New Zealand, that was a massive risk. I'd never even visited the country and then, boom, here I am.'

'Do you miss Ireland?'

'I miss my mam and my brother,' he said, folding his hands in his lap. 'It was brutal leaving Mam. But I couldn't stay there all my life and wonder, what if?'

I adjusted my grip on the steering wheel, a tingling sensation racing down my neck and arms. 'I know what you mean.'

'I'm just up here on the left.' Niall pointed at a small house. A light was on in the front window, and the porch was covered with the wizened bones of a bougainvillea. I pulled the car to a stop and the brakes squeaked.

Niall laughed. 'Sounds like your car needs some physio too.'

I peered out the windscreen. 'My dad used to live around here.' I remembered how Sera had opened the door and that hard look on her face when she saw Bonnie: I'd never forget it. That was the first time we'd come to Auckland as a family — it turned out to be the only time. 'He lives in Mount Eden now, I think.'

'You think?' Niall raised his eyebrows.

'We're not close,' I said.

'That's a shame.' Niall sat still, not moving to open the car door. I didn't mind; I wasn't in a rush to get home. It was warm inside the car, and it smelled faintly of chocolate. Niall spoke softly: 'Nothing better than family.'

His words hit me like a slap. I pushed a finger to the corner of my eye, pretending to wipe away a speck of dust. I asked, 'You're close with yours?'

'Not geographically,' he said, 'but yeah. I miss my mam something fierce, and although my brother and I don't talk much, I know he's always there for me.'

'To be honest, I don't think my dad even likes me.' I pressed my lips together. I'd never shared this suspicion about Teddy with anyone, and I wasn't sure why I'd done so now. Maybe it was because of the wine, or the warm rush of an evening spent with good people, but sitting in the car with him in those secret minutes before midnight I felt as though I could tell him anything.

'Sure he does,' Niall said. 'He probably just doesn't understand you. Not uncommon for parents and children to find the other fucking incomprehensible, and to hurt each other for want of a little understanding.'

'I'm supposed to go to his birthday party. I really don't want to go. Am I a terrible daughter?'

'Nah, not terrible. Just not daughter-of-the-year material.'

'It will end badly, I know it will.' I laughed, though nothing was funny. 'I kind of hope he'll see me and say, Mickey! I love you!' I shook my head. 'I'm deluded.'

'It's good you keep trying,' Niall said. His cheeks were pale in the dim light. 'He won't be around forever. One day you might regret not trying to get along.'

'Do you get along with your dad?'

'My da died when I was a kid,' Niall said, his voice almost a whisper, his brow pinched into a frown. 'My brother found him, in the garage.'

I was seized by a wild impulse to reach out and touch him, but I kept my hands on the wheel.

'I won't get a chance to understand him,' Niall continued. 'I don't remember much about him. Mam said he was a woodworker and a poet who made tables and sonnets of equal beauty.'

'I'm sorry,' I said, and even as I spoke I knew those words were too small and meaningless in the wake of such loss. I was reminded how lucky I was to have had Bonnie for so many years.

'Ah, nothing for you to be sorry about.' He gave me a half-smile and winked. 'I'm a poet myself now, too, or at least I try to write poetry. Do you want to hear a poem about running?'

'Okay.' I wasn't sure I did want to hear a poem — it would be humiliating if I couldn't understand what it meant. Poetry was Shakespeare and Shakespeare, to me, was shame.

'*We swing ungirded hips, and lightened are our eyes, the rain is on our lips, we do not run for prize. We know not whom we trust, nor whitherward we fare, but we run because we must, through the great wide air.*'

The words seemed to hang in the space between us, glittering in the silver light of the moon. After a moment, I said, 'That was beautiful. Did you write that?'

'Jesus, no,' he said. 'That's a classic by Charles Hamilton Sorley. He died in the First World War. Weren't too many women running back then, not like now.'

'I'd love to hear one of your poems.'

He looked surprised. 'Be careful what you wish for, Mickey. You might regret hearing one of my haiku.'

'Haiku?'

'Perfect day for miles, running in rain or sunshine, damn my leg is sore.'

I laughed. 'That's what you write?'

'No, that's a silly joke. Maybe you can hear one of my real poems another time.'

'I'd like that,' I said, and I meant it — I would listen to him say anything.

'Thanks for the ride,' he said, opening the car door. 'Take care, Mickey.'

'You too.' I watched him walk to the house. He paused on the threshold and turned back, lifting his hand in a brief wave before he stepped inside.

THE RACE

WE'RE CLOSING IN ON THE turnaround point at the far end of St Heliers. The sparkling water on our left and the stretch of Vellenoweth Green on our right. There are people everywhere, cheering, and still over that noise I hear my heart thumping, thumping. The sun hurts my eyes. Relief comes now in the welcome shade from the pōhutukawa along the beach and the stretching limbs of the Moreton Bay figs from the Green. Several men have caught us on their hunt for the leaders. I smell them, their singlets soaked through with sweat.

I'm around the turn, facing back to the city. I see the long line of runners streaming out behind us. In this direction, a slight breeze gusts into us — the way to the finish made just that little bit harder. Ruby's ahead, still close.

We're drawing near to the 20-mile mark: Make it a guts race. I don't know if I can do it without the gel. Philippa's two kilometres away, on the far side of Kohimarama. It feels impossible.

But I can see where we started — the mounds of Maungauika and Takarunga over the harbour, so slight from this far away. I can see where I have been from here, and where I need to go.

TWENTY

A BLACKBOARD SIGN SAT ON an easel outside the Duck &
Monkey, and someone had written *Teddy's Gold Card Party. Come
and play!* in a colourful chalky cursive font. A staff member stood
at the door and offered to take my puffer jacket, but I kept it on. It
was chilly inside, the southerly sweeping in through the open doors
and filling the cavernous space. The polished concrete floors smelled
of stale beer and urine. Roxette was playing on the speaker system,
her voice caught with the snap of the snare. A small group of people
huddled around the bar, among them Teddy, his back to the room. I
couldn't see Helen or Bryn.

It was too cold to stand near the door, even in my puffer jacket,
so I moved closer to the group, wary of attracting Teddy's attention
without Helen there. A waitress wandered around the room with a
tray of champagne flutes glittering gold.

A woman in a white satin blouse standing beside Teddy turned to
face me — it was Sera. She wore red lipstick and her black hair was
curled into soft waves, and I was reminded of one of the last times I
saw my mother, her small body in the bed, Teddy sitting beside her,

his head next to her ear so he could speak softly. A severe desire to see her hit me, and I took a breath, as though I were running to the top of the hill. One step, one step, then another.

A young woman next to Sera took her phone from her bag and looked down at the screen. She had Teddy's dark eyes and Sera's black hair. In another setting I wouldn't have known she was my sister Cleo. She was long-limbed and awkward in her pale-yellow dress and black cardigan, her arms crossed over her chest. I felt too shy to say hello — I couldn't remember the last time we'd met. I realised in that moment that I would never know her, that we could go through our lives with family as strangers.

The heady scent of my father's distinctive aftershave grew thick as I approached. I remembered it filling the air when he visited. Sometimes I used to think I smelled it at Rutherford Street, and that he was there, hiding somewhere, and Bonnie would shake her head and pull me in for a cuddle, and say, Not this time, honey.

Teddy turned around and looked me up and down. He wore a crimson shirt and black trousers, his nose shiny with grease. He looked old. Deep lines scored his forehead, and his hair was thin and grey.

'Happy birthday, Teddy,' I said. I held out my hand to shake his — the way we'd done when I was a teenager.

'What, you haven't got a hug for your old man?' He looked put out. I stepped towards him and we came together in a clumsy embrace.

A waitress offered me a champagne and I declined. I had a big run scheduled for the morning and it would be torture if I was hungover. Teddy took the flute from the tray and pressed it into my hand.

'No way you're skiving off without toasting me,' he said. 'This is important. I'm an old man now! The average lifespan of a male in this country is seventy-nine. I'm on the way to irrelevancy. Pale, stale and male, isn't that what they say?' He lifted his champagne. 'Least you can do is raise a glass to the man who's paying for all this.'

I took a sip — it was too dry — and looked around. Most of the women were in heels, and a few men wore shirts with a tie. It was clear I was underdressed in my ripped jeans, dirty white Converse and a flannel shirt.

'Did I hear you got a new job, Michelle?' Teddy asked.

'No,' I said. 'I'm still at the café.'

'You're still making coffees?'

'I like to say barista.' I said it with an appalling Italian accent, trying to lighten the mood. Teddy didn't even smile.

'A fancy job title for what's nothing more than the girl fetching the coffee,' he said. 'It's not too late for you to consider going to university, Michelle, or polytech. Nothing wrong with a polytechnic. You remember my colleague Viv Noone? Her eldest boy Leonard's just gone back to study law, and I thought, a lawyer, wow, she must be proud.'

Someone behind me said, 'God, Mick. You could've worn something a bit nicer!'

I swung around and there was Helen, with Bryn and Wilma. I hugged her, and felt the warm curve of her second child nestled between us.

'I'm joking, by the way,' she whispered. 'God, Mick, you're looking fit!' She held me at arm's length and shook her head. 'Mum would be pleased to see you looking so well.'

She moved on to talk with Sera, and I sat alone at a table with my half-drunk flute. I watched Teddy. He was talking with a woman with silver hair and a man in a gaudy Hawaiian shirt, and his face lit up when Helen tapped him on the shoulder. They hugged. He loved her, I could tell by the way he held open his arms, the way he spoke to her, looking her in the eye.

Bryn came over carrying three glasses, and slid one across the table to me. 'It's only lemonade. Helen will be glad she's not the only sober one here.'

Helen was talking to our Bloom cousins, Marguerite's kids Franca, Lukas and Hans: all of them taller than Teddy, with the same dark complexion and wide smiles. I didn't go over to say hello; I barely knew them. The last time I'd seen them was at the twins' twenty-first.

Wilma was asleep in Bryn's arms by the time Helen joined us. She dragged her chair closer to mine and told me in great detail about the drama of maternity leave, and the house she and Bryn were renovating in Island Bay. 'Two architects,' she said, rolling her eyes, 'and we can't agree on anything.' We talked about Bonnie for a while. I didn't say it, but I wondered if she thought it too: how unfair it was that Teddy made it to sixty-five, and she didn't.

Around nine, the music grew louder. There was a loud smash from near the bar — someone had dropped a glass and a staff member scuttled around with a brush and pan. Teddy waltzed up to our table. He was swaying and his shirt had come untucked. Bryn said quietly, 'Looks like your old man's had a good night.'

Teddy knelt on the floor and rested his elbows on our table. I offered him my chair but he waved me away.

'Zach tells me you've been running again,' he said.

'He's not lying,' I said. 'I'm training for a marathon.'

'You're a bit old for the Olympics now, aren't you, Michelle?' He let out a mechanical laugh.

'I'm not too old,' I said. 'My coach says there's nothing wrong with being an amateur. She says that dedicating myself to the ideal of running for no reward is something to be celebrated.'

'Your coach sounds like a bit of a Looney Tune,' said Teddy. 'You should be careful running such a long way. It's not good for your body.'

I'd heard this before — people were always concerned about the fate of my knees. 'I'll be fine,' I said. 'Philippa places a lot of importance on staying healthy.'

'You want to be sure you can still have kids one day,' he said. 'You might regret all this when you find out about the damage it's doing to your system.'

'Damage?' I wasn't following his train of thought. What system did he mean?

'Dad, I think they proved women are physiologically capable of running without mortal injury a long time ago,' Helen said. 'Mickey's uterus isn't going to fall out or anything.'

Teddy shrugged, and when he spoke again his words were slurred. 'There's a reason people used to think that would happen, Helen. And I suppose you feminists think it's a good thing for men and women to get equal prize money at the Grand Slams, too.'

'Of course they should get equal prize money,' I said. 'They're all playing tennis.'

'Come on, Michelle,' Teddy said. 'Try to think about this rationally. I know this sort of thing is a bit challenging for you. '

I sat up straight and said, 'It's Mickey.'

Teddy scoffed. 'Not this again! It makes you sound like a boy. Michelle is such a beautiful name. So soft and feminine.'

'What's wrong with being like a boy?' My voice was too loud. I wasn't sure I could control myself much longer. 'What's wrong with being a bit different?'

Wilma stirred in Bryn's arms, and Helen touched my arm. 'Mickey,' she said in a low voice. 'It's okay.'

'It's not okay,' I said. 'Tell him he's full of shit. Tell him to call me by my name.'

Helen put her hand over her mouth and looked at Bryn. Teddy groaned as he heaved himself to his feet. 'I can see I'm not wanted here.'

'Dad,' Helen said. 'You don't have to leave.'

Teddy walked back to the crowd of guests. I called after him. 'Stop trying to tell me who I am. You don't know who I am. You don't know anything about me. I'm Mickey. Mickey Bloom.'

He looked back at me. There was an expression of disappointment on his face, a heaviness around his eyes, his mouth turned down. Then a waitress walked through the bar carrying a three-tier cake, one fat candle ablaze on the top, and Teddy put his hand to his chest, faking a heart attack at the shock, his frown replaced by a beaming smile. People began singing 'Happy Birthday'. Wilma woke and started crying.

I thought about what Niall had said to me in the car — that I might regret not finding a way to understand my father. I wasn't sure if I was patient enough, forgiving enough or passive enough to fix things between Teddy and me. There was no way to know if I'd regret how I'd just behaved or if I'd be proud I stood up to him.

Teddy took an inhale, and the flame of the candle flickered in the change of atmosphere. I didn't need to see him blow the candle out. In the excitement, nobody noticed me leave.

THE RACE

CLOSING IN ON 33 KILOMETRES. Philippa, the gel. I'm getting so close. Everything hurts, everything hurts. Seagulls whirl overhead, and their squawking and the cheers from onlookers feel too loud, too spiky. I want silence, softness. Up ahead, people scoot across in front of us to get from one side of the road to the other. I want to scream at them: *Get out of the way* — only I have no space in my mind to force my mouth open, to make the sounds, feel the anger. All I have keeping me going is one foot, then the other. Maintaining the quick pace is my only goal, my feet in time with Ruby's, my stomach a cold rock dropping down, weighing me down.

The breeze has whipped up into gusts, and it's blowing into my face, pushing on my chest, resisting my effort to glide through at speed. I'm tired, so tired. The idea of pancakes is suddenly revolting. Bile coats my teeth in a thick film. My body is warning me. This is a bad idea.

I'm nearly there. I see the table but I don't see Philippa.

CLOSER, CLOSER. FIRST, I SEE her hair, a halo of reddish-brown and silver wild in the sunlight. With each step, more of her comes into focus: the shape of her face, her eyes, the crooked tilt of her smile. There is only one other person I would be happier to see. There's only two minutes, one minute, until I reach her, and it feels like an eternity.

I'm intimate with time. I understand the nature of a second, of a minute, of an hour, how they can metamorphose in my mind. A second feels like a minute, a month feels like a week. Time is elastic, stretching to fit around your movement, your emotions. When I run hills, or along the beach, an hour feels like a minute, the joy of the grind the reason I return to the work. In a race, like now, minutes can feel like hours, like days, the agony of moving forwards seemingly neverending. Sore muscles, oxygen-deprived brain, and every split second continues to split, dividing endlessly, time going nowhere.

When I grieve my mother, or feel rage at my father, minutes I'd rather feel as seconds drag out into weeks, months, and I take a breath: it's just like running up Bullock Track — it won't last forever.

When you think of time like this, you can see the brevity of history. The past thrusting up against the present, not as far gone as we believe. I see people, men mostly, who wish we'd return to — or who want to pretend we've never left — the time when women had nothing. No autonomy, no credit card, no suffrage. I see it in every act of violence against women. Every time a woman is killed walking home. Shovelling snow. On a date. Running. I see it in the way I've been watched, leered at, jeered at, assaulted. I see those who would rather we went back to the time when boyfriends dictated how their women dressed, what they said, where they went. A time when we weren't allowed to run a marathon.

I want the freedom to run in the dark hills.

CAN I MAKE IT TO Philippa? Eat the gel before I fall apart? There's nothing in me, nothing at all. I feel wind on my face, the tarmac under my feet, the body of Ruby so strong, so alive just ahead of me. This is it, my fatal error, forgetting to sort my fuel properly. I have to dig deep, find the nugget of grit inside me — or it'll be all over.

TWENTY-ONE

FIVE HUNDRED AND FORTY KILOMETRES logged in July. Some fast and some slow. A few wonderful; many more — anything but. I loved the winter days when the sky was clear and blue, I loved the days with clouds stretched high as towers, or chubby like marshmallows rising up from the horizon. I loved running along the roads around the west-coast beaches, the creeping dark bush, birds hovering and calling, the grey road my own private highway. Sometimes the phantom steps followed me. I found myself listening for them when I was out there, alone in my work, the sound both a solace and a sinister presence.

It was on one of those crisp winter afternoons in early August that I found myself truly frightened for the first time. I was out for a slow 30-kilometre run. *Real slow,* Philippa had told me. *When I say slow, I mean it.* As I passed a large rimu, its spindly leaves drooping over the road shoulder, I heard the squeak of a pīwakawaka. I made an imitation call, hoping the bird would flit out into the road to investigate, but just as it appeared it was scared away by the sound of vehicles coming up from behind me. The first two cars zoomed by without slowing, but the third car, a black Pajero, slowed almost to a standstill. It was too far away to see clearly inside, though I could tell the interior was dark with bodies. The passenger window lowered, and a head bulged out, emitting a piercing wolf whistle. There was a roar of laughter from inside the car. I clenched my teeth. Fucking men.

The car took off, then the brake lights abruptly flashed red, and I was struck by the memory of another red light, an idling car, the tang of alarm in my mouth — and then the red was replaced with a silver light as the car began to reverse. I stopped running. The car snaked backward closer and closer, half on the road, half on the gravel of the shoulder. My body was still, my legs heavy and hot, yet my heart was racing. I was stuck. I didn't want to pass the car now it had pulled onto the shoulder. A steep, thickly treed slope hugged the roadside; there was no escape route up there. Neither could I cross to the other side; there was a line of cars streaming in the opposite direction. The head stuck out the passenger window again and barked at me, and the rest of the car's occupants barked too, a chorus of insult.

I swore, once, and then again, louder. Fuck. The last of the oncoming traffic passed, but I still couldn't cross the road: cars were whipping by in the other direction, veering around both me and the parked car. One tooted its horn as it swerved. I didn't want to turn around — that would be giving in, letting the Pajero win. I edged onto the road. I would have to run into the other lane to avoid it. There was no other option.

The driver was a young man, probably in his late twenties. Old enough to know better, strong enough to cause damage. He leaned his elbow out the open window and leered at me. He had a thick ginger moustache, and he rubbed a finger under the bristles before he spoke.

'We can give you a lift if you want,' he said. 'Bit late in the day to be out running.'

'No thanks,' I said. I moved past the car, careful to remain more than an arm's reach away.

'No?' he said. 'What are you, some sort of psycho?'

I was clear of the car. I looked back at the front windscreen. Part of me wondered if they would accelerate and run me down. It seemed possible. The driver flicked the headlights on, blinding me for a moment, reinforcing how defenceless I was.

I started to run again. The car's engine growled, and I felt the reverberations through my bones as it raced up behind me. The noise of the men inside hollering and roaring with laughter and the beat of the music on their stereo pricked at my skin. The tyres squealed and spun on the greasy tarmac; the car pulled alongside.

Out of the corner of my eye I saw the man in the passenger seat, his fingers in a V over his mouth, his tongue slicing through the centre. Someone else let loose a whooping cry that seemed to stay in the air for a few seconds before draining away beneath the receding grunt of the double exhaust propped on the rear. I kept running.

THE NEXT DAY I MET up with Hilary at a café in Takapuna. She wasn't alone — a tiny baby, Arlo, was strapped into a carrier. His face was pressed into her chest, his sweet cheeks full and unblemished. I asked how they were getting on, and she told me to shut my mouth. 'I didn't ask you here to talk about the baby,' she said. 'I want to live vicariously through you. Tell me about the running, for goodness' sake!'

The first thing that came to mind was the men in the Pajero, sweat beading on my brow from the exertion and the fear. I cleared my throat and said, 'Do you get hassled when you're out running?'

'All the time,' she said in a monotone.

'Don't you hate it?'

'Of course,' she said. 'It's worse when it's dark and I'm running alone. I try not to think about it, but it only takes one crazy and it's all over.'

All over. That was what had scared me when the car had reversed back towards me. The threat that one moment my body could be running in full flight — and the next, unresponsive and still. Touched and hurt and left for dead.

'What does Ryan say? Does he get hassled when he's out running?'

'Not as much,' Hilary said. 'And I don't get it as much when I run with him, either. It's not an even playing field anyway. If you live somewhere without decent street lighting, it's totally unsafe.'

I held my coffee but didn't drink and looked at the corner of the room. 'Do you ever feel embarrassed about loving running so much? Sometimes I feel too old to be wanting something so desperately. I worry about what people will think if I fail, like, man, she should've stuck with her day job.'

Hilary set her coffee down. 'There's no reason why you need to give up wanting things just because you're older. No one will judge you if you fail. It's brave, what you're doing. Making a comeback.'

'It's easy to say that when you already made it.'

'What do you mean?' She jiggled Arlo.

'I mean, you did it, you went to the Olympics.'

'Some people would say I didn't make it.' She shrugged. 'For every four people telling me how amazing I did, there was always one person who wanted to remind me that I didn't even make the top ten. It bugged me for a while, but now? Meh. Ryan's helped me see that running doesn't have to be about podiums and personal-best times. It can be about community and joy.'

Community, joy. Such simple and beautiful ideals. I looked Hilary in the eye and smiled. Arlo snuffled in the pack and Hilary said she should get him home for a feed. We left the café together, and as I walked back to my car I felt some of my old anxieties return, wondering how those wonderful ideals could sit alongside the ever-present dangers. I thought again about the woman who went out jogging in the hills around Ngāmotu. She'd never returned home. Maybe the ghost steps had always been a warning, a premonition, and not a welcome visit from a spectral friend.

I heard footsteps behind me in that same instant, the same soft thudding of the phantom runner. I expected to turn and find no one there, only when I did look back there was someone: Niall, Hilary and Ryan's physio. His face was pink and glossed with sweat, his curls damp and flat. He looked more athletic than I remembered. His legs were muscular and taut, and he stood with perfect posture. He'd been wearing long sleeves at Hilary and Ryan's house — I saw now his forearms were inked with tattoos. A musical note, a butterfly, half of a fox that must finish up under the sleeve of his tee-shirt.

'You right there, Mickey Bloom?' he said, panting slightly.

'Niall! Hi. Good run?'

'It's tough, to be honest with you,' he said. 'There are worse things, though, than feeling a bit shite while running beside a beautiful beach. You aren't out for a jaunt yourself?'

'No, I just met Hilary for coffee. I'll run later.'

'Lovely,' he said. 'How's the wee one?'

'Very cute. Sleepy. Then hungry.'

'So predictable, these babies.'

'How far are you running?' I asked, stopping beside my car, twitching the keys in my hand.

'Ten ks,' he said. 'Perfect distance for a lunch break. My clinic's down in Devonport.'

'I did what you said.' The words came out quickly. 'I tried to understand him.'

'Who's that now?'

I blushed. 'My dad. You know what you said, to try? I tried. It wasn't a great effort but I really tried. We just don't see eye to eye on anything.'

'Wait, you mean he's a Trump supporter?'

I started to laugh. 'How did you know? Do you follow him on Twitter?'

'Twitter? Jesus, no. If you tried, Mickey, you tried. He's got to meet you halfway.' He scuffed his shoe on the footpath, then said, 'Did you find yourself a physio in the end?'

'Yeah,' I said. 'I did.'

'Got any demand for another one? No need for any actual treatment of course, but it has been said that I'm exceptionally good company on long runs.'

'My long runs are a bit lonely,' I said. 'Let's do it.'

'You got a pen?'

'Hang on.' I unlocked the car and found a black Sharpie pen in my glovebox.

'You got some paper in there too?'

'No,' I said. 'Just write it on here.' I held out my arm.

He hesitated for a moment and then said, 'Fair play.' He snipped off the lid and held it between his teeth and drew the numbers up my forearm with a flourish. 'Flick me a text and we can sort out a time. I better crack on. I've got a client at 1.30.'

I watched him take off round the corner, his blue-and-white Asics flicking up and down, the ink still drying on my skin.

TWO DAYS LATER HIS PHONE number was still on my arm. Every time I looked at it I felt a soaring sensation, like I'd already won the marathon. I hadn't texted him, and I found just the thought of the phone number cleared away my anxiety about the Pajero. The world had good people in it too, the number reminded me.

ON MY NEXT RUN, PHILIPPA suggested I study the course. 'Run a section of it,' she said. 'Feel it under your feet. Get the advantage over others who aren't from here. Learn the spots where the road lifts in a rise, where you can put pressure on, and where the downhill might give others a lift. Understand the variety of wind along Tamaki Drive. How it feels when it's pushing at your back with gusts of salt, how it feels when it's a headwind driving into you and slowing you down.'

So I parked at St Heliers and ran to Ōrākei. Instead of an out-and-back, I decided to loop inland, weave through the maze of suburban streets back to where I started. The world felt strangely deserted away from the water. Dark-magenta magnolia flowers bloomed on bare branches like candles, and a white cat with different-coloured eyes jumped down from a fence into my path. I stopped to pet it, and then settled once again into the gliding rhythm of my body, the tattoo of Niall's number in the edges of my vision, tantalising as a promise.

I saw the rear lights of the car too late — I was down hard, jolted two metres from where the car had made impact. I sat up slowly. Moved my body piece by piece. Nothing felt broken or too bruised, but there was no way of knowing about other, more serious injuries. *This is it*, I thought. I saw the white skeleton bones of the x-ray decorated with tiny black lines.

My ears buzzed and my knees were skinned and bloodied, speckled with dirt and gravel. I brushed my palms clean on my shorts. The driver got out of the car. He was older, in his sixties, khaki trousers turned up at the ankle, dark-brown leather boat shoes. At the collar, his pale blue business shirt was undone to give his Adam's apple room to move.

'What do you think you're doing?' His cheeks were flushed.

'I'm running,' I said. 'What does it look like I'm doing?'

'Well, watch where you're going,' he said. 'You're fucking suicidal if you ask me.'

Blood ran down my shin in a crimson stripe. I didn't know if I could stand.

'Are you listening to me?' He was in my face now. I saw the dark shadow of a beard just below the surface of his skin. When he yelled, the Adam's apple bobbed, up and down. 'You need to be more careful.'

'Yes,' I said. 'I heard you loud and clear.' He examined the rear bumper of his car before he sank back into his vehicle. The white lights of reverse lit up. I sat where I'd fallen and watched him drive away.

My car was at least ten kilometres away. The only way back was to keep running. I couldn't be too hurt; it was simply shock. Nothing worse than shock.

But when I stood my body felt liquid and soft. My hands shook and my legs were unsteady. I let out a long breath and a noise came out of me unbidden — a wavering moan of terror. I took a step, and another. Was I making it worse? My body felt uncontained, as though the impact had shattered me. I had no phone. I was in a neighourhood I didn't know. Meadowbank? It could've been the moon.

I started walking. One foot, then the other. A headache pressed in at the corners of my brain. Eventually, I saw a dairy on the corner of the street ahead. The blue and red signs for milk and Coca-Cola bright against the sky. I stood in the doorway and called to the woman behind the counter.

'I need to make a phone call.'

She hurried to me. 'Oh dear,' she said. 'Are you all right?'

'I got hit by a car,' I said. 'I'm fine, I just need to call someone to pick me up.'

'Do you need an ambulance?' She cradled her cell and asked me again.

'No ambulance,' I said. I couldn't think: the world shimmered down to blocks of colour. The glowing white of the dairy refrigerators. The dark shadows in the corners of the room. The only number I knew by heart was the landline for Rutherford Street; even if it was still connected, no one I knew would answer. I was shivering and I wondered if I might be sick.

'Who would you like me to call?' the woman said. I pressed my hands into my face, and when I let them drop there was blood on my fingers and the black numbers on my arm.

'Call this number please,' I said, extending my arm to her. 'Tell him that Mickey needs a ride.'

I DIDN'T CRY UNTIL I was alone with Niall in his car. He wrapped a picnic blanket from the back seat over my legs, switched the radio off and repeated, 'It's going to be okay, Mickey.'

He took me to the hospital. I said I wanted to go home, that I was fine. A bit shaken, maybe, but fine. I wanted to go home.

'You're not a martini,' he said. 'You need to be checked out properly.'

We sat together in the grimy A&E waiting room. It was busy, and every few minutes an ambulance arrived and a pair of paramedics wheeled in yet another patient. My headache gripped tight and I felt the blood on my cheek drying into a stiff mask. Every few minutes Niall asked if I needed a drink of water; or would I like his sweatshirt as a pillow; or did I want him to call anyone else. It was a long time until a nurse called my name. Niall held my arm and helped me to stand.

'I'll wait right here until you're ready to go,' he said.

The doctor prescribed a week's rest and codeine for the pain. My body was covered in grazes and my hip and thigh were a collage of purple, black and yellow. The worst was the deep cut on my cheekbone, and my face felt tender beneath the bruising. 'You're lucky,' the doctor said, 'to escape with such superficial injuries. No broken bones, no concussion. Take it easy this week.'

Niall drove me home. He turned on the radio, and I fell asleep to the sound of his soft voice singing along to Lana Del Rey. I woke with a start, his hand on my shoulder. We were parked in Titirangi, outside the pharmacy.

'I didn't want to wake you,' he said. 'I don't know where you live.'

I wiped my eyes. There was a stale, almost pungently sweet smell in the car, and it took me a moment to realise it was coming from me.

'Woah, sorry about the stink,' I said. 'I'm particularly rank today. Go up ahead and turn left.'

Niall shook his head. 'I didn't want to be rude, but you do have quite the aroma going on. Eau de athlete.'

'I'll bottle it and sell it on Trade Me.'

'Well, that sounds like a grand business plan. You're an entrepreneur as well as a brilliant runner.'

At home, I went straight into the shower. The water on my sore body felt almost medicinal, and I stood in the spray for a long time. I pushed the tap as hot as it would go, letting the steam billow. The feeling of the impact was still pulsating through me. I could feel the thud of the car, the sickening jolt of flight. I wanted to call Bonnie and tell her. I didn't want to be alone.

Afterwards I stood in my towel, wiped a clear space in the mirror and fingered the bloodied edges of the cut on my cheekbone. This will probably scar, the doctor had said as he'd glued the cut together. Another mark on my body. I thought about Teddy, about sitting in Daniel's car, all the silver lines on my legs. My scars, inside and out, were a message. They said: You are tougher than whatever tried to hurt you.

When I hobbled back into the lounge, I was surprised to see Niall hadn't left. He was sitting on the couch, his body curved with a supple grace. How beautiful he was.

'I called Philippa,' he said. 'Let her know what's happened.'

'Thanks,' I said. 'You can go home if you want. I'm okay.'

'Don't be daft,' he said. 'You're in no state to be cooking, so let me fix you some dinner and then I'll leave you be. Deal?'

I sat down on the couch beside him and propped my feet on the coffee table. 'Deal,' I said.

TWENTY-TWO

BY THE END OF AUGUST, I was back on my feet. An easy week to begin, Philippa told me, and then we were into the grind.

Two weeks later, she met me at Four Loaves after my long Sunday run. I'd done another Waiatarua loop, without Ryan this time, and I was starving. Eggs, bacon, avocado, I told Ginny, and coffee. 'Yes, sir!' she said.

'Tell me about the run.' Philippa was all business.

'Thirty-five ks,' I said. 'I'm getting quicker on the uphill from Oratia.'

It had felt good: the cool air, the feeling of taking my body through the world once again, the insane fun of looping around quiet roads up and down the valleys. No creepy men this time, not even the shadowy slap of the ghost runner's steps. It had been a dream run, all alone on the tarmac, the sunrise a reward for me and only me.

'What was your pace?' Philippa asked, and then came the interrogation — how were my legs? How many gels did I use, and when? How old were my shoes? You need new shoes, she said, and I thought again of what Hilary had said about the privilege of running.

It wasn't just the streetlights: it was the shoes, the gels, the socks, the shorts, the gym, the nutritionist. The freedom of time. I'd been lucky even as a kid, when I thought I had it tough.

Ginny placed our meals on the table, and Philippa changed tack. 'So, Mickey, what are you doing tonight?'

'Nothing. Why?'

'I wanted to invite you over to my house for dinner. It's about time you met my family.'

PHILIPPA HAD TOLD ME VERY little about her personal life. I knew her partner was called Ana, and that was it. We'd spent hours together on the road, or debriefing about training, but seldom strayed into more private territory.

The address she gave me was near Bethells, down the valley near the beach. I almost missed the driveway tucked into the elbow of a tight corner in the road. It veered right and wound up the hill, on and on, until it opened up to a concrete pad outside a simple home. A Lockwood, possibly: brown wood exterior, an L-shaped design. The Subaru was under a carport with two mountain bikes stashed alongside.

The house sat on a small flat plateau at the top of the hill; beyond it, peaks of dense green rose up and, through a gap in the hills, a tiny shining triangle: the sea. The setting sun cast the whole world in a creamy-yellow light — it was heaven. Near the house was a coop, where three brown shavers scraped at the grass, and in the darker, shaded part of the property the murmuring chirp of crickets helped settle the evening into the creases of the day.

The woman who opened the door had long, dark hair and wore a linen smock dress with slippers. Titus padded down the hallway behind her, and put his mouth to my hand. 'You must be Mickey,' the woman said. 'I'm Ana. Philippa's kept you a bit of a secret around here, so I'm pleased to finally meet you. Come in, come in.'

I followed her into a low-ceilinged room crowded with house plants and filled with the spicy smell of cooking meat. One wall was made almost entirely of windows, giving a panoramic view of the hills, the rising and falling of the roads I ran.

'Mickey!' Philippa got up from a white sofa.

'Would you like a glass of wine?' Ana was heading towards the kitchen at the other end of the open-plan room. A large dining table stood between us, with settings for five guests laid out. In the centre, a blue vase overflowed with daffodils.

'Ah, maybe?' I looked at Philippa, who shook her head and waved her hand.

'Of course she does,' Philippa called. 'It's a rest day tomorrow, whether we'd planned it or not. Pour me a glass too, Ana-Lou. I'll only turn sixty once.'

'It's your birthday? You didn't tell me that.'

'Now, Mickey, do I need to tell you everything?' She laughed, and laid a hand on my shoulder. She rarely touched me, and the hand was warm and strong.

'You need to tell her some things,' Ana said, carrying over three glasses of wine. She lifted hers in the air. 'To Philippa, on her birthday, and also to Mickey, who has given our Philippa a new lease on life.'

We clinked glasses. Titus lifted his head from his bed, ears pricked high.

Ana said, 'I bet Philippa also hasn't told you she was one of the first New Zealand women to run an official marathon race in the seventies?'

I looked at Philippa. She blushed, her crinkled and tanned cheeks reddening even in the low light.

'It was a long time ago,' she said. 'It was a different time.'

Ana returned to the kitchen, stirring pots on the stove and chopping coriander on the board, the woody scent strong in the room. 'She was very good,' she called, and lifted the knife and pointed it at Philippa. 'She was an outstanding runner. Did you know she was one of Barry's Beauts?'

'Stop it,' Philippa said.

'I won't stop it! It's your birthday. I will scream your attributes from the rooftops!'

'Well, I didn't know that,' I said. 'And I also don't know who Barry is.'

Philippa slapped her hand on her knee. 'You dare call yourself a runner and you don't know who Arthur Barry Magee is? Tell me you know Marise Chamberlain?' I shook my head. 'Millie Sampson?' I shook it again. Philippa raised her eyebrows and took a drink. 'I have to say I'm disappointed in you, Mickey. I can see we have a lot of catching up to do. Starting tomorrow.'

There was a knock at the door and someone called out a cheery hello.

'Lauren!' Ana put the knife down and wiped her hands.

A couple entered the room, a tall, bearded man and a pregnant woman with wild auburn hair. 'Happy birthday, Mum!' She wrapped Philippa in a hug.

Philippa had a daughter? I couldn't believe I didn't know. I drank more wine, taking deep gulps. I felt suddenly out of place, unnecessary.

'Dad says he hopes you've had a great day,' the young woman said. 'He's sorry he can't make it.'

Philippa gestured for me to come over. 'Lauren, this is Mickey. I'm helping her with her running. Mickey, Lauren's my daughter. And this is her partner, David. And this —' she patted Lauren's stomach — 'is going to be my grandson.'

Lauren looked between her mother and me. 'You're coaching? Well, you kept that quiet. It's nice to meet you, Mickey.'

Ana called us to eat, setting a glass of wine for David by his plate. I sat next to Lauren, who made a joke about how far she needed to sit away from the table. I felt tense, uncertain, despite their easy welcome. I knew families and what could happen when they gathered together.

Ana placed large dishes of food in the centre of the table. Lamb with pomegranates, a large green salad with pine nuts and avocado, flat breads, a bowl of hummus, potatoes with chorizo. The sounds of serving spoons on plates filled the room, and in a pause David asked if I was training for anything special.

'The Auckland marathon.' It still sounded mad, but it was thrilling to say it aloud.

'You know what I heard?' Lauren said. 'Some athletes are taking this stuff calcitonin, this nasal spray.'

Philippa looked confused. 'A nasal spray?'

'Sometimes they use it for like arthritis and bone things. I guess it's to promote bone density and avoid stress fractures. People do crazy stuff.'

'For heaven's sake!' Philippa said. 'Those girls just need to eat properly, and rest properly, and have some bloody fun. There would be far fewer of these stresses, and they wouldn't need to spray arthritis medicine up their noses.'

I felt my cheeks grow hot. It was insanity, this nasal spray, just as all the other drugs were. I also knew I would've taken the spray when I was eighteen, nineteen years old. I would've taken anything Bruce or Alain or Yuri offered. Running with North Lynn hadn't been about the love of it: it was about the result. I knew that, but what was I running for now? To win? For love?

'Well, good luck for the marathon,' David said, and then the conversation meandered to Philippa's birthday; Ana's work as a pottery teacher at the Ceramics School; Lauren's due date, and predictions about birth weight; David's new car; Titus; the shrinking size of the *Herald*: ordinary, day-to-day conversations. There was no bitterness, no passive-aggressive jibes. We ate together, we drank, and we laughed.

Lauren and David said goodbye around 10.30. We watched the

headlights of their car grow smaller along the roads in the black hills. I'd had too much to drink to drive home, and Ana said she'd make me a bed on the couch. Philippa, though, wasn't ready for sleep, so we sat and continued talking.

'Why did you stop running?' I asked.

Philippa sighed and rubbed her palms on her thighs. 'I didn't ever stop running,' she said. 'At least not in my mind. I did leave the United States, and I did stop racing. Once it's in your blood, geez, I don't know if you ever stop, even if you can only run in your mind. I spent three years in the States. Running and training with the best. God, it was a great time. I thought I was going to the world champs, to the Olympics. I might have, too, if I hadn't been stupid.'

I let the moment sit between us before I asked what happened.

'I fell pregnant with Lauren, that's what happened.' Philippa tapped her feet and shook her head. 'I don't regret having her, of course I don't. I just won't ever know how far I could've gone. I wasn't one of those superstars; no one was interested in helping me get back into it. There wasn't the sense that I could have her and keep doing the running — not in those days. My parents told me to come home. I thought I would leave the baby with them, go do the Waiatarua on Sunday with the boys. I couldn't have been more mistaken if I'd tried. It's different now,' she said, looking at me. 'So don't let that put you off having a family if you want to. Just plan it better than I did.'

'I thought you were a lesbian.'

Philippa laughed. 'I have a partner who is a woman, that's true. I suppose you could say I'm bisexual. Lauren's dad is a good man, he's just not the man for me. And I was lucky, I found Ana, so I didn't have to raise my daughter alone.'

In the moment of silence between us I heard the booming of the waves, and I thought of the roads, my roads, empty and waiting for my footsteps. When she spoke again, Philippa's voice was sad.

'When I ran, I felt invincible. Hell, I miss it. Running in the summertime, the smell of cut grass, the smell of my sweat. Magical.'

'So it's a rest day tomorrow?'

'It is, my Mickey, it is. I'll see you in the morning.'

I lay on the couch under the blanket, Titus at my feet, and I slept a long, dreamless sleep.

NIALL STOOD ON THE CORNER of New North Road and Kingsland Avenue, where we'd agreed to meet. It was already dark, but I spotted him straight away, his body lit by the cold white streetlights and the warmer yellow light from the bars and restaurants along the strip of shops. There were people everywhere, heading out to dinner or drinks.

We'd texted nearly every day since the accident. Every time my phone buzzed I felt dizzy for a moment, hoping it was a message from him. When at last I plucked up the courage to suggest we meet up for a run, he replied within seconds with a date and a time. And there he was, exactly where he'd said he'd be. I called his name, he turned, and we both smiled. Neither of us said a word, and I wondered if this had been a bad idea.

Then he spoke: 'I planned out a route. It's about 9 ks. Be gentle with me, I'm not as fit as you are.'

I gave a faux chuckle. 'Be gentle with me. I'm recovering from a car crash.'

We started running, heading towards Morningside. Once we were past the main village, the footpath emptied and the noise of the evening dimmed. The road was ours. The night air cleared and grew quiet, and I settled into the run. I could hear him breathing, even and calm. Our footsteps were almost perfectly sychronised.

We ran under the pooling light on the dark streets, the sound of our feet echoing against the house fronts. Niall talked about work and how he got busy in the weeks leading up to the marathon, lots of people doing too much too fast, but that it was good, he said, to see so many people out there giving it a go, trying to do something new. We talked about Hilary and Ryan, and he told me more about Ireland, how he moved to New Zealand and his brother moved to America, and that it had been five years since they'd last been together.

'There's no bad blood,' he said. 'Just lives moving in different directions.'

We started talking about my family, my friends, my work, bad dates — I said nothing about Joel. The conversation felt almost like flirting, skirting alongside the idea of romance without talking about it directly. Although it wasn't clear whether he was attracted to me, there was no doubt how I felt about him: even when he wasn't in my line of vision, I felt him running beside me. The heat of his body, the smell of his skin.

We turned right onto Carrington Road. A car drove by, the exhaust rattling and smoking. We paused to let it drive through the intersection before we crossed, and Niall cleared his throat and said, 'What's your idea of a perfect date?'

'Let me think about it. Probably October twenty-ninth. Not too hot, not too cold. Low chance of rain. Perfect marathon weather.'

He laughed. 'That wasn't quite what I meant.'

'I know,' I said, and took a breath. 'To be honest, this is my idea of a perfect date.'

'This?' he said. We looked at each other for a moment, and then I looked away, concentrating on the cracks in the path, eyes out for cars reversing from driveways. I pressed my thumbnail into my lips, resisting the urge to bite. It had been a stupid thing to say.

He slowed to a stop when we came to the shops of Point Chevalier. Garish light and noise spilled out of a pub on the corner, and for once I didn't feel as if I was missing out, standing on the outside looking at the rest of the world while I ran alone. I turned to face him. The space between us was filled with the exhale of panting breath, and he said,

'What if we went for a beer and a pizza after our run? Would that spoil your perfect date?'

'No,' I said. 'I think that would be an acceptable addition to the evening.'

We ran through to Grey Lynn, looping around to Bond Street, and back to Kingsland. We ran slow, and didn't stop talking. The black of the night settled in and we ran in our own private darkness.

THE RACE

THERE'S PHILIPPA AND ANA, I'M there beside them again. My brain feels strange, shrunken somehow.

'Gel!' I shout at Philippa.

She starts to run with me, fishing out a gel from her pocket. It's in my hand, I'm squeezing it into my mouth. The sticky salted caramel tastes of chemicals. Is it too late? Will I be able to rally for the hardest part of the race? I feel wretched and filled with an inexplicable sadness. I take the drink bottle and swig to wash away the residue on my teeth.

Philippa pulls up and yells, 'It's just you out there, Mickey, don't forget that.'

THE SUN IS DIRECTLY OVERHEAD now. My stride is shortening, I feel the lethargy of the lactic acid kicking in, and also the energy of the gel sliding around in my stomach, snaking its way through my bloodstream. I deliberately work to keep my stride long and my posture upright. Tuck my elbows in. Efficient. Clean. Don't waste any energy.

There's a change in Ruby too; now we've hit 33 ks, only nine-and-a-bit to go. There's a tension in her, I can feel it. It's the wall, and I'm hitting it as well — and I have to find the other side.

Ruby looks like she wants to die, and I feel a rush up in my chest. One of us is going to make a move, and I don't know who. One of us will be victorious.

TWENTY-THREE

DEEP IN THE SWAMP OF marathon training. Always hungry. Always exhausted. Only four weeks to go. The taper wasn't far off — but it wasn't time for it quite yet.

Philippa rang me at work one day. I'd run 15 ks that morning, a tempo run, and I assumed she wanted to hash out the details.

'Today you will go for a second run,' she said. 'Learn to run on tired legs.'

'A second run?' I hadn't done that since the days with Bruce.

'Another run. You'll do that twice this week and the next, until we taper.'

'I thought you said this wasn't about punishing myself?'

'It's not about punishment! This is about the last 7 ks. Now, no matter what, those legs of yours are going to start to hurt around then. All of you is going to hurt. Think of these second runs as your dress rehearsal. You're role playing the sensation of running on tired legs.'

So out I went, back into the streets. New shoes on my feet to break in for the marathon. Ryan had helped me choose them. 'These aren't your workhorse shoes,' he told me. 'These are the wings for race day.'

PHILIPPA CAME OVER IN THE evenings while I did my stretching and foam rolling to give me a crash course on New Zealand long-distance running history. John William Savidan, Cecil Matthews, Noel 'Snow' Taylor. Dick Quax, Lorraine Moller, Anne Audain, Allison Roe.

'Millie Sampson was a legend,' Philippa said. 'She would run from Sandringham to Western Springs and bolt up Bullock Track eight times. Eight times!'

So I started to do that too. Parked my car on Jason Ave, and ran up Sandringham Avenue, left onto St Lukes Road. Followed that up and around, past the darkness of Fowlds Park, over the motorway, choking on exhaust fumes. Left onto Great North Road — then the terrifying Bullock Track. The steep road was always clogged with traffic in both directions and the footpath was ridiculously narrow. Uphill once, twice, heart about to explode, chest bursting with agony. Three times, four. Ragged exhales, oxygen-starved muscles crying out to stop stop stop. Never stop: eight times, I had to do it. Five. Six. Slower, though still trying, pushing, up up up. Seven. Jogging back down hard on the joints, but a marvellous rest before the last and final ascent, breaking through to Old Mill Road, looping around Western Springs, down Motions Road, the roar of the lions from the zoo, loud in the evening air.

THREE WEEKS OUT FROM THE race. Sunday morning, out running my final Waiatarua Loop. I was so deep in the tunnel of marathon training, by turns tired and calm, then anxious, almost manic. The race was creeping closer and closer, and I wanted it over — or for it never to happen at all.

I ran alone that day. Ryan was busy with Arlo and Hilary, a family man now. The ghost runner's steps were loud on the climb up West Coast Road, the sound echoing in my head. It seemed surreal that there was no one there. From there I turned sharp left to Scenic Drive:

I'd broken the back of the beast, and now it was all downhill.

The Subaru was parked up on the verge. We'd planned this — Philippa had a bottle with electrolytes for me to drink on the trot. Just as I would in the race.

I stopped, sat down on the roadside — and started to cry.

'I don't think I have anything left,' I sobbed. 'There's nothing left. I can't do any more.'

Philippa put on the hazard lights, got out of the car and sat down next to me. I retched and spat bile onto the small flowering weeds that grew up between the bitumen and the clay.

'There's always something left,' Philippa said. 'Always. That's what you've come here to find out. What's there, right at the bottom of you, when everything else is worn away. Do you just want to get in the car and go home? Or is there that hard kernel of determination to keep going, no matter how bloody difficult it might get?'

A car drove by fast, swooping around the station wagon. From the back seat, Titus barked at the fading tail-lights that took the next corner without braking.

I wiped my mouth and rubbed my eyes. My body felt spaced out and disconnected. Fleshy and not my own. My skin pimpled from the chill breeze on my hot body, cooling quickly from inaction. I felt done, completely exhausted. What was there, now that I'd run myself down to the very bottom? It wasn't the first time I'd felt ready to stop. I knew what it felt like to be emptied of desire and excitement, to want to disappear. This wasn't that — but what was there?

There was hunger. There was grit. My body felt like teeth ready to grab hold of anything that might satisfy it.

'I don't want to quit,' I said. 'I want this so bad.'

'Then don't stop,' Philippa said, her voice strained. 'It's a certain type of person who keeps trying even when they know they'll probably fail. Don't turn away from that feeling, Mickey. Use it to keep going.'

I tightened my ponytail and looked at her. Her face was creased into a sad smile, her hazel eyes soft at the corners. She asked, 'You ready?'

'I'm ready.'

Philippa stood and reached out her hand. I took it, and she asked again if I wanted to just climb into the car. 'I hate to see you hurting, even when it's partly my fault.'

'No,' I said. 'I'm all right. I'm going to run from here.'

I started on the final stretch. Eleven kilometres to Titirangi, to my home. I knew the hills that rolled in around me like the back of my hand, and I settled into their rhythm. The sun was setting, and the sky was swathed in patches of watermelon pink. The air was damp and smelled of salt. I breathed it in, taking it down into the very core of myself.

The run home didn't feel like flying. My body was a sack of concrete hitting the tarmac. Each step sounded like a thundering in the back of my head, and it didn't matter. I still loved it. My stomach churned and I spat more bile onto the road. I didn't stop, though. I kept putting one foot in front of the other.

And I wasn't alone. Philippa drove past, tooting the horn. I saw Titus's head out the window, his mouth open and panting, fur rippling in the breeze.

THE RACE

IT'S GRAVITY I'M FIGHTING NOW, and many other heavy things besides.

Ruby and I are heading back along Tamaki Drive. We're doubling up on landmarks — Bastion Point again, Kelly Tarlton's, past the brick toilets of Okahu Bay. I watch all the runners still on their way to the turnaround, some quick, some slow — it's an extraordinary sight. There's a young girl, short, miniature compared to the people around her, and I know what I want to say to her:

It doesn't matter how far you run nor how fast — a step is still a step. Running should be a movement to inspire joy, not a tool for punishment, because nothing about you needs to change beautiful girl, unless that change is learning how to love yourself even more.

I would say to her, let running be what it should be, a passion. Let yourself love the work. Understand that it won't all be good days. Running is a constant battle between comfort and discomfort. When things get hard, don't question your worth. Don't let other people's opinions about your running steal your joy.

WE'RE NEARING THE FINISH LINE. In the distance, the city skyline grows larger and larger. Back past Mechanics Bay and Judges Bay, and it's a guts race. I'm giving it everything. My mind begins to drift from the moment — I need to focus. Stay on the now. Keep it together, keep pushing. We run past the mini-golf with the dinosaurs, past the overbridge to Parnell. I think of who is waiting for me at the finish line.

TWENTY-FOUR

TWO WEEKS OUT, PHILIPPA ANNOUNCED that Wednesday's training session would be at the track, and my first reaction was to say no way in hell.

'What do you mean, no?' Philippa said. 'It's important to do some speed work. Ryan will pace you.'

'I know how to run track,' I said. 'Go fast, turn left.'

'That's not quite how I look at it. It's not only about pace and turning left. When was the last time you worked out on the track anyway?'

I shrugged. I thought of the cool air on the track in the evenings, the play of the orange against the green pines beyond, and I thought of Daniel, of Benji. Yuri, Alain and Bruce. I thought of racing and winning, and standing there, calipers pinching my skin.

In the end, I did what she asked. I drove there straight from work, my hands still black with coffee grime. Niall and I had gone to the movies the night before, and he'd given me a gift: a pair of pink socks. His lucky colour. I pulled them on, hoping they'd give me some luck on the track. He'd kissed me, too, in his car. I thought of my hands in his curls, his hand holding my head close to his.

There were a few people on the track, and the lights were already on, bright squares of white against the last of the day's blue. A group of young men were sitting on the grass in the centre, listening to Kendrick Lamar. They were laughing and stretching, and every so often a couple of them would get up and do a lap all out, their form loose and sloppy. I knotted my laces, pulled up the pink socks and waited for Ryan.

He was late but told me he was amping to run, though first I needed to see some videos of Arlo, three months old now. I could see how proud he was, how engaged with the baby's every new milestone, and I felt sad then, for me and for Teddy, for everything we missed out on and everything we would never have. Eventually, he put the phone away and asked about the plan for the session.

I listed the set: 'Two sets of three 1,600 metres. 5:20, 5:15, 5.10. Then 5:15, 5:10, 5:05. She said we weren't to go under five minutes.'

Ryan nodded, and swung his arms around. 'Shall we go for a warm-up first?'

As we were running a few laps in the outer lanes, a tall man came over and stood near our bags. His chest was bare, a running singlet tucked into the waistband of his yellow shorts. Ryan waved to him and we eased to a walk, stopping beside the newcomer.

'Mickey,' Ryan said, 'this is my mate, Clark.'

'You guys doing a session?' Clark stared at Ryan, before taking a quick look at me.

Ryan told him the plan. 'Join us. I'm pacing her.'

'That's ambitious, Mickey,' he said, and laughed. I didn't want to go into it irritated, so I closed my eyes and took a breath. It would be an intense workout, a quick pace only getting quicker. Perhaps Philippa had sent Clark down as well: an annoying companion as yet another exercise in patience. I would run with him, but I wished he'd put a shirt on.

'I'll time,' Ryan said, holding his watch. 'I'll go first, then Mickey, and then Clark, you at the back. That good?'

Clark looked put out, but he didn't seem inclined to argue.

We jogged to the starting line, to the inside lane. Ryan's hand went to his watch — and we were off. I pushed and tried to keep my breathing steady. The track was empty now, the group of younger guys were all sitting in the grass. I concentrated on my form, keeping my head up, chest out, focused on Ryan's shoulders, the shifting purple fabric of his tee-shirt as his arms moved in time with his feet. The sounds of the music faded as we moved around the far side, and for a few moments all I could hear was the sound of six footfalls, the soles of our shoes hard on the track, the light rasping intake of breath from Ryan in front and Clark behind, the thudding rise of my heartbeat into my neck and head. I'd forgotten the thrill of this, speeding around.

We ran the next slightly faster. Ryan's shoulders moved in front of me again, only he ran on the outer edge of lane one this time, and I sat closer in behind him, drafting in his wake.

We came through the second in 5:13. We jogged back in the other direction, preparing for the third, and I heard Clark cough and clear his throat. His face was pink, and red splotches had appeared on his chest and back. I smiled — he was finding it tough. It was only going to get tougher.

On the third, my breathing was shallower and I realised I was clenching my teeth. *Relax,* I told myself. *At least pretend to enjoy it.*

Five minutes 10 seconds. Right on the money, Ryan said. We agreed on a two-minute break between the sets of three, and walked around to work through the lactic acid. I stopped by our bags for a drink while Ryan and Clark kept walking near to the guys sitting with the music. One of them called out, 'Is she a professional runner?'

I heard Clark snigger, and Ryan said, 'No, but she should be.'

Second set: we went through the first in 5:14. Slow jog, heart rate thumping, and then slower, slower, deeper breaths. Turn around, go again. Next one, 5:08. Fatigue was settling in, so I jumped up and down to freshen my legs. My mind felt clear. There was no chatter, no mist or worry. Just open space. My body knew what to do, I just had to let go and enjoy.

'Last one,' Ryan said. 'You good to go?'

'You bet,' I said. Clark coughed again and nodded. We jogged in a line to the start, Ryan's hand to his watch.

Quick this time. Some hair had come loose from my ponytail and blew back from my face. Relax my jaw, drop my shoulders. Elbows in. Let my legs swing, hinged from my hips, core tight and strong. I'm nearly there, at the point where the motion feels like flying. Both feet are off the ground — and it's as if the moment lasts forever.

Two laps, three. The guys on the grass began cheering and whistling. I knew why: we were quick, the three of us in a line, zipping around and around. I kept my eyes ahead. Clark's heavy breathing just behind me, the sound of his feet keeping me going. Eleven days to go. It would feel like this at the end of the marathon. Like my stomach was in my throat, my legs tired and heavy. I might not win — there was very little chance of that. But I would give it my best shot. *Your best is all I ask.*

WE SAT ON THE GRASS after we'd finished the session and ran through our results.

'So what time are you aiming for in the marathon, Mickey?' Clark asked.

I didn't hesitate. 'Two hours thirty.'

There was a pause, as though the men were considering the folly of my ambition. 'Interesting, I shall keep that in mind,' Ryan said.

'That's pretty quick,' Clark said. 'Have you ever raced a marathon before?'

'She is quick,' Ryan said. 'But you'll have to race your skin off, Mickey, you know that.'

'I've run the distance,' I said. 'A couple of times. I've never raced it.'

'Find the pacer,' Ryan said, looking me direct in the eye. He stood up. 'I'm going to run a final 400,' he said.

'See if you can go under a minute,' Clark said. 'Then I'll run and see if I can beat your time.'

Clark set his watch as Ryan started to run, then he turned to me and said, 'If I don't see you again before the day, good luck for the race. You're going to rip it.'

'Thanks,' I said, a bit stunned by his compliment.

Eleven days to go.

THERE WAS A STACK OF books on my doorstep when I got home, along with a note from Philippa: *Read these*. I set them on the floor next to my foam roller. *Born to Run. Once a Runner. Running with Lydiard.*

I hadn't told Philippa that I hated reading, or why. I felt ashamed even looking at the books, so I pushed them to the corner of the lounge.

I showered and changed into jeans and a tee-shirt, and checked the time. Niall was coming over for dinner. I picked up some dirty socks and stacked the unwashed dishes in the sink.

He saw the books as soon as he came in. He picked up *Born to Run* and flicked through the pages. 'Are you going to read this?'

I sat down next to him. 'I want to but I'm not going to.'

'Why not?'

'Why not what?'

He tapped the book on my knee. 'You know, it's okay if you find reading difficult.'

I felt nauseated, too visible. Niall read literature and wrote poetry — he would be shocked that I didn't read.

'It's obvious you aren't dead keen on reading,' he said. He put the book down on the couch between us and touched my face. 'I saw how tricky it was for you to order pizza last week ... Hey, don't worry.' He seemed to sense my discomfort. 'It's okay, Mickey. I'm not attracted to your reading ability.'

'I can read if I want to,' I said. I looked at the book. Behind the white words was the small figure of a man running along a dusty yellow trail. Rust-coloured rocky hills smouldered in the distance. Above him the sky darkened from pale pink to deep cerulean blue. It looked dry and flat and magnificent. *Born to Run*. If only it were that easy! My mouth was dry. 'I can read,' I said again. 'Slowly and with lots of mistakes. My brain is fucked up, what can I say?'

'Don't say that,' he said. He pulled me to him, and my body slackened into his. I felt his heartbeat, the warmth of his skin.

I opened the book and tried to read the first page aloud, then shut it again. 'It's no use. I'm officially stupid.'

'If there's any word I could use to describe you, it wouldn't be stupid. Reading is an astonishingly tricky thing to learn. I'm sorry it's been so hard for you, Mickey. Writing was created so we could put our thoughts down on paper, so someone else could read them — from anywhere, at any time — and hear our voices. I can't wait until you can read that book, and the others, and hear what these people have to tell you.' He took the book from me and opened it again to the first chapter. The pages made a soft rustle at his touch. I closed my eyes and he began to read: 'Chapter one. For days, I'd been searching Mexico's Sierra Madre for the phantom known as Caballo Blanco ...'

WE ATE DINNER, THEN WE sat on my couch, no books this time. We kissed and undressed. His chest was thin, and I saw the fox in full, its head up on his bicep. He touched my shoulders and kissed the ridge of my clavicle, up the side of my neck. I took his hand and led him to my bedroom.

'Are you sure?' he said, and I nodded, and he moved inside me, and it was better than running.

THE RACE

WANDERING MIND, PROTECTING ITSELF FROM the immediate agony, and another memory comes unbidden, my mind a frayed VCR tape skipping from one part of the movie to another—

'You don't need to read the recipe,' Bonnie said. 'You can if you want. I can teach you. We'll start with something simple. My favourite: custard.'

It wasn't really cooking, I knew that, but I'd told Mum I wanted to learn. I saw how much joy she found in sifting flour, stirring pots, putting food on the table.

It was dark outside, and our faces were reflected in the kitchen window, with Mum's light-brown, chin-length hair, my own darker head. The others were in the lounge, waiting for Teddy. I stood on a stool so I could reach the wooden spoon and stir.

'Now, two tablespoons of custard powder, and one tablespoon of sugar.' She let me scoop the powder and sugar into the saucepan. 'That's right, good girl. Now, a bit of milk to get it started, then we turn on the heat and add the rest of the milk.'

I stirred, and slowly the mixture came to the boil, and what was once watery became thick. With the heat and the gently stirring spoon, it changed from one thing to another.

THERE'S LESS THAN 5 KS to go. I go to check my watch — and then stop. I listen to my body instead. Our pace is quick, though slowing. There's more push now, more effort, less grace. Ruby's arms are off balance, one shoulder pulled up to her ear, each arm swinging in front of her on an uneven beat. She's still fast. Her panting breath sounds louder than the cheers of the crowd alongside the course. I follow her up the hill towards the port. Pressure builds in my head on the uphill strain. This is the point when I might once have said there's nothing left, and that I'm ready to stop.

I won't stop. There is something left. It's the will to go on, even though I can't know the outcome. I'm giving it everything, and still I might lose. A cloud drifts out of the sun's path, and the morning light hits bright now. I can't see the finish line, but—

It's close—

TWENTY-FIVE

SEVEN DAYS OUT FROM THE race. My last long run came too soon. Niall ran with me, an easy 10 ks before breakfast. There was the feel of summer in the air, and on every inhale I smelled the sweet damp earthiness of the bush, the brackish bite of the sea on the wind. The sky seemed to loom over the road, and as we ran it began to shift, colours merging and reforming. The clouds were grey floating in a wash of peach. Birds began their chorus in the trees, and I couldn't think of the last time I'd heard the ghost runner's footsteps.

'How do you feel?' Niall asked.

'Like I could fly,' I said. It was true. The taper was kicking in. I felt like I could conquer the world. My legs and stomach, my arms and the back of my skull — when I ran, it felt as though the whole inside of my body and mind were filled with white light, and that soon I might evaporate into a million pieces and float up into the sky. It didn't happen, of course, yet the feeling remained, a full charge. We curled through the streets, weaving around rubbish bins on our way to the open road. Hanging over the fence of one house was a cherry blossom, the bare branches drenched in pale-pink flowers, a perfect match for the morning sky.

Niall spoke then, in his soft, measured tone for reading aloud. 'The sky ablaze with red and pink, the sweet grass wet with dew, one month melts into the next, the winter thaw has begun.'

The words matched the metronomic beat of our cadence, and he continued. 'In the eyes of man it may not be a church, but the road it is my temple, the long run is my service—'

The road rose up a hill and we breathed together, slowly making our way up to the crest. At the top we paused, looking down at the road ahead. The silver ocean spread out before us.

'That was beautiful,' I said.

'Running and poetry are more similar than you might think,' Niall said. 'Consider the beat. Your heartbeat, the rhythm of the poem, both pushing you onward. Like the iambic pentameter of Shakespeare.'

Shakespeare. I thought of the long afternoons in the classroom at Mangorei College, the heavy textbook open on my desk. *King Lear.* That consuming dread I'd felt when someone stopped speaking and they turned to look at me, the Cordelia, trying to read the words. I said, 'I don't want to think about Shakespeare. Who wrote that poem you just said? *The road it is my temple.* I love it.'

'I wrote it,' he said. 'That's one of my poems. It's about running in springtime, in case you couldn't tell. I may not be a great poet, or a great runner. I just love to dedicate myself to the pursuit of beautiful things.'

'That poem was more beautiful than running can ever be,' I said.

'Do you really think that?'

I wasn't sure. I looked at him, and thought he was the most beautiful thing in the world. More beautiful than running, than poetry. I loved the shape of his thighs, curving up under his shorts. I loved when he read to me in bed, his glasses on his pointed nose. I loved the way he told me, *Since he touched you when he shouldn't have touched you, every cell in your body has died and new ones have replaced them. The girl he touched can no longer be hurt by anyone, because she no longer exists.*

There is only you, Mickey, the woman.

I had nothing to hide from him, no reason to pretend to be someone I wasn't. It was nothing like how it was with Joel. Niall saw the insane burning fire of competition inside me and he liked it. He knew the reason my legs were striped like a silver tiger, and he wasn't frightened. Instead, he kissed me, and said he hoped I'm never so hurt on the inside that I feel I must make it plain on the outside.

We set off down the hill, and he continued to speak a word of a poem with every step we took. I listened to his voice, to his breath, and felt a clench of the muscle in my chest moving forward to a destination, a place of understanding.

FIVE DAYS TO GO, FOUR. Then three, and two.

Philippa came over on Friday night to have dinner with Niall and me. Niall cooked spaghetti, and I made custard for dessert — from scratch, just the way Bonnie had taught me.

Philippa drank a beer and talked again about what to expect in the race. 'You know what they say … Running a marathon's a lot like living your life,' she said. 'It's easy to get bogged down in it. Some of it will be great. Some of it might even be incredible, if you get lucky. A lot of it will be utter shit — more of it than you thought you could tolerate. And when it's over, Mickey, I bet you're gonna say, *Goddamn. Can I do that again?*'

Niall laughed, and said that sounded about right. I let out a breath and told them I was nervous. More nervous than I'd ever felt before.

'You've learned a lot about running in the past few months,' Philippa said. 'But what you've really been learning about is much more important than just running. Any fool can lace up a pair of sneakers and put one foot in front of the other. That's not the hard part. The hard part is the rest of it.' She tapped her head. 'Patience. Dedication. Trust. Gratitude. I believe you understand a lot more about those things than you did a year ago. So no matter what happens on Sunday, no matter if you crash and burn or if you finish in a record time, you will have that.'

'I know,' I said. 'I'm trying not to fixate on the outcome.'

Philippa leaned forward. 'Now Mickey, I know your natural inclination is to hang back, try to claw your way back to the lead. I don't want you to go out guns blazing, but I do want you to hang in behind your main competition, Ruby Bright. She isn't going to be expecting you. She's going to think she has this in the bag. What you need to do is stay with her. Keep close to her. And then, at twenty miles, I need you to push her harder than she wants to work. Make it a guts race, as old Prefontaine would say. You'll get her then.'

'Right,' I said. 'Sounds vicious.'

She shrugged. 'Strategy is all about perverse intent, my dear girl. You aren't out there to make friends.'

THAT NIGHT I DREAMED OF my family. I dreamed of Kent in the river, my arms around his neck, and the feeling of him slipping down under the surface. I dreamed that I woke then, and Helen was there, and she said, *It's only a bad dream, Mickey,* and I reached out, and there it was, her hand, waiting for mine in the darkness between our beds. *It's okay,* she said, *I'm here.* I dreamed about Zach, waiting for me at the end of the relay on the field by the beach, the dry brown grass spiky underfoot. I dreamed I ran to the win, and he caught me, and lifted me high into the sky, as though I truly were a bird, and Bonnie was there, and she said she was proud of me.

I woke in the early hours of the morning, overcome with sorrow that they weren't here, that I was by myself. Then Niall woke, and asked me if I was all right. He kissed me, and I remembered that this was how it was. You grew up and left your family behind — and it was okay, because there could be a new family, waiting for you somewhere.

THE DAY BEFORE THE RACE I stayed at home, resting my legs. Helen called to say good luck, and Wilma said in her squeaky toddler voice, 'Good luck Aunty Mickey.' Kent sent a message from London, saying Knausgaard the cat hoped that I ran a good time. Zach texted me the eloquent **break a leg.** I didn't hear from Teddy, although Helen told me he knew I was running.

'Maybe he'll surprise you at the finish line?' she said. 'Maybe Cleo will be there, too.'

'I won't hold my breath,' I told her. 'For fear of suffocation.'

Philippa came around in the afternoon for a final pep talk. 'Set your alarm,' she said. 'Hell, set two alarms. Get into your race gear and eat your breakfast, with a hot Milo or coffee, then go back to bed for half an hour. Use the toilet when you get up. Is Niall driving you to the starting line?'

He wasn't — I was going to stay at his flat in Cheltenham for the night, and I would walk to the starting line.

'Aren't you clever?' Philippa said, shaking her head. 'You never cease to amaze me. Found yourself a man with a place within walking distance of the start line. Tell me, do you have all your drinks and gels sorted?'

'Not yet.'

Philippa rolled her eyes.

'It will be ready!' I said, laughing. 'Where will you be on the course?'

'I'll be near the support station for 29 and 33 kilometres. Then we'll see you at Vic Park. Remember, Mick, it's only 26 miles. Barry used to say that anyone can run 20 miles, it's the next six that count. Go make them six miles count, my girl.'

She turned to leave, and I felt my hands shaking. I watched her as she walked to the car and unlocked it.

'Wait!' I called, and ran out to the road.

'What's the matter?'

A gust of wind lifted her hair, which shone auburn in the light. I didn't know what I wanted to say. There were no words that seemed suitable for the moment — none that would capture the feeling of wanting my mother back, and also how she was as close to being my mother as it got.

'I wanted to say thank you. I wouldn't be here without you.'

'Oh, Mickey,' she said. 'Of course you would. Don't underestimate yourself.'

I wanted to tell her what I had learned in the past few months. I'd not been able to grasp any of it when I was younger, but I knew it now: that while running was my own journey, an adventure I took on alone, even when someone was beside me, running was also about the community I surrounded myself with. The people supporting me, carrying me when I couldn't carry myself. All this — it was impossible to do it alone. People loved to say that stupid thing: you just need a pair of shoes and you can be a runner! It isn't true. You need so many things. The most important is people, giving you their time and their love. Everything I'd achieved — everything I was still to achieve — was built on the sweat and effort of many.

Philippa reached out and took hold of my hand. 'Hey,' she said. 'You doing all right?'

Nerves, and years of wanting, dreaming, the failures, the terrors. All the parts of my life that had led to this moment, what I hoped this race might then lead to, came rushing to my head like blood, and I began to cry. Philippa pulled me in, her arms around me in a tight embrace.

For five months we'd worked together. All the hours on the road, more hours meeting at Four Loaves, hundreds of text messages and phone calls, discussing run routes, hill repeats, foam rolling, the weight of the dumbbells for strength workouts, drills, eating plans, expectations. In all that time, Philippa hadn't hugged me, not once. There'd been a strict professional distance. Touch was only to demonstrate a movement, to grind a tight muscle with a thumb.

I didn't mind. Daniel and Bruce and his minions had touched me enough for a lifetime, appraising my body with their eyes and their hands and their scales and their measurements and their judgements.

And now there was this: a hug, into the warmth and softness of Philippa's body. She smelled of sugar and lavender, and I closed my eyes. I could almost pretend I was no longer standing on the road outside my brick unit, that I was now in Bonnie's arms inside the Rutherford Street house, the smell of scones browning in the oven, the sound of rain on the roof above, the voices of my brothers and sister talking in another room.

'You know I'm proud of you, Mickey,' Philippa said, pulling her head back and looking me in the eye. 'Like Yoda says, you've been training yourself to let go of everything you're terrified of losing.'

'Yoda said that?'

'Something like that.' She opened the car door and got in, and when she drove off she tooted the horn twice.

'I'LL SAY GOODBYE BEFORE YOU go,' Niall said before we went to sleep. 'Then I'll see you further into the race.'

'Where will you be?'

'It's a surprise,' he said. 'You see me when you see me.'

'I'm scared, Niall. I'm scared of looking like a fool.'

'Sometimes you gotta risk it for the biscuit,' he said. 'And the biscuit, in this case, is the satisfaction in all your hard work. And I'll still take you home, fool or no.'

'When this is all over,' I said, touching his face, 'I'm not going to remember all the runs, or the agony of training. I won't remember which shoes I wore and what my split times were. I think I'll just remember who was there for me when I got home.'

THE RACE

CLOSER TO THE FINISH LINE with each step. Along the course, people jostle to see us. Their faces blur as I race past. Above us the clouds are thin and streaky, wandering off into the horizon above Victoria Park as though on a race to a finish line I will never see. The crowds are cheering, loud and as one: I feel the noise like a physical thing.

I think I hear my name as we turn the last corner. The end is tantalisingly close. My body aches and I want to lie down. Somewhere soft and warm, in a place where I don't have to move ever again and my tired muscles can drift away into nothingness. Then, my name again, a voice clear against the throbbing racket of the onlookers, clear over the sound of the man on the loudspeaker naming the runners of the 10-kilometre and the half-marathon as they cross the line.

I glance around quickly to see who it is, but I need to focus on the last 50 metres. This is what it boils down to — a mad dash. Ruby's arms pump, her legs look fresh again, renewed at the sight of the finish line. I sense that she's kicking into a last-minute sprint. My heart is loud in my ears. A sharp taste of vinegar on my tongue. Then I see them, Philippa, Ana, Hilary and Niall, together at the barrier on my right, near the finish line. Their faces are bright and happy. I turn away from them to do what I must.

The race has taken so much out of me, not just from my body but from my mind and the part that might be my soul; I think of Marcus, sitting in the gutter at 33 ks. Roadkill. Tears staining his cheeks, his long skinny legs bent crooked, his knees bloodied from the fall.

I'm not giving up, I'm not emptied of all I have to give. There's always something more. That's what I've found over the years, if you hang in there long enough everything will change. Bonnie might be gone but I feel her with me. Teddy, Helen, Kent, Zach — the family I seem to have lost along the way, through mistakes and lies and hurt. The journey to the starting line has been so much longer than the one to the finish line.

I've got Philippa, and Ana. Hilary and Ryan. Niall. I inhale deeply through my nose, hold my head high, and I run faster. Lungs screaming, legs hurting, and still I push harder. Everything is beautiful and everything hurts, and it's perfect. I'm running to the finish line, and I don't know what I will find when I get there.

END

ACKNOWLEDGEMENTS

Everything is Beautiful and Everything Hurts was inspired by many things: my own experiences in sports and stories I've been told or discovered through research, but it isn't a biography; it is a work of pure fiction. Though I've tried to create a believable world within the New Zealand running and athletics scene, there were times when the novel's narrative meant I took liberties and changed dates or locations of actual events or omitted things entirely. For all errors, I beg the reader's forgiveness.

I want to acknowledge the book *The Kiwi Runners' Family Tree, Volume One: 1800s–1999* by Dreydon Sobanja, published by Inspired Kids Limited, 2020, for providing me with background on the incredible running history of New Zealand and for grounding information so my novel can honour the outstanding runners who've taken on the roads of Aotearoa. I would like to credit Christopher McDougall and Profile Books for the quote from *Born to Run* and Charles Hamilton Sorley for the quote from his poem, *The Song of the Ungirt Runners*. I'd also like to thank all the hilarious running meme accounts on Instagram for invaluable running jokes like 'the perfect date', and to so many runners from around the world — Mary Cain, Molly Seidel, Alexi Pappas, Kara Goucher, Lucy Bartholomew, Lydia O'Donnell — for sharing their lives on social media and helping me understand the pressures unique to female runners.

I want to say a million thanks to my publishers, Allen & Unwin, especially the panel of judges for the Commercial Fiction Prize: Michelle Hurley, Jenny Hellen, Leanne McGregor, Leonie Freeman and Kathy Callesen, plus the rest of the team, especially Melanie Laville-Moore, Abba Renshaw and Nyssa Walsh. Winning the prize has changed my life, and I will always be so thankful you fell in love with Mickey. I'd also like to thank my editor, Jane Parkin, for her incredibly generous and considered help on the manuscript and Lawrence Patchett for his encouraging and thorough assessment of the manuscript.

Without this wealth of expertise, my novel would be a lesser work. More thanks to my master's supervisor Paula Morris, and my cohort of 2018, for the invaluable lessons in storytelling and craft. Thanks especially to Sarah Ell and Erica Stretton for your daily support, advice, and friendship, which kept me through the toil of creating these words.

To my parents, Tim and Valerie, thank you for always letting me read whatever I wanted while growing up. To Paul, Ann, and Kim, thank you for your support and care, which made writing while parenting possible. And finally, to Lee. Thank you for giving me the time to write and follow my dream. I love you and I couldn't have done this without you.

JOSIE SHAPIRO has a Masters in Creative Writing from the University of Auckland, where she was awarded a Wallace Arts Scholarship for her work. Her writing has appeared in journals and anthologies, and she writes book reviews for *New Zealand Listener*, the Academy of New Zealand Literature and ketebooks. co.nz. She lives with her husband and two daughters in Tāmaki Makaurau, Auckland.